One Weekend in May

Gordon F.D. Wilson

 FriesenPress

One Printers Way
Altona, MB R0G 0B0
Canada

www.friesenpress.com

Copyright © 2024 by Gordon F.D. Wilson
First Edition — 2024

All rights reserved.

No part of this publication may be reproduced in any form, or by any means, electronic or mechanical, including photocopying, recording, or any information browsing, storage, or retrieval system, without permission in writing from FriesenPress.

ISBN
978-1-03-830492-6 (Hardcover)
978-1-03-830491-9 (Paperback)
978-1-03-830493-3 (eBook)

1. FICTION, LITERARY

Distributed to the trade by The Ingram Book Company

1.

She was dressed in her best tweed coat and matching hat, her gloved hands gripping the handle of a small leather suitcase with the name Lena Murshid, written in indelible ink, taped to the lid. She tilted forward, as if pulled by an invisible string, concentrating on each step.

She pushed away the biting pain from her blistered feet and focused; left foot, right foot, one in front of the other down the narrow dirt road.

This would be her final parade.

Like golden confetti, the early morning sun bounced off the drops of dew falling from the branches of the alder and poplar that stood tall to her left and right, uniformed in sliver bark leggings and spring-green coats, gently swaying in the breeze.

Song sparrows and juncos sang in chorus from the thin branches of late-blooming wild cherry trees, while black-capped chickadees danced within the dark green foliage of low-growing salal, and the bald eagle whistled applause from the tallest fir trees.

She offered a demure smile and gentle nod to the blurry blackness of the ravens hopping alongside her, and if not for the grip of both hands on the suitcase handle, she would have acknowledged the windy cheers and the rustle of leafy applause with a wave of her hand. Her tired and increasingly shuffled steps were made lighter by the birdsong.

This was the triumphant return she had hoped for when planning her escape from captivity and return to Uruk. She knew that throngs of her loyal subjects would line up along her route home. It was a most fitting tribute.

"Well," she stated aloud, "you really have put on quite a show for me today. But you mustn't mourn for me when I am gone. Just know and remember, as harsh as my rule over you may have seemed, I ruled in this manner because of my love for you all."

It was a short address, spoken as loudly as her breathless lungs allowed, yet despite her exhaustion and growing pangs of hunger, she had no intention of stopping—nor did she know how long she had been walking. It had been a long time, because she had to admit that, while she had been thankful for the warmth of her coat when she had begun her journey in the chilly darkness of the night, it now seemed too warm, a burden on her frail shoulders.

Perhaps it was time to eat the egg salad sandwich she had wrapped in a napkin and put in her coat pocket.

No.

Despite the remoteness of the narrow dirt road, she felt quite sure that she was close to her destination, and tried to visualize where she was going. But she quickly shook her head at such a bad idea. The mental void that met her each time she tried this only served to make her anxious, so she shuffled on and on.

Lena's ears filled with the rapid drumbeat of her heart, while her lungs choked out their objection as she crested a low but steady rise in the road. She swayed slightly on her now-rubbery legs.

She stopped and put down her suitcase, thinking it might provide a temporary seat, and had she the confidence to sit down, she would have. But her inner voice warned her, as it had done several times before on her journey, that if she sat, she would be unable to get back up. Instead, she opened her stance slightly, using the suitcase to help secure her balance, and waited for her heart to calm and her lungs to refill with air.

It was then that she heard the barking—deep and full of conviction.

Her eyes followed the sound, but the distant road blurred into shapes and shades of grey. There was a time, she had to believe, when she could see the horizon. She tapped her head with her left hand to nudge the blocks of memory into line, to restore that ability, but instead heard only the early steps of panic entering her mind. So she decided to shuffle on toward the deep but friendly bark beyond.

Thankful to be walking downhill, her heart skipped a beat when a rare moment of visual clarity revealed a lush, sheep-filled field through the thinning trees. The source of the barking was a large, white dog, tail wagging, his nose pressed against the wire fence that ran the perimeter of the road.

"This is it." She was certain of her destination, and saying it aloud comforted her. Revitalized, she continued along the road with her now-happy companion bouncing and barking along the other side of the fence that lined the road toward the farmgate.

***

Ken Graham cursed the arthritis in his now-bruised right hand as he pushed it beneath the pelvic bone until his fingers finally felt the unborn lamb. For her part, the once-cooperative ewe, now in the agony of a breached birth, bellowed for it all to stop.

The ewe lay prone on the floor of the lambing pen, half-straddled, her head pinned down by Ken's fully extended leg.

He closed his eyes and let the touch of his fingers guide the image in his mind. He felt the curve of the back, and ran his fingers over the curled vertebrae to determine on which side the neck and head rested.

Then the contraction.

A crushing pain shot through his hand as the unborn lamb pinned it against the groaning ewe's pelvic bone.

When the contraction stopped, he carefully pushed the lamb back into the uterus sliding his fingers along the spine until he felt the head and ears. Cupping his throbbing hand over the head, he gently but firmly rotated the lamb to the left until he felt the nose and teeth.

The next contraction pushed the head forward.

Ken slipped his hand along the underside of the neck until he felt the lamb's chest and shoulders.

When the contraction ended, he untangled the long, thin front legs, pulling them forward beneath the chin of the unborn lamb, then slipped his fingers over the fragile carpal bones, gripped them, and pulled in rhythm with the next contraction. Using his left hand, he gently guided the lamb's head into the world.

One Weekend in May

It was a large female, lifeless at first as it lay in the straw. Ken lifted it by the hind legs, and with his gloved hand, removed the birth mucus from the creature's nose and throat. The lamb took its first breath, causing her to jerk her head as the remaining mucus bubbled from its nostrils. The ewe, in shock, lay still until Ken presented the lamb to her. Smelling her baby for the first time, she offered it a murmur, raised her head, and started to clean her newborn.

Kneeling in overalls soaked with birth fluids, his heart filled with the happiness that a successful outcome always brought him. Ken wiped his hands off with a towel while watching the newborn lamb struggle to find her feet.

He could hear Toby, his Maremma guardian dog, barking somewhere in the fields outside the barn, but he waited until he was sure the ewe and lamb had formed a bond before leaving them. Satisfied, he headed out to see what had caused Toby to be so vocal.

Ken was very familiar with the overtones in Toby's bark, and knew despite the dog's welcoming tone, he was about to have unwelcomed company.

I really don't need this. Whoever you are, go away.

He was in no mood for company—although judging by the dog's friendly tone, Ken felt it must be someone that Toby knew.

He stepped through the barn's Dutch door, shading his eyes with his arm from the sudden, blinding sunlight.

Toby was at the fence by the entry gate at the end of the driveway. He had raised himself on his hind legs and planted his meaty front paws on the top rail of the fence. The shadows beneath the bending bows of the giant green willow beside the gate made it hard for Ken to see who Toby—his tail wagging furiously—was greeting.

"Who the hell is this?" Ken muttered, walking a little faster. Judging from Toby's effusive welcome, whoever it was wasn't a threat.

A few feet from the gate, a woman came into clear view; a frail soul who, had she been on a city street, might have been mistaken for a homeless person.

Ken stopped abruptly.

The woman, dressed in a tattered tweed coat that appeared two sizes too large, was speaking to him—but her voice was swallowed up within the baritone of Toby's bark.

Ken stared at the figure outside his farm gate. An outdated tweed golfer's cap crowned her tangled, shoulder-length grey hair, which framed a regal face: high cheekbones, a straight nose above cracked, trembling lips, and sad, sunken eyes—which betrayed her attempt at assertiveness, just as her shaking frame belied the regal posture she tried to present.

"Why are you here?"

"Well, that seems rather rude," the woman said, taking a step back from the gate. "Do you not know who I am? Perhaps my long quest has changed my appearance."

Ken's shoulders dropped as an all-too-familiar feeling of futility swept over him. He squeezed his eyes shut for a moment. "Uh … OK, right … I am sorry."

"Much better," the woman said. "It is me, Gilgamesh. I have returned from my travels, and presently, I am looking for somewhere I might eat my egg salad sandwich."

Ken sighed, pushed Toby off the fence, and unlatched the gate. "I am Kenneth. If you can manage a short walk to the house, I will make you food. Please, let me take your suitcase."

Lena stepped through the gate, stretching out her right hand—not in a handshake, but fingers-down, the gloved back presented.

Ken looked at her hand, not quite sure what to do with it. Then, thinking it safe, he gently took it in his. He bowed in a manner he had only seen in period movies, and in doing so, noticed her scuffed shoes and the dust-crusted blood on her ankles and heels.

"Nice to meet you, Kenneth," she said. "I cannot let you take my luggage. It stays with me. But please, lead the way—I really am quite hungry for that sandwich."

***

The loud barking caused confusion in her mind. She wanted to believe that the noisy dog was just part of a group of happy men and women with their loud children, waving flags and yelling their support as she walked along the road. She felt safe enough, as the wire fence that lined the road was on the opposite side of a deep drainage ditch. Nevertheless, she thought it best to walk on the opposite side of the road to provide more distance. But with every step that brought her closer to the gate came more uncertainty.

Once she walked into the driveway, the fence, now cedar-railed, was no longer opposite a ditch. And the barking became louder, more frantic, demanding, and unpleasant—the dog was now close enough for her to realize she had been mistaken.

Standing on hind legs, his two front paws on the top rail, his neck stretched forward, the image in her mind was clear enough. This was that wretched, fat, bad-tempered bitch who had leaned against her bedrail each morning, yelling for her to wake up! It was a routine that she knew well. With every foul-smelling breath, the woman would scream, "Are you still with us, or have you finally died?"

She was consumed with panic, and she clenched to try to stop the thin trickle of pee, warm against her legs. Fear twisted her shaking fingers as she tried to unlock the gate. Despite her clouded vision, she could see that she would be safe on the other side.

Then a figure appeared through the mist in her mind, and she called out. "Stop her! Don't let her near me, please," but her voice was weak—too soft, she feared, to be heard above the barking.

The approaching figure of a man seemed to fall into slow motion as he came closer. He whistled a command that she be left alone, and the noise stopped as the aggressor backed off in compliance. A welcome calm came over her.

She put down her suitcase, tidied her coat, adjusted her hat, straightened her back, and lifted her chin. First impressions mattered—a lesson that she thought this gentleman might consider. This long-haired creature was filthy.

Despite his kind tone, she was shocked at the audacity and rudeness of this unkempt man when he asked her why she had returned. Was it possible that this wild-looking yet vaguely familiar creature had come to challenge her?

Unnerved, she took a step back from the gate, stood as tall as she was able, and told the man he was rude. But he had asked a question that demanded an answer. Yet when she considered an appropriate response, she drew a blank. She searched for that comfortable, less defensive place in her head that helped her control the anxiety that always accompanied her unclear thoughts. *Who is this demanding man? Does he not know who stands before him?*

"Do you not know who I am? Perhaps my long quest has changed my appearance," she replied, stiffening her resolve not to let this man intimidate her. *After all*, she thought, *who greets a person of my stature in such a manner—wet, slimy pants and a damp, filthy shirt, with sleeves rolled up to the elbows and all covered in wood chips and hay?* It was outrageous, really. Anyway, judging from the quick change in the man's posture and his apology, she was satisfied that her stern rebuke had worked, and with as much dramatic flair as she could manage, she accepted his apology.

Having accepted that this man didn't know who she was, she thought it proper to introduce herself—but that task also drew a momentary blank. She tapped her forehead with her fingers. She had been afraid that this might happen. After all she had been gone from this place for a long while, hadn't she?

Your credentials are in the documents within the suitcase, the voice in her head reminded her. She remembered rehearsing the line so many times in the planning for this journey. *Of course, I remember now. The contents of the suitcase.*

She tightened her grip on the handle. There was no more precious cargo than that within this small, leather suitcase—truth in all its confirmations, scribed for posterity within the writing in the book. She was reminded of her identity—and this scruffy man would not have grounds to challenge her assertion. After all, in this moment at least, she knew who she was.

"It is me, Gilgamesh. I have returned from my travels, and presently, I am looking for somewhere I might eat my egg salad sandwich". Her hand had found the egg salad sandwich in her pocket. Then, she realized that she was owed a name. She was relieved when the man offered it.

The man's name meant nothing to her, but she repeated "Kenneth" over and over in her mind, for fear that she would forget it. That would be impolite. As soon as she had the chance, she would write it down.

He really is quite filthy and smells awful—quite wild, actually—but there is a kindness in his face, and a melancholy within those kind eyes that leads me to believe that, contrary to my first impression, he does not seek to harm me. I will offer him my hand and see what he does with it. Manners are all-important, yet they are too little practised.

Lena stepped through the gate and offered Kenneth her outstretched hand. If he tried to shake it, that would prove him common; if he tried to kiss it, that would prove him untrustworthy. When Kenneth took her hand, gently bowing, that was perfect. A long-lost feeling flickered alight deep within her—a tiny and uncertain flame, but alight nonetheless—and the warmth it provided her did not go unnoticed.

2.

Asher Mirza sat upright in the worn leather chair in the sparsely furnished office of Dr. Sonja Chopra at the Caring Hands Hospice and Palliative Centre. He took a deep breath and tried to manage his emotions.

"I understand you're angry," said Dr. Chopra, with a faint, nervous smile. She adjusted her wire-rimmed glasses on the bridge of her olive-skinned nose. The lenses enlarged the doctor's youthful, light brown eyes, which belied her mid-fifties age. "However, your anger does nothing to help us find your mother."

"I am beyond angry," Asher growled. "I withdrew from presenting a paper at an important astrophysics conference in Copenhagen to come here to attend to my mother in her last days, and instead of finding her bedridden and gasping for her last breath, you tell me that she is missing! The incompetence of this place is staggering. How do you know she didn't stumble into a closet and get herself locked in? I refuse to believe that she could have just walked out of this place."

"Mr. Mirza, our security personnel have thoroughly checked the saved closed-circuit TV footage from inside the facility, and those cameras that capture the perimeter of the building. The footage clearly shows that at 1:12 am, your mother got out of bed, dressed herself, and pulled a suitcase out from under her bed. She put on a hat and coat that hung in the closet, reached under her mattress for something that she stuffed in the pocket of the coat, and then, suitcase in hand, walked down the hallway to the red exit door and opened it with a pass key card. The external CCTV confirms she left the property."

Asher clenched his fists, his anger rising again. "I don't believe this!"

"I can arrange for you to review the footage for yourself if you would like to see it," Dr. Chopra said curtly.

Asher stared at a framed, embroidered meme that hung on the stark white wall behind the doctor. He found it infuriatingly taunting.

A bad attitude is like a flat tire; you can't go anywhere until you change it.

"So, am I to believe that my mother, in her current condition, just got out of bed and went for a walk?" Then, in a voice as calm as possible, he said, "I was told that she was close to death. How is it possible that she could wake up at one in the morning and randomly decide to get out of bed and walk out?"

"She didn't," Dr. Chopra replied.

"Excuse me?"

"There was nothing random about this event. Your mother had *planned* to leave. Her actions were clearly pre-meditated," the doctor responded.

"That's ridiculous. My mother was in your care! She is in no fit state to plan and execute her escape like some incarcerated inmate!" Asher's voice was now at full volume. "Why in God's name would she do that?!"

"Mr. Mirza, I know how stressful this must be for you, but I must ask that you lower your voice. As the managing director of this facility, I not only completely understand your concern, but share it. The facts are as they have been shown on the CCTV. Your mother had a dress, along with a coat and hat, hanging in the closet in her room. That is unusual, as they are generally in a locked central closet in the hallway. She had a suitcase under the bed, which somehow—and I am investigating this—went unnoticed by her attending nurses. She pulled something from under her mattress. I am guessing it was food of some sort that she must have put there from an earlier serving. Finally, she not only had a pass keycard, but knew exactly which door it would open."

"I know what you are doing, here, Dr. Chopra."

"What do you mean?"

"You think that if you can prove that my mother acted in a premeditated fashion, it will somehow absolve this institution of negligence and malpractice." Asher hissed the endings of *negligence* and *malpractice*, as a snake would hiss toward its prey.

"That is untrue; I merely referenced her premeditation in the hope that you might have some idea where she might have planned to go. Is there somewhere or someone she would want to visit badly enough to make her take such risky action?"

"What are you talking about?!" Asher barked back. "My mother is nuts ... OK, let me rephrase that: she is mentally ill. She can't remember who I am, let alone hold a memory of a place or person she longs to visit!"

Dr. Chopra pushed her reading glasses up the bridge of her round nose until the rims rested upon her plump cheeks. She opened a file that lay before her on the desk, took a moment to read from it, then peered above the lenses at Asher.

"Your mother's condition is extremely complicated, which makes her activity difficult to predict," she said. "As you have been told, your mother suffers from frontal variant frontotemporal dementia, known as fvFTD. The condition is quite rare. It causes behavioural anomalies that, as I have just told you, are difficult to predict. But sadly, as you also know, she has a tumour lodged deep within her brain that is interacting with the frontal lobe degeneration. We have seen her swing from periods of relative lucidity to what seems to be complete fantasy. Lena lapses into a delusional realm, and I believe they cause her to do these impulsive if seemingly impossible things." Dr. Chopra paused, her eyes locked on Asher.

"Mr. Mirza," she spoke again, this time more softly, "you need to know that it will not be the fvFTD that will cause her death; it will be the tumour, and based upon her latest CATSCAN, which I have here, she does not have very long. There is a chance that when we find her, and we will, she may be —"

Asher put up his hand and stopped her from saying the next words. He shook his head and blinked away tears. For a moment, he said nothing, looking at the peeling paint on the muntin of the paned window still coated with winter's grit. The window diffused the beam of morning sunlight spotlighting the coffee stains on the tattered carpet.

"She was brilliant, you know. She would have been one of the world's most preeminent historians if she hadn't been seduced from her academic calling."

"I understand that she has been published," Dr. Chopra said softly.

"Five books on the great civilizations of Persia. The greatest civilizations that ever ruled, yet rarely studied or emulated since the rise of the Judeo-Christian farce upon which our modern Western world is based; to the detriment of all of us, I will add." He spoke with melancholy, but his words were acrid.

"I am very sorry," Dr. Chopra sincerely offered.

Asher stood up. "Yeah, well, sorry doesn't cut it, doc. Nothing you have said has answered any of my questions. I know what my mother's condition is; I know she is dying." He put on his coat, his damp eyes glaring. "I just didn't think that she would take her last breath alone, lying in some ditch."

When he reached the door, he turned to Chopra.

"Expect to hear from my lawyer!"

3.

"Nice to meet you, Kenneth," she said, taking her hand away from him. "I am afraid that I cannot let you take my luggage. It stays with me, but by all means, lead the way; I really am quite hungry for that sandwich."

She walked a few paces behind Kenneth, silently repeating his name so as not to forget it. He urged her to follow him along a narrow path of uneven paving stones, so she had to be particularly mindful of each step.

Her torn, blistered heels had started to bleed again, but she refused the pain and dutifully followed, looking down at each footfall until they reached a wooden gate. She lifted her head and gasped as her eyes sharpened to a fleeting moment of focus and clarity.

There before her, beyond the sun-silvered cedar gate, was an emerald field, lush with green grass, all dotted with tiny pink, white, and yellow daisies. Rising toward the light blue sky, cedar centurions grew tall, armoured in green tunics and spaced in a formation, guarding a castle-like house built high off the ground. Some distance beyond the house, a forest phalanx of fir, hemlock, and spruce stood at attention. She placed her hand on Ken's shoulder.

"Behold the high tops of the cedar, the entrance to the wood," she said, excitement now coursing through her as though it were a tonic that might bring her immortality. "Where Humbaba goes in on lofty tread. The ways are straight, and the path is wrought fair. See the cedar mount, the dwellings of gods, the sanctuary of the Imini." Pointing as she spoke, in awe of what she saw, she paused a moment before tugging upon Ken's rolled-up sleeve.

"Before the hill stands the cedar, abundant and tall. Her good shadow is full of rejoicing. It covers the thornbush, covers the dark-hued slope. And beneath the cedar, the sweet-smelling plants." The words flowed from her, her eyes wide and her mind swirling as the images faded back into the grey shapes with which she had become so familiar. "Sanctuary!" She repeated, "Yes, Sanctuary!"

She sucked in the air, inhaling the sweet scent of jasmine, which cleansed her nostrils of the lemon-scented Lysol. The rush of full freshness cleared her sinuses, which had been plugged by the dander of death she had inhaled every day in that place where the aged awaited their moment of eternal silence.

She turned and faced the man who called himself Kenneth, desperately trying to refocus her eyes. Somewhere in the deep recesses of her mind, his name evoked an odd comfort, like a faded memory—perhaps of someone she once knew.

She gently beat the palm of her hand against her forehead as if to shake the memory loose, and she was struck by an exciting thought. *Could he be … ? Of course, it makes sense now that he wouldn't share his real name—but is he not dead?*

Confusion, that all-too-familiar incoming tide, flooded and muddled her exhausted mind and prevented her from asking the man his true identity. It was as if she were under the crashing waves, her world swirling, everything in motion. She felt herself starting to fall until the man's strong arms wrapped around her, and her feet, worn raw from her journey, left the ground.

***

Ken couldn't believe his eyes. The fact that his ex-wife, Lena, who he had known to be in palliative care, was standing alone at his farm gate was shocking enough, but her emaciated appearance alarmed him—as did the anger he felt at seeing her outside his gate.

For a fleeting moment, he actually considered turning her away, but the guilt of thinking such a thought prevailed, and he introduced himself, then extended his hand to carry her tattered suitcase. His heart sank when she introduced herself as Gilgamesh, and refused to give it to him.

Seriously? He shook his head lightly, so as not to be noticed. *Gilgamesh.* He had heard the name many times before, when Lena had been researching the epic Persian poem, but that seemed like a lifetime ago.

Obviously, he had to let her through the gate—and judging by her condition, he needed to get her to the house. He studied her, trying to determine if she had the strength to walk up, or if he should have her wait while he went to get the pickup truck.

A wave of sadness washed over him as he pushed Toby's paws off the railing and commanded that he stay down. It would be in his best interests to just play along. *Gilgamesh, then—let's go with that. God, she's so thin and frail.*

Ken took the path that led to the rear of the barn and a narrow gate that opened into a large field. He turned to see Lena trying to navigate the uneven flagstone path. *I really should run up and get the truck and drive her to the house.* He was just about to suggest doing so when he felt her hand on his shoulder, and she broke into verse.

"Behold the high tops of the cedar, the entrance to the wood, where Humbaba goes in on lofty tread. The ways are straight, and the path is wrought fair. See the cedar mount, the dwellings of gods, the sanctuary of the Imini."

He knew she was quoting the poem; a shot of adrenalin pumped through him when he saw her eyes widen and heard her tone become more elevated. This behaviour had become too familiar to him, quoting from the poem, then snapping into a rage, clenching her fists, and pounding on his body.

She pulled on his shirt sleeve, and he braced for the blows that he felt sure would follow, but none came. Instead, she paused. Her pallid cheeks blushed pink, and she gazed at the field before her, and he looked along with her.

"Before the hill stands the cedar, abundant and tall. Her good shadow is full of rejoicing." As Lena continued to recite the poem with a sing-song rhythm, Ken looked at the cedars growing at the top of the green field, shadowing the white-flowered, wild blackberry that seemed to rejoice at spring's return.

"Sanctuary!" She repeated, "Yes, Sanctuary!"

He didn't take issue with her calling the farm a sanctuary. That's without a doubt what it had become. A place where he could shut out the madness of the world. Where, except for his dreams at night, he could leave unpleasant memories packed and stored away, where he might be safe from the pandemic that was humanity.

She startled him by suddenly turning to stare at him. Was that recognition? He wasn't sure, and the uncertainty put him on guard for what might come next. But then he saw her legs wobble, the momentary blush of colour fade from her face, and her eyes turn upward, and he caught her before she fell.

***

Layers of mist fogged all rational thought, leaving her unable to determine if she was up or down, and she melted into the strong arms that prevented her fall. The name that had caused her excitement was *Enkidu*. She tried to shake it away, because Enkidu was dead, fallen into the underworld—perhaps at the hand of the gods, for his role in slaying the monster Humbaba.

There were those who blamed her for sending him after fallen sticks, and she groaned in response to the internal pain. It was so unfair to be wrongfully accused. Maybe this man who smelled like an animal was Enkidu—and if so, then perhaps … but as hard as she tried to focus on the images, the lines were all blurred.

She had seen the gate, and she had seen the forest, and she was determined that she would not suffer Enkidu's fate. Her mission to find the secret of immortality depended on it. She would triumph, no matter if she was called to use trick or trump; it didn't really matter. She would defeat the hand of death.

Her body felt fully supported, but she was not on her feet. Where, then? She felt the rhythm of a gentle rocking from one side to the other, and concluded that she must be on the boat. But where was the boatman?

She struggled to find focus, but her inability to do so only served to heighten her anxiety. The sharp, striking pain within her brain was becoming more frequent, and with each strike, the less clear matters became.

An end to her need to cry out came when she felt herself gently fall onto a receptive, soft landing, and her head came to rest upon a soft pillow, and she felt warmed by a heavy blanket that wrapped her in a calm embrace. She sighed, feeling relief from her aching fatigue, and the pain in her head subsided as sleep gently turned off her mind.

***

The moment that Ken saw her eyes turn upward, he knew that she would faint. He caught her fall and looked to see where he might let her rest. Despite her heavy coat, his fingers could feel her ribs, and when he lifted her, he was shocked at how light she was. There had been a time when her full and curved figure had made carrying her challenging—but not now.

Ken looked up toward the house, trying to judge how hard it might be to carry her all the way without having to put her down. "You're so thin and frail," he said to her, knowing that she couldn't hear a word. *Come on, then—let's get you to the house and off those feet.*

When he lifted her, the pungent odour of shit-soiled clothing made him gag. He would have to deal with that as soon as he had her safely in the house. But, as bad as that smell was, it was the sickly scent from the perfume off the back of Death's hand that concerned him. He knew the stink all too well—the marinade used on all animals in preparation for Death's arrival.

Holding her close to him, he carried her toward the house as she rested, semiconscious and crying out in anguish, in his muscular arms. There had been a time when the two had walked this path hand in hand, happy as they crossed the green field and passed beneath the tall cedars that crested the gentle slope, serenaded by cedar waxwings and yellow warblers.

But not all were happy memories, and many times in the last few years, he had walked the same path as though cast in the role of Giselle, in some twisted version of the ballet—only in his version he, not she, had been driven mad by the unmasking of the woman he had fallen in love with, seeing for the first time she was no longer who he thought she had been.

As he carried her to the house, he recalled that fateful evening when, walking the very same path, he had tried to hold her hand, but she pulled it away, and her once warm, loving eyes had turned cold and distant.

He looked down at Lena, curled in his arms, and a sadness swept over him. This was the woman with whom he had made a life—the joyful highs and the hurtful lows, along with every emotion in between.

Reaching the house, he struggled to climb the steps up to the timbered entryway, unlatch the tall front door, and get Lena inside, where the warmth from the embers left from the last evening's wood fire and the lingering smell of warm, early morning coffee on the top of the airtight stove seemed to alert her senses. Her eyes opened for a moment as Ken carried her along the wainscoted hall and into the guest bedroom. As gently as he could, he laid her on the bed, then removed her hat, coat, and shoes.

"I'm going to clean you up and treat those blisters," he said, noticing how her head melted into the soft goose down pillow and her eyes closed once again as sleep carried her away.

In the mudroom at the rear of the house, Ken took a 3M Coban wrap used to bind the legs of injured sheep and a jar of zinc oxide from a wall-mounted cabinet. He placed a bar of lye soap into a bowl and ran warm water over it, creating a bubbly broth of soapy water. With hands washed thoroughly, he dried them and pulled on a pair of disposable latex medical examination gloves from a box kept in the same cabinet marked "Sheep Medications."

Armed with his jar of zinc oxide, a bowl of warm water, and a facecloth, he went to Lena, whom he judged, from the rhythm of her breathing, had found peace in sleep. He administered to her feet before turning his attention to the source of the fetid fecal stench.

God almighty, this is disgusting. He peeled the diaper away from her crepe-paper-like skin and saw new and wet defecation layered upon old. *Clearly, it's been a while since this has been changed.*

Ken took a thick, large bath towel from a closet in the adjoining bathroom, and returned to the bed. Then, he gently lifted her legs and slipped the towel under her. Softly, he cleaned her, trying not to further enrage the angry bedsores that lined her lower back, inner thigh, and buttocks.

"You need to be properly bathed," he said to his sleeping patient, "but in lieu of a bath, this will have to do." Ken unhooked a long terrycloth robe from his closet and laid it out on the bed next to Lena. As gently as possible, he removed her dress and the backless medical gown over which the dress had been worn.

So much bruising—what the fuck? This is deplorable. He looked at strips of finger-width bruises on her upper arms and shoulders. Then he examined the fiery intertrigo on her body, and he could feel his anger. Her skin was raw beneath her armpits, and within the folded creases of her beasts.

Washed and patted dry to prevent bleeding, Ken applied zinc oxide and some coconut oil to Lena's skin, hoping that would bring her some relief. He had nothing like the adult diaper she had worn, so he wrapped her groin with a towel, pinning it as he would an infant's cloth diaper.

He looked down at Lena's thin body and brushed away a tear that had welled up in his eye. "You are going to need something to eat," he said, although he knew she was deaf to his comment. *I'll thaw the rest of that homemade soup.*

He lifted her onto the robe, slipped her arms into the sleeves, wrapped the robe snugly around her, and looked at the woman who had for so many years been his partner, lover, and best friend. *Life can be pretty strange*, he thought as he stroked Lena's hair. *You're safe now.*

He covered her with a down comforter before heading to the kitchen, where he removed leftover vegetable soup frozen in a yogurt container from the freezer. It wouldn't take long to thaw and be heated on the stovetop, and he was quite sure that, in her condition, it would be more satisfactory than the squished egg salad sandwich he had taken from the pocket of her coat.

4.

Ken felt quite exhausted from the morning events, and the smell of warm coffee reminded him that he had only managed a half cup before he had sensed he needed to check on the pregnant ewe in the barn. He walked over to the pot on the stove and poured himself a cup, then headed toward the leather armchair that furnished the sitting area in the open-concept kitchen, dining room, and living room.

He had furnished the sitting area with his favourite leather armchair and matching couch, both draped with tanned sheep skins. Every wall had a built-in bookcase filled with an eclectic range of books, making it appear more like a library than a conventional living room.

He dropped into the welcoming armchair and glanced at the large, antique clock on the wall—8:30—then checked his phone.

This has been a morning of the unexpected, unwanted, and bizarre. He sipped his coffee and flipped to his email inbox. The email he had received from an old Oxford colleague, Julius Omondi, had definitely been unexpected. And having to assist number 8, Red, a veteran ewe, to deliver her lamb had certainly been an unwanted event. He took another sip of the warm, rich, dark roast and shook his head. But Lena had been standing at his farm gate, and that was bizarre.

In his seventy-sixth year, Ken found the routine of the farm a necessary part of his life. It gave him reason to rise in the morning, with a mostly predictable set of challenges he would face during his day, which then led to a certain serenity each evening. A solitary existence, to be sure, but he had long ago convinced himself that he would never admit that being alone was the same as being lonely.

But this Saturday had not been routine.

Ken held tightly onto the warm mug and took a deep breath, setting his mind to the upcoming call with Julius. Seeing an email from Julius Omondi at six that morning, when he routinely checked his email, had shaken him. He hadn't heard from his former Oxford University colleague for over twenty years, and when he read the urgency of Julius's request for a Zoom meeting, it brought back old and well-boxed-up memories that he would rather not unpack.

Thinking of the eight-hour time difference between them, he set the time for 1 p.m. PST, hoping that 8 p.m. in London might prompt Julius to set a time the following day. A time that Ken had no real intention of accepting. Instead, Julius had immediately responded with a link for Ken to connect to.

His cup now empty, he rose from his chair, walked over to the stove for the last refill, and wondered how long Lena would sleep. What the hell was he to do now? Lena had not been well cared for, that much was obvious. Still, it didn't take much for him to admit to himself that he was not equipped to give her the care that she would require.

Filling his cup, he tried to remember exactly what Dr. Jessica Gunn, one of the attending doctors at the palliative care centre, had told him about her condition.

She had some kind of dementia that was not Alzheimer's. But there was more to it. Something that had more to do with the frontal lobe. He remembered it had a long name, so he picked up his phone and Googled "dementia affecting the frontal lobe," and immediately found it.

Frontal variant frontotemporal dementia was what he had been told Lena suffered from, though he couldn't really recall the details, as he had become more intrigued with Jessica Gunn than what she had been telling him.

He searched the options that Google provided, avoiding those that had "promoted" below the heading, until he came across a research paper on frontal variant dementia authored by a group of doctors who had received the Brain Prize two years earlier. Feeling confident that he could trust the source, he started to read it and refresh his mind on the details of Lena's disorder.

Midway through the paper, the ringtone on his phone played the opening guitar riffs from "Bad Moon Rising." It was the ringtone he had assigned to his daughter, Sheena.

"Hi, sweetie."

"Hi Dad, how are things?"

"Everything is fine, thanks," Ken replied in a measured tone, looking down at his right hand, where the redness was turning into a dark grey bruise. "Number 8 Red Tag had a large female; I had to assist her with delivery." He refused to name the sheep for two reasons: first, he didn't like to eat anything he had named, and second, he likely wouldn't remember all of the names anyway. "Both are doing well, but it was a good thing that there was only one. The lamb was breached, so it was a difficult birth."

"I am pretty sure you are getting too old for that kind of stuff, Dad," Sheena said—and then, before he could respond, she added, "I really worry about you out there all on your own. What if something happens … ?"

Ken chuckled. He knew exactly how this conversation was going to go—the same way it always did. "You and Ethan have a standing invitation to move onto the farm and take on some of the load. There's lots of room in the house."

"Ethan is only five years old; he is hardly going to be delivering lambs. Besides, we have been through all this before."

We certainly have! He kept his thought to himself, and said, "You brought it up."

"Anyway, it's roast chicken dinner today, complete with stuffing, Greek potatoes, and brussels sprouts—your favourite. I'll pick you up around 4:30, right after you have finished the day's chores and will have you home by 7, promise."

Right, well, that wasn't going to happen today—not with his unexpected guest, whom he decided would remain his secret, at least for now. Besides, he did have a legitimate excuse. "Sounds delicious—and my favourite meal, for sure—but no can do this week, kiddo. I am sorry; I should have mentioned that Janis is delivering a truckload of hay this afternoon. We likely won't finish stacking much before six."

"Oh well, don't let me get in the way of your time with Janis!" Sheena said, her voice lilting so as to leave no doubt as to her inference, which made Ken sigh.

"She is bringing some hay, Sheena."

"Hey," Sheena played on the word to punch the pun, "I am happy she spends so much time out there. You know, I bet if you made the offer, *she* would move onto the farm in a heartbeat."

"I think you have the wrong idea about Janis."

"Really? She is single, a few years younger than you, loves farming and animals … and I have seen the way she looks at you, Dad."

"Janis has a farm of her own—and anyway, if I were interested, which I am not, I am pretty sure I play for the wrong team, Sheena."

"I guess it will just be Ethan and me enjoying that chicken dinner."

"Sorry about that; I didn't remember our Saturday night dinner date when Janis and I made the delivery arrangements."

"Well, don't overdo it. Those bales are heavy. By the way," Sheena said with a hint of apprehension in her tone, "I've had four missed calls from Asher this morning. I don't like to speculate, but I have a sinking feeling he is calling to tell me that Mom has passed. Have you heard—"

Ken abruptly interrupted his daughter. *Talk about burying the lead!* "I haven't talked to Asher in a very long time, and, as you know, I would be the last person he'd call."

"To be honest, I am in no rush to return his call; there is always so much drama with him. He's always so angry about everything. He is so rude to me, even though we have the same mother."

"And Sheena, you know the reason for his anger. He believes that your mother's pregnancy with you was the reason she left his father to be with me. He is wrong, but there is no dissuading him from that point of view." Ken sighed.

"I will call him this afternoon, and if it's what I suspect, I will of course tell you. But if it is that, I would much rather tell you in person."

When she had been young, Sheena had had a very strong bond with her mother. But that hadn't lasted through Sheena's teenage years, despite great efforts by Lena to stay close to her daughter. When Sheena wrote from university that she was pregnant with Ethan and had no intention of marrying the child's father, that had been, for Lena, a step too far.

The fact that her mother had such a negative reaction to Sheena's choice to raise a child as a single mother was, from Sheena's point of view, in complete contradiction with her mother's vocal activism for the emancipation of women.

Her mother had flown east, to Sheena's university, to meet with her to discuss the situation. But that meeting resulted in a terrible fight, where Sheena had accused her mother of being a hypocrite, still caught in the inflexible cultural web of tradition that had been woven by her Persian grandfather, a man she had never met, except through her mother's idolatry toward him.

Ken knew exactly why Asher had been calling. He never communicated with either of them, unless to launch some grievance. And it didn't surprise Ken that Asher had chosen to call Sheena and not him.

Ken was quite sure that, as the holder of Lena's legal guardianship papers, the centre had contacted him and told him that his mother had gone missing. Ken held no doubt that Asher, in true passive-aggressive fashion, somehow would first lay the blame at his feet and then start a lawsuit against the hospice.

A distant warning bark from within the main field pulled Ken's attention away from the conversation. *Now what?* The day had been eventful enough.

"I would appreciate you calling me back after you have spoken with him," Ken said. He had not felt entirely comfortable with his decision to say nothing about her mother's presence in his home.

"If Mom has passed …" Sheena paused. "I doubt that Asher will want you involved in any way. How will you manage that?"

"I think you're getting ahead of yourself, Sheena," Ken said—but his focus was on the white Ford Bronco he could see through the window, making its way slowly up the driveway toward the house.

He recognized the signature blue, red, and yellow stripes of the RCMP along the side of the vehicle. Was it possible that they knew that

Lena was there? No. It was more likely that they were out looking for her and, given his relationship with Lena, sent an officer to the house to determine if he knew she was missing and, if so, whether he had advice as to where they might find her. *Time to end the call.* "Let's talk after your call with Asher."

"Sure, if you say so, Dad. Take care. I love you. Talk soon."

5.

Ken knew most of the local RCMP, and got along with them by keeping to himself on the farm and minding his own business. The recent proliferation of commercial marijuana growing on a number of neighbouring farms had increased the amount of traffic on the otherwise isolated road that passed the farm, and with it came the much more frequent presence of the RCMP, who kept a close eye on the goings-on.

Not wanting this officer, whoever he was, to come into the house, he went outside and saw that Toby, his tail wagging, was getting his head rubbed by the uniformed officer.

"Hello Alice—er, I should say, Constable." Ken greeted the female officer. "I understand that congratulations are in order now that you have graduated from the rank of cadet."

"Hiya, Ken. Yeah, I am pretty proud."

"No doubt. I read in the paper that you get to stay in your community—are you happy about that?"

"I am posted near my nation during my probationary period. Get to police the reserve quite a bit. It's what I wanted, but it turns out it's not really ideal."

"No?"

"On reserve, I am still 'Alice Joe' to my elders, who remind me of my life as a kid anytime I try to exercise authority. And quite a few of my friends kinda shun me because I am no longer one of them. They call me 'Alice Joe the cop'—and not in a good way."

"What brings you here?" Ken thought it best to let Alice tell him why she had made the trip out to the farm.

"Your ex, Lena," Alice said, looking intently at Ken, and offering him nothing more.

"OK, what about Lena?"

"There is a silver alert issued. It seems she walked out of where they were keeping her." Alice spoke slowly, not removing her eyes from his. "Wondered if you might have seen her?"

Ken tried not to flinch when the question was directly put to him. There was something about the way that Alice asked the question that made him think that she knew Lena was inside the house. But if she did know, why the charade? What should he tell her?

Ken was not a good or well-practised liar. In fact, being lied to was a huge deal for him. He detested being lied to for a host of legitimate reasons, not the least of which was the deep hurt he had experienced when he had discovered that Lena, the one person he had always trusted to be truthful, had deceived him.

For Ken, honesty was more than a virtue; it was the only path to open and productive dialogue. And yet he didn't want to tell Alice that Lena was in the house. Well, *Gilgamesh* was in the house. So it was a soft lie, and he swallowed hard.

"This farm is a long way from the care home. As I understand it, she is quite sick. That's a long way for her to walk."

Alice Joe kept her eyes focused on Ken. "Yup, a long way and I understand she is very sick. Making her last journey before she crosses over, I suspect."

"What makes you think she would come here?"

Alice looked at Toby, who sat obediently at her feet, and she rubbed his chin. She looked back up toward Ken, then turned her eyes toward the sky, where a number of mature eagles rode the updraft thermals in a circular glide. "You don't often see that," Alice said.

"Eagles are special birds," Ken replied, looking up and counting the aerial merry-go-round of eagles silently circling above them. "Five of them," he said.

"Odd," Alice replied.

"You mean the number?"

"The eagle is the wisest of all birds, and has a special and direct connection to the Creator," Alice said. "They mate for life and are a symbol of lasting love and dedication. You don't usually see them in odd numbers when they soar before the Creator, like they are doin'. One of the mates is missing—or maybe just hidin'."

Her words unnerved him. "I can tell you, Alice … I mean, Constable Joe, Lena Murshid, as we both knew her, is not here."

Alice didn't move, just looked intently at him.

What the hell is she thinking? Ken stood his ground. Seconds seemed like minutes.

"Alright then," she said, turning and walking back to the police car, where she stood motionless for a moment.

She doesn't believe me. Ken watched the police constable open the rear passenger door and take out a suitcase from the rear seat.

"I figured you might have been down at your barn when I first drove up, so I looked for you there. I found this suitcase by the gate behind it. You must have left it there by mistake, hey?"

She walked the suitcase over to Ken and put it at his feet. "I thought I would bring it up and save you the trouble of going down for it. You can't be too careful these days, especially with all these weed farms popping up all over." She tilted back her chubby face, eyes looking to the sky. "You never know who might show up at your gate."

Ken glanced up. A sixth bird had joined the circling eagles.

"Six, Ken. One was hiding, just like I thought," Constable Alice Joe said.

She walked to her car, climbed in, and drove down the driveway and away from the farm.

6.

"Dad! I called Asher back!" Sheena sounded out of breath. "Mom is missing from the care home. They have put out a silver alert!"

"Slow down," Ken replied, hearing Sheena's rapid breathing.

"Asher is wild! He claims that Mom was permitted to just walk out of the facility in the middle of the night. He told me they had CCTV footage that showed her getting dressed and walking out. He has already contacted his lawyer. It sounds like he plans to sue the centre."

"Calm down, Sheena."

"Dad, I am really scared! Mom will die out there."

"Your Mom is here. She is safe. And as for Asher, that is typical. Get a lawyer hired and go for the jugular first; look for his mother second." Ken replied.

"Wait, what? Mom is with you?"

"Your mother is resting. She's fine."

"What?! How?!" Sheena's incredulity resonated.

"Right now, it doesn't really matter how she got here, just that she is safe and resting. I am sorry, but I have to get off the phone or I will be late to get onto a Zoom call."

"I'm coming over, Dad."

Ken heard the rising panic in his daughter's voice, and knew only too well where that would lead. "Please don't. Everything is under control. I told you so that you wouldn't worry or go looking for her, but I must insist that you not tell Asher just yet. Can we keep this between us for the time being? Let's see how things are in the morning, OK?"

"Seriously? In the morning, Dad? We are talking about my mother. Why and how did she get there? Did you go pick her up? She is sick, Dad. Does she even know where she is? Does she know who you are?"

"No, I didn't go and pick her up. I know that she's sick, and you know from your visits with her at the care home what her mental state is. I will give you a call in the morning. I think it might be good for you and Ethan to visit then."

"Does the care home know she is there? Does Jessica know?"

Ken took a breath. The mention of Jessica gave him an idea. Would Jessica Gunn help him? He really wasn't sure how things were between them, given the way things had ended the last evening he and Jessica had been together. Still, she was a doctor—and who better to see to Lena's needs than a palliative care physician who had treated her and knew her file?

"They will; I will give them a call. Now, I really must get onto this Zoom call. Do *not* worry, OK? I love you lots, and give Ethan a big hug from Granddad." Ken ended the call with his daughter.

He walked down the hall and quietly opened the door to the small bedroom where he had put Lena to bed. Satisfied that she was fast asleep, he closed the door, stepped across the hall into his office, and sat at his wide oak desk. The fragrance from the bloom on a tall, potted Mandarin, bathed in a column of sunlight that streamed through the tall floor-to-ceiling windows, filled the room.

A prompt flashed on his desktop screen. Julius Omondi had invited him to join the meeting. He accepted. The familiar, chubby, joyful face of his former colleague, who was much older than Ken had remembered, appeared on his screen. Despite the thinning grey hair, the sparkle in his eyes and toothy trademark Omondi smile were unchanged.

"Kenny, my friend. It is good to see you," Julius said, his rich, throaty voice loud over the computer's tiny speakers.

"Oh my God, Julius, you are an old man," Ken chuckled, then, thinking better of his comment, added, "but handsome as ever."

"Ha, you are too kind. I was not at all sure you would accept my invitation. How are you?"

"I am keeping well, thanks. How many years—?"

"Twenty-six," Julius responded before Ken could finish his sentence. "But, in some respects, it feels just like yesterday."

"And I hear that you are now a retired gentleman of letters," Ken said.

"Professor Emeritus, actually," Julius said, and roared with laughter. "It was a way for me to keep an office here at Oxford."

"I see, you have risen to éminence grise at Oxford University—well, bravo to that!"

"I do keep my hand in academics by reading for a few PhD and post-doctoral students. That's actually how I came to track you down," Julius said. "I have a postdoctoral student, Rehema Tanui. She is quite brilliant, and like me, is Kenyan-born—which is likely at the root of her brilliance," Omondi said, with a chuckle and a wink.

"I don't doubt it for a moment," Ken responded. "But what does this student have to do with me?"

"She is fixated on your work, Kenny. She has read everything you have ever written in the field of demography and global development, and has become especially attached to the paper you presented at the '94 Cairo conference," Julius said.

Julius's mention of the Cairo conference made Ken sit back in his chair. An uneasy feeling as to where this conversation was heading began to form.

"I am surprised she was able to source a copy," Ken said, trying to hide his bitterness. "I hope that you have advised her against pursuing it, and have directed her to a more promising career path."

"On the contrary, my good friend," Julius replied. "Contrary to what you might think, given the controversy that surrounded your work, your publications are not only available in the library but have recently been digitized."

This news came as a shock to Ken. He had long believed that his research and subsequent publications on the serious consequences associated with unmeasured population growth had been relegated to the conspiracy trash can.

"It seems that in electronic format, your work has become quite popular," Julius continued. "And that isn't surprising when so many of the predictions made as a result of using your algorithm seem to have come true."

"Because it analyzed sound primary assumptions and not political wishful thinking, hidden state agendas, and outright hypocrisy," Ken said abruptly.

"When Rehema approached me, wanting to use your algorithm for her post-doctoral work, I spent some time re-reading your work. You have been seriously misjudged," said Julius.

Kenneth's anger was palpable. "I don't recall hearing your voice in my defence when I first presented my research!" He hoped his smile would hide his bitterness. "What has brought you to this epiphany now?"

The African man took off his glasses and rubbed his eyes before returning them to his wide, flat nose. "Fair comment, Kenny; I'm sorry. I wasn't there for you at the time. Your work was so controversial, and to be honest, I was too focused on my own rise up the academic ladder to risk supporting your work," he said. "But I didn't ask for this call to beg your forgiveness—though I would like it."

"So why did you ask me for this call, Julius?"

"Rehema has a brilliant mind, Kenny. She would give you a run for your money!" said Julius, his eyes wide. "So many of the predictions made in your research have happened, from climate change to global viral pandemics to the looming shift toward a radical change in the global order of things." Julius paused and leaned toward his screen as though trying to get closer. "Rehema saw the value of your work immediately. Not because you wrote it all down almost twenty years ago, but because it provides a blueprint for global populations to retain some measure of coexistence and not destroy the planet. That blueprint is the foundation of her thesis, Ken."

"The global power base and influencers don't want to hear it, Julius. Their faces may have changed in the last twenty years, but their agenda has hardened. They made sure that I became a pariah in academia and the brunt of endless jokes. I was treated as a racist." Ken took a breath and resisted the almost overwhelming urge to terminate the call. "My own colleagues challenged my research methodology and called me a fraud. I lost my tenure at Oxford, and the Internet, which you say has provided a platform for my work to be resurrected, has defined me as an eccentric nutcase. I couldn't even get a position at a community college, let alone become, as you have, a professor emeritus. Go ahead, Google me, and see for yourself."

"I have. Or more correctly, both Rehema and I have read it all, my friend," said Julius. "I can only imagine how hard that must be for you. But here is a chance for your work to be revisited and vindicated. Properly republished, it will take on a new and important role in finding solutions to this global crisis."

"Julius, look around you. You and I are in a generation that nobody listens to."

"True, our youth is often too quick to dismiss their elders—and along with them, the wisdom they have to offer." Julius sighed.

"I think you missed the memo, Julius. We are to blame for all the ills of this world. Well—perhaps not you, my handsome black friend, but certainly this white-skinned colonial is, along with the rest of his kind." Ken laughed at his own comment. "The only other sin, beyond my whiteness, would be if I were filthy rich."

For a moment, neither spoke. It seemed to Ken like they were in a game of chess, and Julius was considering his next move.

"Kenneth, don't you see? You predicted the rise of the racial divide. Where others painted a racially homogenized future, you were the one who, at the 1994 Cairo conference, spoke about the new tribalism. You coined the phrase 'identity politics,' and you were the first to warn how it would threaten constitutional authorities all over the world; and you were right." Julius leaned back in his chair. "That is exactly why I am asking you to give permission for Rehema to dust off your work and shine some light on your conclusions. Will you grant her an interview?"

Ken squirmed in his chair. On the surface, it wasn't an unreasonable request. He pushed his fingers through his hair. "It's a bit late for that now, Julius."

"On the contrary," said Julius. "This is exactly the time that your work and predicted outcomes need to be examined. By understanding root causes, we might actually be able to institute real solutions and prevent a century of civil conflict."

Checkmate!

One Weekend in May

Ken couldn't argue the point because, fundamentally, he knew that Julius was right. He had no move to make, though he felt apprehension about agreeing to meet this student. "Have your student contact me, and I will at least grant her an interview. But I am only doing this for you, Julius. I need to go now."

"May we speak again soon?" asked Julius. "It has been wonderful to reconnect."

"Yes, sure. Let's do that."

Ken hit the end button and stared at the blank, black screen. The call had churned up old memories—and not good ones. More pressing on his mind was the phone call to make to Dr. Chopra. And before he did so, he wanted to check on Lena.

Quietly opening the bedroom door, he stepped into the room. Lena was exactly as he had left her. A shiver coursed through him before he noticed the gentle rise and fall of the terrycloth robe, which confirmed that she was still with him. He walked to the side of the bed and gently stroked her hair, pushing down the memories of much happier times.

"I have to go and let them know you are here," he whispered. "But don't worry, you are safe."

7.

"This is Dr. Chopra." The rhythmic lilt and extended vowels made that clear.

"Hello, Dr. Chopra. This is Kenneth Graham."

"Ah, Mr. Graham, it is good to talk with you. I have been expecting your call."

Her comment caught Ken off guard.

"Excuse me … ?"

"I had a call from Alice," Sonja Chopra broke in. "I am aware that Lena is with you. I was hoping that you would call to discuss her return. Alice was not sure if you would make the call or what your intentions might be in this matter."

"I was calling to let you know that she is safe and that the search can be stopped. I think that she needs to be here." Ken used a polite but stern voice. He was quite unsure how this was going to go, and knew that Chopra was a no-nonsense woman who would likely reject any thought that Lena should not return to the care of her facility.

"Mr. Graham, that is both impractical and impossible. Ms. Murshid is a patient here. She was admitted by her son, who is also her legal guardian. Beyond the legal ramifications, your request is quite impractical. Lena is an extremely sick woman who requires specialized care." Dr. Chopra spoke with a measured tone, causing Ken to stiffen his resolve. This wasn't going to be an easy conversation.

"Let's discuss those legal ramifications, Dr. Chopra. I am aware that Asher has already engaged legal counsel and will sue your facility for a large sum of money. He is like a dog with a bone when he sets his mind to doing something. I am sure you would like to avoid such a lawsuit."

"How will letting his mother stay with her ex-husband, his stepfather—who, I gather from past conversations, is not his most favourite person—do anything except aggravate an already bad situation?"

Ken thought it a legitimate—not rhetorical—question, which gave him some hope that the promise to rein in Asher might be an avenue toward a resolution.

"Why not leave that with me? But I am quite sure that I know what Asher needs to have him drop any thought of legal action."

"That would be helpful, but as I have said, what you are proposing is impractical on several levels. Lena is—"

"Dying." Ken fought to keep his patience and not lose his temper. "She isn't extremely sick, doctor; she is dying."

"Yes, Mr. Graham, your wife—sorry, ex-wife—is dying, and that may come faster than you think. Her latest brain scan shows that her tumour is growing quickly now, which has unpredictable outcomes. She may experience anger, with wild outbursts, in which case she will require restraints. After that, in short order, she will lose all motor functions and be bedridden. The fact that she had the strength to walk out of here and to your farm underscores how unpredictable her behaviour is. Frankly, I am astonished she was able to do so in her condition. Beyond that, we have no way of predicting what level of pain she may experience. You simply are not equipped to handle those eventualities."

"And if she was in your facility, what would you do? Sedate her? You would tie her down and give her morphine to manage the pain. I have seen the bruises caused by those restraints, Dr. Chopra. All grist for Asher if he goes forward with a lawsuit. Whatever you would do for her there, I can do for her here."

"Mr. Graham, I simply cannot allow that to happen. You do not have the training or knowledge. Far from solving a potential lawsuit, I believe your plan would more likely open this facility to an aggravated lawsuit. If your stepson thinks he has a case for willful neglect against this facility, your plan will more likely give him cause for a case against both you and us."

"Leave Asher to me. He can be very hotheaded, but I think I can get him to see reason," Ken replied, although he was not at all sure that he could actually manage his stepson.

"'Hotheaded' is your term, Mr. Graham; I would say *litigious*. He was furious at what had transpired. Beyond his concern for his mother, he apparently has had to forfeit travel to a conference, which I gather was important for his career."

"Oh, did he say as much?"

"Yes. He said he was to present a paper in astrophysics at a conference in Copenhagen but withdrew after I called to tell him his mother had only a few more days at best."

"I see." The cogs were whirling in Ken's brain. He knew Asher only too well, and presenting a paper in Copenhagen would have been a very big deal. "What if I were to have assistance?" Ken offered. "If Jessica Gunn were to oversee Lena's last days?"

There was a pause on the phone connection.

"Have you spoken with her?" Sonja asked, her tone hesitant.

"Not yet, but I expect that if I asked her to help, she would do so." It was a shot in the dark. He had no idea how Jessica Gunn would respond to such a request.

"Well, if Lena is still under medically supervised care, I suppose … but this will require the consent of her legal guardian."

"I understand that. Can you at least give me until the end of the day to try to sort this out?" Ken tried not to sound like he was pleading.

"I must hear back from you by six this evening, Mr. Graham; that is when I will have to face my board of directors. I have already spoken with Asher and told him that his mother is safe."

"Did you tell him that she was here?"

"No, I was not sure quite how to handle that matter, so I am going to rely upon you to inform him that his mother is with you and that you, not this institution, are keeping her there."

"Understood, thank you."

Ken ended the call.

8.

Asher accelerated the treadmill, pushing himself harder, faster, trying to outrun the anger in his body.

The alarm on his Garmin watch beeped a warning: 172 beats per minute. Part of him didn't care—the part that loved his mother. Gasping for breath, he yielded to the part that loved himself more, and lifting himself on the handrails, he dropped both feet on the framework, allowing the whirling belt to race between them.

He stripped off the sweat-soaked terrycloth headband and stepped off the machine.

It wasn't fair; none of this was. He hated that this was happening to him.

He should have been at the Astromeet in Copenhagen, delivering his cutting-edge paper on the sun's steady source of high-energy gamma rays, not in a sub-standard fitness room in the basement of a crappy hotel in this godforsaken, crappy little town, waiting for his mother to die. It was appallingly unfair.

He flicked the off switch and the belt slowed, unlike the thoughts in his head. *Shit, they told me she had a few days at most. That's why I came. To settle the matter. Why couldn't that have been the reason for the call? Fuck!*

The belt stopped, and Asher leaned on the handrail, drying his face and neck with the towel provided by the hotel. And if they had found her, why had Chopra been so vague about the details? He was pretty sure he knew why. *Because they are trying to protect their asses from a lawsuit, that's why.*

Riding the elevator back up to his room, he flipped through the messages on his phone. He had hoped to find a return email from Ido Schoenberg, his lawyer, but there wasn't one. *That's OK; there will be time to bring him up to speed. Ido will shred that bitch, Chopra, in court.*

The elevator doors opened. Asher had almost reached the door to his room when his cell phone rang. He glanced at the screen, and what he saw stopped him in his tracks. *Why is that fuck still in my contacts?*

"You have to be fucking kidding me," he said aloud. He needed to vent his anger, and gave the door to his hotel suite a punch before he swiped the key card. As he stepped into his room, he debated whether he should answer the call. *I might have known this fuck would be involved in this.* He swiped up on the answer tab.

"Hello, Ken," he said, and flopped into a wingback chair.

"Hello, Asher; it's been a long time since we spoke." Ken's voice sounded measured and assured, and that angered Asher even more.

"What do you want?"

He came directly to the point. This wasn't a social call.

"I want to tell you that your mother is safe, and resting here at the farm."

Asher bounced up out of the chair. "You son of a bitch! I knew she didn't just walk out of that place."

"Listen to me, Asher. I had nothing to do with her coming here. She just showed up at the farm gate this morning. I was as shocked as I am sure you were to hear that she had left the care centre."

"I don't fucking believe you. My mother is dying. She has a brain tumour the size of a tennis ball in her head, and on top of that, she has dementia. Do you expect me to believe—"?

"I don't care what you believe! That's the truth, and is the first reason I'm calling—to let you know that she is safe and as comfortable as possible here."

Asher glanced at the wall mirror. A wild-eyed man looked menacingly back, perspiration dripping from his forehead beneath curly, black hair that rose from his head like small springs. He had to get a grip, so he started to pace the room, his phone on speaker, lying flat on the palm of his right hand.

"Are you still there?" Ken asked.

"I'm here," he replied, forcing a calmer tone. "OK, so telling me my mother is with you was your first reason to call. What's the second?"

"You are her legal guardian, Asher. I need your permission to have her stay here."

Ken's directness shocked him, and he dropped back into the chair. "Is this a joke? You've got balls—I'll give you that."

"No, I am quite serious." Ken's voice remained calm. "I am not sure how much longer she has, Asher, but I believe she has chosen to be here when she passes."

"Well, that's bullshit!" His anger caught fire again. "She divorced you! Finally came to her senses and realized that she needed to be free of *you*! Yes, *you*, Ken. My mother rejected *you*. So, why would she go back to you to die? Not content that you fucked up her career, choked off her independence, and cast shade on her brilliance during life, now you want to control her death?!"

"If you don't want her to stay here"—Ken's calm voice infuriated Asher—"then please arrange to pick her up this afternoon and take her back to the centre."

Asher sat upright. He hadn't actually considered that he might be responsible for getting his mother back to the centre. "The police, surely, or someone from the centre will come for her, won't they?" It was Chopra's responsibility to go and get his mother. Surely, that's what he had been paying them for.

"Your mother is *your* responsibility, Asher. You are her legal guardian. You insisted that you and you alone fulfill that role, remember? Besides, I have already spoken with Dr. Chopra and suggested that your mother remain here—with some medical help, obviously. Under the circumstances, I thought you might not want her to go back."

"Why would you think that?"

"You're a pretty smart guy, Asher. Dr. Chopra told me that you have contacted a lawyer and are planning to sue the centre for negligence and possible abuse. I thought that if you really believe there has been negligence and abuse, it would look pretty odd to a judge if, having a suitable alternative, you insisted she go back to the very place you are suing for neglect. But obviously I was wrong."

Asher's hand scrubbed his forehead, trying to stop his whirling mind. Part of him was outraged at the very thought of his mother being back at the farm, but Ken had a point. How would that look in court? How could he explain that he would rather have his mother returned to the place he was suing for neglect than have her with her ex-husband? That's what a judge would ask.

"Look, Asher." Ken's voice took on a more compassionate tone, which twisted like a worm in his ear. "I get that this is a really difficult time for you. You lost your father a few years ago, and you are about to lose your mother. I know that your life with your parents hasn't gone the way you would have liked it to. I know you think I am a wife-stealing jerk."

"You've nailed that one, Ken."

"And you have chosen not to see Sheena as your sister, despite your mother giving birth to her just as she did you. And then there is Ethan, your nephew, who you have not let into your life at all."

"Sheena is your progeny, Ken. Not my father's."

"She is also your mother's," Ken argued.

"Yes, out of wedlock. You were fucking my mother while she was still married to my father, and Sheena is the result of your seduction and my mother's infidelity. You ruined their marriage and broke my father's heart!" Asher felt the bile rise within him.

"We have had this discussion too many times, Asher. That all happened twenty-six years ago. Your father led a very fruitful life during those years, until his death. He died of a heart attack, not a broken heart, I assure you. But then, you know this. Only you know why, for all these years, you have latched onto a pretty twisted view of the truth. It was your choice to do so, but that choice has been very hurtful to a lot of people."

Asher was immediately back on his feet, his temper raging within him. "Don't talk to me about being hurt."

"Look, I didn't call to have a fight with you." Ken said. "I don't know what possessed your mother to walk here, much less how she managed to do so. But she is here, and she is dying. There is nothing more that you can do for her, and I can take care of her here. Dr. Chopra mentioned you were scheduled to go to an astrophysics conference. If it's not too late, I suggest you go."

Ken's words were like a sudden blast of arctic air, and they chilled him to the bone, unmasking a raw emotion: guilt. He'd felt it when deciding not to cancel his flight, and again when he asked the conference organizers to keep his slot on the afternoon of the second day open in case his mother died quickly and he could still attend and deliver his paper.

Asher took the phone off speaker mode for fear that his thoughts might be heard, which would betray the overwhelming guilt he harboured for feeling disappointed that his mother's death hadn't come quickly. He had thought that would be the case when Dr. Chopra called to tell him his mother was dying. *This is all so damn inconvenient.*

He had booked a flight to this coastal backwater, Brockhurst, to settle her estate and pay his last respects, not to engage in an indefinite vigil over his mother as she died. After all, she no longer held any memory of him. He hated that. How do you say goodbye to someone who can't remember ever saying hello?

Asher wiped away a tear; "I will call you back."

Abruptly terminating the call, he threw his phone onto the quilt draped over the hotel bed. "Ahh, shit," he said to his image in the mirror. "What the fuck am I supposed to do?" He stared into the dark brown eyes that glared back.

Go have your shower, but don't take too much time to make up your mind, or we won't make the flight to the conference.

He looked away and headed toward the shower.

9.

Jessica Gunn, her shoulder-length auburn hair pulled tightly back into a ponytail, removed the wire-rimmed reading glasses that had been perched upon her tiny nose. Her warm, light brown eyes smiled at the drawn, umber face turned ashy by age and pain. She tucked the glasses into the fabric case in her breast pocket and handed the tablet to the tall, very thin, slightly hunched nurse who had accompanied her on her rounds.

"I have updated your prescription. This will increase the strength of your pain management regime and let you rest more comfortably." She smiled at the patient, who responded by raising a calloused, twisted finger from the hand that scratched the curly grey stubble upon his chin, made damp by the constant drizzle from the corner of his lips.

Jessica walked with the nurse toward the ward reception. "There is nothing else that I can do for him." It was a statement directed toward the nurse, but she knew she was reassuring herself. Cancer, a nasty business, almost always won in the end. Her father's death had been proof of that. "Has the man's family been updated on his condition?"

"Charlie has no family that we know of," the nurse replied. "He talks of a brother, who I think is still in Jamaica, but we have not had any success in locating him."

"Friends? Is there anybody who cares about this man?!" Jessica reigned in her emotions, and the nurse looked away.

The phone in Jessica's pants pocket vibrated. She had ignored it three times before, trying to conceal her irritation during rounds. Jessica didn't like interruptions, which is why she always turned off the ringtone.

"Sorry," Jessica said, putting her hand on the nurse's shoulder and ignoring the buzzing vibration against her leg. "Wasn't directed toward you or any of your staff. It just seems wrong that a man can walk this Earth for sixty years and be so anonymous during his last hours."

The nurse placed her hand over Jessica's and said, "We will look after him. Seems like someone is really keen to talk!" The nurse smiled, nodding toward Jessica's pocket.

The buzzing stopped.

"Whoever it is can wait," said Jessica, pulling out her phone and quickly scrolling through the log of missed calls. *Sheena Graham? Why would she be calling?*

Jessica forced herself to focus on finishing up the paperwork required to write out the prescriptions for each patient that she had typed into the tablet. *Sheena never calls me. Not even when her dad and I were ... whatever we were.*

Fearing that the calls had come because something had happened to Ken, Dr. Gunn said a hurried goodbye to the nursing staff and walked quickly down the long hall, past the main reception, and out the exit door. The fresh spring breeze that provided rhythm to the dance of late-blooming daffodils, narcissus, and tulips in the planted border in front of her car was a most welcome relief from the still, stale air of the hospital.

Seated behind the wheel of her Ford Escape, Jessica took a breath. The fact that her patient, Charlie Brown, lay dying in a hospital bed without anybody knowing, much less caring, that his life was about to end, really bothered her. She wasn't at all sure why it had caused such a surge of emotion. He certainly wasn't the first poor soul to pass unnoticed, and, as God was her witness, he wouldn't be the last.

And why had this dying man resurrected all that emotion that surrounded the death of her father? Both were men in their sixties, both taken by prostate cancer—which, had either of them been paying attention, might well have been caught early enough to be treated.

But that's where the similarity ended.

Jessica tapped on the leather phone cover. She knew she should call Sheena, but found her mind seized by events ten years earlier, when her father had arranged the timing of his death with a doctor who practised medicine in Aberdeen, Scotland.

It was the second day of her third-year term as a medical student at St. Andrews when she received the phone call. It had been her father's instruction to the doctor that Jessica not be told until after his death, for fear that she would try to intercede.

She banged the palm of her hand on the steering wheel, thinking of the letter he had left her. *I am going to be with your mother*, he had written. *My biggest regret is that I did not see you married, nor bounce a grandson on my knee*—words written in his own handwriting expressed how much she, his only child, had disappointed him.

She opened the case of her phone called up the log of Sheena's last call and pressed redial.

"Sheena, it's Jessica. You were trying to reach me?"

"Hi, Jessica. I really hope I haven't caught you at a bad time, but I just didn't know who else to call."

"Slow down, Sheena, and tell me what this is about."

"It is my father."

"Has something happened to him?"

"My mother has happened to him. I called him because of the silver alert that was put out about my mom, and guess what? He has her out at the farm and wants to keep her there."

Jessica was confused. "OK, back up a bit ... I know nothing of a silver alert. Is your mother not at the care home?"

"No—apparently, she just walked out, and has shown up at my dad's farm."

"Your mother is very ill, Sheena. I doubt that she had the strength or the mental capacity to walk out of the centre and find her way to your dad's farm."

"And yet, according to my dad and Asher, who is livid and threatening to sue the centre, that is exactly what has happened. Now my dad wants to keep her at the farm."

One Weekend in May

"None of this makes much sense to me, Sheena. Let me call Dr. Chopra at the centre, and I will get back to you." Jessica ended the call and checked the time on her phone. She had enough time before her next appointment to stop by the centre. *This is bizarre. I had better speak to Sonja directly.*

Her thoughts tumbled around in her mind as he drove toward the senior centre. She knew Lena Murshid's diagnosis, having been part of the team that had determined it. Lena was a strong-willed woman, but didn't possess superhuman strength. On the other hand, Jessica conceded that the brain was a powerful and complex organ, and the impact of that tumour on her particular form of dementia was unpredictable.

Traffic was light, and she made good progress. Why would Ken take her in? That didn't make any sense. Her mind drifted to the last evening they had spent together. Both had agreed that what had transpired had been a mistake, assuring the other that it wouldn't affect their friendship—and yet it seemed to have done just that. After all, at the end of the night, nothing had really happened—but surely that was the point, wasn't it? She turned into the driveway of the centre and parked directly in front of the small sign: "Reserved: Dr. Gunn."

10.

Ken watched from the open barn loft doors, his leather hat pulled down to shield his eyes from the afternoon sun, as Janis Lieberman's dark blue Ford F350, stacked high with bales of hay, backed up to the barn. It stopped at the base of the hay elevator that reached, like a fireman's ladder, to where he stood.

This supply of local hay was a critical part of Ken's farming operation. He knew how fortunate he was that Janis had not only wanted to lease the hundred-acre farm property from the de Jong family after Frankie, the patriarch, had finally lost his battle with cancer, but that this big-city girl had learned to manage the hay production so well.

The driver's door opened, and Janis jumped out of the cab, landing with a bounce and a broad smile on her face as she slapped her leg with a leather Australian outback hat, She flipped it onto her short, white-grey hair, which was swept up in tight, natural curls like a finely whipped meringue.

"Hey there, good looking," she called up to Ken, "I got thirty bales here." Seeing Janis always cheered him up.

This self-effacing woman, with sparkling, light brown eyes didn't look almost sixty years old. She was dressed in jeans, legs rolled up atop steel-toed work boots, broad leather belt around her narrow waist pulled snug to accent her hips. A red plaid shirt that strained against her ample bosom.

"Fantastic. I am really grateful that you would take time to bring them over," Ken called down to the ruddy, freckled face, which responded with an electric smile.

"Just another day to me, Ken. You ready? I'll fire up this puppy, and we can get these lifted and stacked. I brought six of Denmark's finest, chillin' in the cooler for when we are done." Janis walked to the elevator and pulled the starting cord, firing up the Briggs and Stratton engine on the side of the hay elevator, which, with a puff of blue smoke, roared to life.

The rubber belt on the ladder's pullies squealed, and the teeth on the steel chain jerked, rattled, and rolled upward. "I am so happy it's not raining. It's such a pain when I have to tarp the load," she shouted. "OK, you be ready, old man, because when I start these moving, they're coming fast and steady."

"Keep in mind I have to stack at this end," Ken shouted back, a little worried that he wouldn't be able to move as fast stacking the bales as she could loading them.

"Just keep them free from the end of the elevator so we can lift the whole load, then I will come up and help you stack," Janis called back. With a bale hook in each hand, she climbed up to the top of the hay and started to carefully drop each bale onto the elevator.

Ken pulled up a mask to cover his nose and mouth. In his younger days, the dust from the hay would cause him no concern, but it did now. He plunged his bale hooks into the first bale as it toppled off the top of the elevator and, as quickly as he could, carried the seventy-pound bale the short distance to the dunnage laid on the loft floor, ready to receive the hay.

He worked as fast as he could, stacking the bale at the furthest end first, just managing to get back to the elevator in time to meet the next bale, which toppled off the elevator and onto the floor with a thump, but by the time the thirtieth bale landed and Janis shut off the motor, he was well behind, and found himself dragging the bales out of the way for the next to land.

He heard Janis climbing the steps to the loft.

"Hey, good job." She grinned at him. "You've got your half stacked already." She unhooked the cooler bag strap from her shoulder and placed it on a few bales stacked by the wall. "Why don't you just take a seat, and crack a beer? I'll stack my half, then join you."

"I can't do that." Ken found himself puffing out the words, his lower back throbbing with pain, his knees tightening up. The beer sounded great, but he was not about to have Janis show him up, even if he was quite a few years her senior.

He was not quite sure when it had happened, but recently, people seemed to view him differently—especially those closest to him. And as much as he liked Janis, her constant reference to his age annoyed him.

Still, he had come to recognize when the eyes of the onlooker defined him as a senior or old man, and he knew that platitudes and sometimes condescension followed. So, having something to prove, he matched her bale for bale as they finished stacking the hay.

With the last bale kneed into place, Janis jumped off the stack and tossed her hat on top of the hay. "Now, about that beer," she said, pulling a cotton hanky from her hip pocket and wiping the sweat from her brow. "You care to do the honours?" she asked, taking a seat on an available bale.

Ken unzipped the cooler bag, took out two ice-cold Faxe Amber beers, and handed one to Janis. "Again, thanks for your help. All that snow over the winter meant a lot more hay had to be fed in the fields. This will hold me until I get the first cut off the back pasture."

"Hey, no worries," said Janis, emphasizing her own pun and laughing before taking a gulp of beer. "Mother Nature is all fucked up. The whole world is fucked, Ken." She swigged her beer, then, looking directly at him, asked, "So … I am guessing that you have heard the news about your ex. It's been all over the radio; there was a silver alert to go look for her. Did you know that?"

Ken could tell by her tone and the tapping of her foot that Janis wasn't too sure how to broach the subject, or even if she should at all. "Yeah, I heard."

"Well, I guess they must have found her, since they have pulled the alert. But still, that's pretty messed up, right? I mean, they said she just walked out of a care home. I mean, that's got to be bullshit, right? They probably locked her in a closet by mistake and said she walked out to cover their asses. I mean, she is pretty sick, right?"

"Just add it to your list," Ken replied, and noticing she didn't clue into *your list*, he said, "of fucked up things, Janis," and he was pleased to see that made her laugh.

"I guess I shouldn't laugh," said Janis. "It's a shitty way to go, don't you agree? I'm hoping no one tries to put me in one of those PWDs. Crap, I feel sick just thinking about it."

"PWD?"

"Places to Wait to Die. I mean, I can understand that you probably don't have a lot of schmaltzy feelings left for her. Not after the way she treated you at the end, but Jesus, she is a lot younger than you, right? I mean to be going first, and in this way. Life can be pretty harsh." Janis drank her beer while still looking at him.

There it was again—but Ken let her reference to the age difference between Lena and himself slide. What he was thinking about was the obvious question: should he tell her?

"Are you OK? Did my reference to your saviour offend your Catholic sensitivities?" She laughed. "Now *that* would be fucked up! So, talk to me."

"No offence taken. I simply chalk it up to the words of an ignorant Jew," Ken replied, smiling at his curly-haired, freckle-faced friend.

"Ouch! Jew for sure, but ignorant—now, that hurts." She grinned before taking another gulp of beer.

The cold beer washed away the particles of dust from Ken's dry throat. Janis was right; the whole situation *was* fucked up. His dying ex-wife had, in the early morning hours, simply walked out of her care home and come to the farm. Why would she do that? This was the woman who, five years earlier, had walked off the farm and wanted nothing more to do with him.

Still, he felt compelled not to send her back. He felt that it must be Lena's last wish.

What really shocked him was the realization of just how much he still cared for her. He hoped Lena was peacefully asleep at the house. He was going to need help. Would Janis be the person to provide it? *Then again, what if I told her that Lena was up at the house and she didn't support her staying?*

"Hey," said Janis, and she waved a hand in front of his face. "Are you having a senior's moment? Talk to me."

Ken rolled his eyes at her comment. "You and I are pretty good friends; would you say that?"

"Oh shit, here it comes. What the fuck have you done?"

"I haven't *done* anything, but I do need to know if I can trust you."

"OK, I'm listening."

"Janis, can I trust you?"

"To do what, Ken? How long have I known you? Twelve—no, more like fourteen years?" Janis went for another beer, taking two cans from the cooler, opening one, and handing the other to him. "Here, keep up. You should know you can trust me. What kind of schnegger do you think I am?"

"Schnegger … ?" Ken chuckled.

"Yeah, someone who bails on friends. You are dangerously close to insulting me, Ken. Have you forgotten what went down five years ago? Lena walked out and demanded a divorce. Does that ring any bells with you? You were a fucking mess, my friend. Not that I hold that against you; after thirty years of marriage and all the hurt you've gone through, I get it. And that's my point. Who was there for you then, and has been every day since? Who has pitched in to help with the farm? Who held you when you cried like a fucking baby? Oh, that would be me—so don't be such a fucking putz."

"You *have* been a really good friend, Janis. I wasn't trying to insult you," Ken replied, looking at Janis sitting half-reclined on a bale of hay, her back resting against the barn wall.

"Yeah, well, you did. We all have our shit, Ken, and you were certainly there for me when I arrived from New York, pretty broken. I have never questioned your friendship or trust, so why don't you tell me what the fuck's going on?"

"She's here. Up at the house." Ken waited for a reaction that came almost instantly as Janis sat suddenly bolt upright, choking on her beer.

"Are you shitting me?"

"Nope, she walked up to the gate this morning right after I delivered number 8 Red's lamb. Except the woman who is now asleep in the house says she is Gilgamesh, not Lena, and I am quite sure she doesn't have a clue that I am the man she was married to for thirty years."

"Gilgamesh, as in the character from the poem?"

One Weekend in May

"Yes. She thinks she is Gilgamesh, the main character in that Babylonian poem she did so much research on. She was quoting from it when she passed out, and I carried her up to the house."

"Wow, that's crazy—but then again, the study of the poem was heavily featured in Lena's last book," said Janis. "Maybe whatever messed up her brain left that poem as the last remnant of sanity."

"Maybe, who knows? Anyway, it seems she is caught up in it and thinks she is a he. Gilgamesh was male, not female."

"Well, there's no shame in being gender-fluid, is there, Ken?" Janis laughed.

"She has no knowledge of Lena, doesn't act like her—nor, it seems, does she have any memory of Lena's life. That's why when Alice Joe stopped by to let me know that Lena had walked away from the care centre and that the police were looking for her, I could tell Alice that the woman I knew as Lena Murshid wasn't here."

"What the fuck, Ken? Alice is a cop; even though she's a rookie, she's still a police officer, and she is looking for your ex-wife."

"I know."

"I don't get it. The cops have called off the search, so they must know she is here. So, if you didn't tell them, who did? And how much shit are you in now? You can be such a fucking meshugener."

"Alice somehow knew that she was here. She found Lena's suitcase when she came snooping around. Anyway, I called the rest home, and Dr. Chopra has agreed that for the time being, Lena can stay here."

"What?! Ken, give your head a shake!" Janis jumped to her feet.

"Yeah, it's all pretty weird. But it's not just her mind. Lena is not in good physical shape. She has not been well cared for, and I think that she chose to come here for her last days. I won't send her back."

"Are you fucking kidding me? You just told me that the woman doesn't know her earhole from her butthole. She doesn't know who she is, who you are, or where the fuck she is. You are seventy-six years old, and have a farm to manage all on your own. You can't look after Lena—how the fuck does any of this make sense?"

"I don't deny it sounds really bizarre, because at least outwardly, she doesn't recognize where she is or who I am," said Ken, getting to his feet.

"And yet, she knew enough to walk twelve kilometres, most of it in the dark, based on the time she arrived at my farm gate. Of all the places she could have wandered off to, why did she come here?"

"Ken, it's been five years, and you have not heard a peep from this woman. From what you have told me, she has been in palliative care for the last six months. What the fuck are you thinking? Do you seriously think that she is coming home to you?" asked Janis.

The exasperation in Janis's voice made Ken regret telling her anything, but he needed her help. He finished the second can of beer and refused her offer of a third.

"So, we are going to call the police right now and ask them to pick her up and take her back, right?"

"Janis, I need your support in this. I am going to find a way for her to stay for as long as she needs to be here—which, according to Doctor Chopra at the care centre, will not likely be very long."

"You aren't making sense right now," replied Janis, her eyes darkened by anger. "You mean until Death opens your front door, walks in, and snuffs her out? He's not good company, Ken; you don't want him in your house." She drained the beer from the can, crushed it with her hand, and then tossed the crumpled remains into the cooler.

"Look, I don't know why she walked here, but I know that she didn't just happen upon the farm in some random walkabout. She came here for a reason, even if she did so as somebody other than Lena. She is in no danger, or in any obvious pain, at least at the moment. She is resting quietly after having a solid meal—which, by the look of her, is probably the first solid meal she has had in a while." Ken responded.

"Shit, Kenny, why do you want to do this? This woman has done you no favours, at least not recently. She fucked you over. When you were most vulnerable and under attack professionally, she walked out the door. Shalom, schmuck, the divorce papers will be sent by special delivery!"

"Because I care about her, Janis."

"For fuck's sake, grow a set, Ken."

"Someone else's life, seen from a distance, can appear quite different than it actually is, Janis. There are always two sides to every relationship," replied Ken.

"I don't even know what the fuck that means, Ken," said Janis, pacing the rough fir planking of the loft floor. "Look, I am not saying that Lena didn't have her good side. Shit, when I first met her all those years ago, I thought she was pretty hot. Not only beautiful, but really intelligent, kind, and open." Janis leaned toward him. "As I have told you before, had she been so inclined and not married to you, I'd have taken my shot. But, Jesus, Ken, toward the end, it was pretty bad. Have you forgotten all that?"

"Not for one minute," replied Ken, "and as God is my witness, Janis, if that person had showed up at my farm gate, I wouldn't have opened it. But the woman who has arrived is different, and I cannot shake the feeling that she has come home for a safe place to die. If that's true, I have to give her that."

The two were startled by a voice that called from outside the barn.

"Ken, are you here?" It was Jessica Gunn's accented voice that shouted from the entry door below the hay loft.

"Expecting someone?" asked Janis, and Ken caught the surprised look on her face.

Jessica Gunn stood, hands on her slender hips, her wavy auburn hair brushing against the shoulders of her snug-fitting brown leather bomber jacket.

"Up here, Jessica. I will be right down!" Ken called, and waved.

"Who is that?" asked Janis.

"Dr. Jessica Gunn," replied Ken. "I was going to call her, but it seems that somebody beat me to it. Come on, I will introduce you if you promise to be nice."

"Be nice?" With her right hand, Janis flipped the rim of Ken's hat, lifting it off his head and over the edge of the loft. "I am always nice."

Ken chuckled and climbed down the steps to the barn floor, where he gathered his hat, with Janis only a few steps behind.

11.

Wrapped in warmth and fragrance long past familiar, Lena drifted in a mist. Through the haze, she recognized the body of her most loyal and loved companion, prone, with no pulse and no breath, and her heart ached for Enkidu.

Their triumph had been grand indeed. Against all odds, the weak and faint of heart said they would not succeed but instead be trampled under the hooves of the Bull of Heaven, whose snort would slay a thousand. They had truth on their side, having called out the corruption of Ishtar, scorned her seduction, and refused to join with those pernicious malcontents who, in the name of the Gods, imposed their will upon imprisoned souls.

Drifting backward, Lena saw the Bull of Heaven roar through the mist. Snorting, the massive animal charged at Enkidu, who narrowly escaped impalement by dodging aside, leaping upon the Bull's back, and seizing it by the horns.

The Bull of Heaven foamed through snorting nostrils and whirled, trying to brush Enkidu off with the thick of its tail.

"Stand with me, my friend, for we have truth on our side," Enkidu called to Lena, who lay restless as Gilgamesh beneath the robes that wrapped her. "Thrust in your sword between the nape and the horns," he instructed.

Feeling all the power of Gilgamesh, she did so by seizing the thick of the bull's tail, and when the giant head turned, she thrust the sword she wielded in her fog between the nape and the horns and slew the Bull.

At first, the crowds cheered them, hoisting both of them on their shoulders. They were heroes among the people. But the fog started to clear from her mind, and the warmth turned to chills. She didn't want her mind to travel there, but she was powerless to stop it.

Through the darkness came four Gods. They were the Council. She didn't know how she knew that, but she was certain they had power over her, and they were seething with anger.

"You shall be punished, for there is no greater threat to our authority than when the people believe they have power over those who rule them."

The words were clear enough to her. She needed to escape, to flee, and so she rose and steadied herself by her hand, which she let slide along the wall. She made her way down the narrow passage, through the furnished room, and out the large door, where her nostrils were filled with the fragrance of a hundred blooming apple trees.

Fearful that she might fall, she descended the steps upon her bottom, bumping down one at a time until she reached the ground and stumbled toward the smudged pink shapes, unaware of the sharp blackberry thorns that bit into the cotton robe, pulling strands from the weave as she pressed on. These were the talons of the Beast, she thought, before banging her legs upon an unseen bench, whereupon she sat, trembling beneath the soft pink bloom of a golden noble.

Death had been summoned; she knew it now. It was only a matter of time before Enkidu would slip away, and she would be left alone to face her fate. He had told her as much when she had last seen him.

The beast had come, his face sombre like the black bird of the storm. The sharp talons would tear into his skin and lift him into the air, carrying him off to the Queen of Darkness, Irkalla, who resided within the palace from which none who enter ever return.

Through the fog, all smudged and whirling, she saw the figure approach. No, not one, nor two, but three of them. *These will be my judge, jury, and executioner.*

***

Jessica Gunn had insisted on driving up to the house, so Ken had jumped into the front seat beside her, with Janis taking a seat behind him.

"Pull up in front of the greenhouse," Ken told Jessica, pointing toward a long, glass-framed building. "Lena, believe it or not, is right over there in the orchard, sitting on that bench."

Jessica stopped the car and looked at Lena Murshid, wrapped in a terry towel bathrobe, rocking her frail body in a rhythmic motion forward then back, her sunken, dark-ringed eyes wide in an open stare, mouth agape. "Good God," Jessica whispered to herself as she climbed out of the car.

She led the others in a slow approach toward Lena—Ken and Janis a few steps behind her. "Lena, it's Jessica Gunn; I am a doctor, and I am here to help you," she said quietly. But Lena did not blink or show any response; she just rocked herself more furiously back and forth.

"Ken," said Jessica, not taking her eyes away from Lena, "in the trunk of my car you will find a folded wheelchair. Please get it out, unfold it, and lock it open. We need to get Lena back in the house."

"I will give you a hand," offered Janis. The two made short work of freeing the wheelchair from the car, locking it open, and wheeling it toward Lena. Jessica reached out her hand.

"I know you!" Lena's cracked, frail voice called out. "You have come to judge me."

"I have come to help you, Lena," Jessica reassured her. "We need to get you back into the house."

But Lena became more agitated as Janis and Ken approached with the wheelchair.

"Oh, so the executioner wheels the chariot to haul me off to Irkalla, to the house from which none who enter return. You will have me stand before the Queen of Darkness." Lena seemed at first fearful of Janis, but then her dark brown eyes switched from fear to a menacing glare. "She," Lena's bony, arthritic index finger wagged toward Janis, "is the juror you have hand-picked to do your bidding and pronounce a guilty verdict! She will shout it out for all to hear."

Lena was rocking back and forth fast now, and Jessica moved quickly toward her, fearful that she might fall off the bench.

Lena put her hand up, as if to stop Jessica from touching her. "And what is my crime? Having been born at all and being bold enough to live life?"

Her voice became shrill, her words a wheezing pant, despite her effort to shout.

"We who walk the earth are not like you gods, who emerge from the light to live an everlasting life," Lena continued. "Our birth inflicts pain. Mothers scream with agony." Tears started to well up in Lena's eyes. "And you gods will gleefully remind us of our punishment for the original sin, and you will rub your hands together in delight at the knowledge that each will endure dark days of suffering like bleak winter nights." Lena paused, dropping her gaze from Jessica, and looked toward the ground. "And then Death, a most unwanted guest, will invite himself to sit at my table, where he will feast upon my memories—like spring and summer days filled with the love of family who brought joy into my heart—until all are consumed. Gone forever." Lena started to sob, a flood of tears rolling down her puckered cheeks. "They are gone, all gone, and all that is left are the bones from the skeletal remains of shame and regret."

Jessica put a hand on Lena's shoulder as she covered her sobbing eyes with her thin, contused, bony hands.

"Do you have any idea what she is talking about?" Janis asked Jessica.

"She couldn't be clearer," Jessica replied, turning to Ken. "Help me lift her into the wheelchair."

12.

"Do you want help with the farm chores?" Ken heard Janis ask as he closed the door to the bedroom, leaving Jessica to attend to Lena, who the three had managed to lift back onto the bed.

"I am sure you have chores of your own to attend to," replied Ken, his hand on her shoulder as they walked back into the living room.

"You're such a putz," said Janis. "Sure, I have things to do, but nothing that will stop me from helping you."

The sun lingered longer in the evening sky each day as it journeyed toward the June summer solstice, its light streaming through the west-facing windows and bathing the dining and sitting areas of the house in a gold and amber warmth.

Ken knew he could use the assistance, but it wasn't in his nature to ask or readily accept an offer, so he stood for a moment looking out the window at the mackerel sky, the white fleecy clouds beginning to turn purple with the setting sun.

"We'll likely have some rain tomorrow," he said to Janis, who shrugged and walked into the kitchen. She opened a cupboard, took out a large bag of Lays chips, and helped herself to a handful.

"By all means, please help yourself," he laughed, and in response, Janis raised the bag as one might gesture "cheers," hiding a raised middle finger behind the bag. She returned to the sitting area, dropping into a large armchair and swinging her right leg over the burgundy leather arm.

"Tell me about Jessica," said Janis through a mouthful of potato chips, digging into the bag for another handful.

"Not much to tell," replied Ken, a bit surprised by the question. "I first met her when Lena was admitted to Caring Hands; she is a geriatrician and works at the centre as part of her practice."

"Geriatrician," Janis chuckled, nodding. "A good person for an old fart like you to know, that's for sure. How come you have never mentioned her to me before?"

Ken processed the question for a moment and, thinking that Jessica might like a cup of tea before she left, filled a kettle with water and put it on the gas stove above a dancing blue flame. "Why would I mention Jessica to you?"

"Because we're best friends, schmuck. And she seems to know you pretty well; she knew exactly where to go when she came into the house, and she doesn't look at you like a doctor looks at a relative of a patient. I suspect, *wink, wink*, in your head at least, there's more to Jessica than just caring for Lena." Janis emphasized the wink with an exaggerated closing and opening of her left eye.

Ken looked at Janis, who had melted into the large chair and all but demolished the entire bag of chips. He wasn't quite sure what to make of her remark. If he didn't know better, he might think she was jealous of Jessica.

"But, to be honest with you, Ken, I don't get the vibe that she and you are a good fit. Do you know what I mean?"

Ken's mind, for one fleeting moment, recalled that evening when he and Jessica had thought about having a sexual relationship, but he quickly extinguished the thought. "How is whatever relationship I have with Jessica any of your business?"

"Like I said, we are best friends, and best friends share these details, Ken."

"Why are you so interested in Jessica?" Ken asked.

"No particular reason; I'm just surprised that I haven't met her before."

Ken could think of no reason why Janis would have had the occasion to meet Jessica. Anyway, it was of little consequence, so he returned to the subject of the chores. "It would be a big help if you don't mind putting out grain and hay in the main barn and then letting the main flock in. I will head down after Jessica leaves, and check on the newborn."

"I am happy to help," she replied, and, seemingly having had her fill of the Lay's chip bag, she climbed out of the chair, folding over the top of the bag and tossing it onto the dining table. "I left the broken bits for your chickens; they will love them," she said, walking to the kitchen sink to wash the salt and chip grease from her hands, then wiping her hands dry on the legs of her jeans. "I'll head down now."

"I'll give you a ride down if you wait a minute," said Jessica, entering the room. She turned to face Ken. "I don't think she will be getting up again."

Ken knew exactly what Jessica was saying, and the concern floating within her eyes underlined her statement. The realization that Lena's death was likely only a few hours away made him nauseous, and that surprised him. He had grieved too many times, for different reasons, and knew it was pointless to hope for a return to the years he had spent with this remarkable woman.

Jessica's words had such a finality about them that for that moment, he thought that she might as well have been talking about him. What had it been all about? In that instant, in some deep recess of his mind, he saw so very clearly the dream of growing old on the farm with Lena by his side, their lives filled with the laughter and the play of grandchildren, snuffed out.

"Are you OK?" asked Jessica. She took his hand.

Ken pulled himself together, taking a deep breath. "I'll be OK."

"I am sorry, Ken, but she is declining rapidly. She is going to need an intravenous feed to help her manage. I will come back after the evening rounds and set one up if that's alright with you. For now, the sedatives will work, but pretty soon she will need both."

The words jumbled in his head, and he found himself just nodding at Jessica. There really was nothing more to be said.

"You don't have to put yourself through this, you know," Janis piped in. Ken glared at her.

"Janis is right, Ken," said Jessica. "I can arrange to have her moved back to Caring Hands. It will be much easier on you."

Ken didn't want to hear any talk of moving Lena. "No," he said firmly. "She went to a great deal of trouble to get here; I don't plan to send her back. How long do you think?"

Jessica was gathering some of her medical instruments and tucking them into a black bag. "Well, that in part depends upon how she is medicated from this point forward. With only pain management, I would estimate twenty-four to forty-eight hours. Not much longer."

"Or, she could be put out of her suffering painlessly and more quickly," Janis chipped in. "You wouldn't let one of your sheep suffer the way she is, and you know it."

Ken bridled at Janis's comment, partly because it was true and partly because in all his academic work, he had written about the need for planned death and a change in the attitude that held the view that medical science should be used to keep a person alive for as long as possible, regardless of the circumstance. But somehow, this felt different.

He hated his own hypocrisy.

"Why don't you and I go do the chores and leave the good doctor here? By the time we come back up to the house, it will all be over, right, Doc?" said Janis, pulling on the brim of her hat.

"What the fuck, Janis?" Ken snapped. "Are you asking Jessica to kill her?"

"She's dying, schlemiel," Janis pushed back. "I am not saying Jessica should do anything unethical. She doesn't strike me as someone who would. But you should consider that Lena might need a little help to get over to the other side."

"OK, let's not go there right now," interrupted Jessica. "I have to get to my evening rounds. I'll come back and check on Lena, and on you, Ken. Lena is sedated sufficiently to get her through the night, I think, and an intravenous feed will help with that. Let's see where we are when I get back. Now, Janis, do you want a ride down to the barn?"

Ken watched the two women gather their things and head toward the door, and as they were leaving, he heard Jessica ask Janis, "What's a schlemiel?"

"A fool," Janis replied.

"Ah, a dobber," said Jessica, letting her Scottish accent blossom, and they laughed as the door closed behind them.

13.

Ken sat in his favourite garnet-coloured leather chair, inhaling the fumes from the two ounces of single-malt whiskey that beckoned him seductively from a crystal glass he held in his hand. It had been almost four years since he had tasted Highland Single Malt. It had been a reluctant choice, but an essential one to close the door on depression.

The nectar of the gods, as he affectionately called it, had become all too inviting after Lena had walked away from him. Sitting in the absolute quiet and darkness of the unlit house, he tried to make sense of why he had poured the drink, or even why he had kept the bottle from which he had poured it.

The full moon, peeking out from behind the clouds, shone through the tall living room windows, lighting the otherwise dark house and casting gentle shadows. The success of his house design was a source of joy for Ken.

In designing the house, he took great care to make sure that the orientation and open concept would capture every phase of the moon through the large windows, which, on a cloudless night of a new moon, provided a grand vista of stars. It was supposed to be their shared space—a place where the romance they had shared would rekindle.

The sedative that Jessica had given to Lena had done exactly what she had said it would. Ken had watched the frail remains of the woman he had been devoted to for so many years drift into a coma-like sleep, and that same crushing question lay upon his mind: what had it all been for?

Quietly closing the door, he had gone to the liquor cabinet, taken his special glass reserved for the nectar, and poured himself a healthy portion of the golden liquid, the smell of which set his taste buds on fire, even though he had not yet sipped it.

He looked at the wall clock: 9:30 p.m. Jessica had said that she would drop back after her evening rounds at the Caring Hands Hospice, and he wondered how soon she might arrive. Time enough for at least a couple of drinks, he thought, staring into the glass, struggling with the strangeness of the panic that was growing within him, and trying to fully understand its origin.

The years since Lena had left him had just rolled on by, and he struggled to think of what he had done in the time that had passed, much of it spent alone. He pushed back the tears that started to well in his eyes, and his mind pulled him back to the soft sound of his mother's breath and the gentle beating of her heart. He was a small boy again, his head resting on his mother's chest in the moments before she would tuck him into bed. Together, they would say a prayer.

His house had been noisy for as long as his siblings had been at home. His sisters, Mary and Shannon, fussed over him as older sisters did, while his older brother, Thomas, born a war apart from Mary and eight years older than him, was an untouchable hero figure who seemed to be able to do everything well except spend time with his little brother.

He had often wondered how different his life might have been had he known his father, though he hadn't thought about that for many years. Somehow, in the quiet darkness, his current circumstances conjured the only memory he had of Tom Sr., his father: a sepia photograph of a uniformed man sitting atop a battle tank.

Tom Sr. had been a member of the Fife and Forfar regiment, a hero in the eyes of his mother, who would tell Ken he had been a national hero who had done his part to stop the rising tide of Nazism from destroying the free world.

But, six months pregnant with him, his mother received news that the coal mine had done what the Nazis couldn't do, and taken the life of her husband, his father.

He put the glass of whiskey back on the small table beside his chair. He could still hear his mother's voice tell him in her soft Irish brogue, "Now, you listen to your mom, me boy, it is family that will keep company with you when you're elderly and infirm."

But that wasn't true for Patsy O'Toole, who after the death of her husband had retaken her maiden name, packed up her four children, cashed in her life savings to buy passage across the Atlantic to find hope in the New World, and sought out her sister, who had made the voyage several years earlier.

The death of his father seemed to have a profound effect on his mother. Ken found himself chuckling, remembering his mother's fiery temper, scarf tied over her hair, cigarette hanging from her lower lip, railing on through the circling bands of smoke about "how that bastard had left me alone to deal with you unruly brats," as though Tom Sr. had planned his untimely death in a collapsed coal mine.

In the moonlit silence, it occurred to Ken how much of his life had been spent alone—working, studying, and writing. It was in that moment that it occurred to him how alone his mother must have felt, her four children notwithstanding, for most of her life.

His mother's sister had apparently "taken up with a Godless bunch in New York," and she wanted nothing to do with them—or perhaps it had been the other way around, he couldn't be sure. But by Ken's sixteenth birthday, she had honed the blade she used to cut through life to a very sharp edge, and at fifty-one, she decided it was time to make *her* dreams come true.

"I'll provide for you 'til you're eighteen," she had told each of them; "after that, with mine and God's blessing, you're on your own." *And she kept her commitment*, Ken thought, *except for me.*

"You're the smartest," she had told him. "You'll do fine."

He remembered how tired his mother had looked most of the time—waitress by day, office cleaner by night—earning enough money to feed, clothe, and provide, in moderation, gifts on birthdays and at Christmas.

But the image that replayed most in his head was his mother walking into the kitchen, suitcase in hand, to tell him she was going on a short trip. It was a birthday he would never forget. He was spreading jam on a piece of buttered toast that he had made himself for breakfast when his mother walked into the room, uttered those words, and then walked out the back door without so much as a goodbye.

Ken reached for the glass of whiskey and brought it to his lips. He really wanted to drink it, but the insubordination of his hand and mouth prevented him. He took a deep breath; he couldn't be sure that one sip would not lead to a night of drinking, and he wondered why he had poured the drink in the first place.

As he looked into the glass of whiskey, he thought that perhaps he was slowly losing his mind. Was that the source of his panic? He hoped not, but there was no denying that his once visionary mind, that had been able to project well into the future, had become myopic, able only to see the demands of each day, or week at most, able to manage each hour as he previously would have orchestrated a year.

A loud knock on the door snapped him out of his contemplation, and he replaced the glass of untouched whiskey on the small table beside his chair, rose, and walked to open the door for Jessica.

14.

"Why are you sitting in the dark?" Jessica asked as she returned to the living room, where Ken still sat in silence. She had been all business after arriving, declining Ken's offer of help carrying in the apparatus required to set up Lena's intravenous feed. "Mind if I turn on some lights?"

Ken rose from his chair as Jessica, not waiting for a response, turned on the living room lights. "How is she?" he asked.

"As comfortable as I can make her, and that's all that can be done at this stage." She glanced at the glass on the table next to Ken's chair. "I thought you were off booze."

Ken smiled and said, "I am; I haven't even taken a sip yet."

"Then why did you pour it?" Jessica asked.

"I thought I might need a drink, but I didn't trust myself to drink alone, I guess."

Jessica smiled at him. "OK, in that case, if you are offering, I would love a glass of wine."

"A glass of old vine zinfandel—your favourite, I believe—is coming right up."

Jessica unzipped her bomber jacket and hung it on the back of a dining chair. Zinfandel wasn't really her favourite, but she didn't have the heart to say anything.

The night he first served her a glass of that particular wine was etched in her mind. She had raved about how good it was and drunk more than she should, both to make Ken feel good about his choice of wine and to find the courage to overcome her all-too-familiar discomfort over the possibility he would want to take their friendship to the next level.

It wasn't that she didn't like Ken; she did. She liked him a lot. He had a fine wit, was obviously intelligent, seemed kind and thoughtful, and his good looks had weathered well with age.

The reason for her discomfort was her fear that Ken might misinterpret her friendship, thinking that she would welcome having sex with him. It wouldn't be the first time that a man had acted on that assumption, and the shame and the anger she felt toward her younger self for having yielded to their advances rather than standing her ground had led her to bury her sexual desires altogether, choosing instead to bury herself in her studies, and later, her medical work.

As an adolescent, she repressed her deep feelings, thinking they were wrong. She felt sure she had been successful at hiding them from her father, although her dying mother let slip one night during the months Jessica had nursed her: "There is no shame in loving those you choose to love. It would make for a very dull garden if every flower within it were the same."

But Janis had seen it right away, and when Jessica had driven her from the house back to the barn, Janis had called her on it. It was the first time anyone had openly confronted her with what she knew to be true.

"So, I'm guessing that you're a lesbian, but not out, am I right?"

"That's a very forward question," Jessica responded, unable to hide her discomfort.

"And that, my lesbian friend, is a very backwards answer," Janis replied, and then chuckled. "Ken doesn't have a clue, does he? He is such a putz—loveable just the same, as much as any lesbian can love a putz." Janis burst into laughter, and, not familiar with Jewish slang, Jessica was left to assume there had been a joke in there somewhere.

"Well, whatever your reason, your secret is safe with me," Janis continued, and Jessica was happy to hear her say so. But she chose not to respond, and dropped Janis off at the barn.

"I hope I will see you again," Janis said with a smile, as she opened the door and stepped out of the car, leaving Jessica to immediately wonder when and how that might happen.

"We'll see," she offered in clumsy response. They had just met, and while there was an attraction, Janis was, well, unlike anybody Jessica had known. "Nice meeting you," she said, and she immediately regretted the way it sounded.

Her interaction with Janis had replayed in her mind a few dozen times since she had dropped her at the barn, and for some reason, Ken getting her a glass of wine had caused it to replay again.

As she watched Ken bring out a bottle of Zinfandel from the pantry, take a corkscrew from the drawer, and uncork the wine, she wondered. *Is Janis right? Does Ken really have no idea that I am a lesbian? Surely he's figured that out by now.*

"I am sorry if Janis made you uncomfortable earlier; she can be pretty blunt," said Ken, and Jessica felt a blush rise to her cheek. *So he does know,* she thought.

"She seems to be one of a kind, that's for sure," Jessica replied, assuming Ken was referring to her discussion with Janis in her car. But how would Ken know what the two of them had discussed? "Did she say something to you?"

"Janis can't help being Janis," replied Ken. "She has no filter; just says what she thinks. Come on, let's get comfortable." He handed Jessica the glass of wine and offered her a seat on the couch, and Jessica felt relieved that he chose to sit in the adjacent chair. "I can't tell you how much I appreciate your help with Lena."

"It is what I do, Ken, and I am happy to help you. Are you OK?"

"I know that's your profession. It was one of the reasons I was reluctant to ask for your help."

"I don't follow."

"Well, if you were an electrician, how would you feel if I asked you to come over on your own dime and fix the wiring in my house?"

Jessica laughed. "I am not an electrician."

"Obviously," Ken said. "But you know what I mean, right?"

"I do, and I appreciate it. Thank you for the wine. Cheers." Jessica raised her glass and took a sip. "So, what's another reason?"

She watched Ken swirl the scotch in his glass, wondering if he was actually going to drink it. He seemed reluctant to answer, or became lost in thought.

"Ken, are you still with me?"

"It's not really important now, is it? You are here and helping, and I am appreciative." Ken took the tiniest sip of whiskey.

Should she just let his comment go? After all, he was right; she had come to help and was happy to do so, whatever the reason for his reluctance to ask her. *So why is it not important now? Janis must have told him the real reason for my rejecting his advances the last time we sat on this couch drinking Zinfandel.* She was quite sure that Ken would not have forgotten, despite the fact that they had never discussed that evening.

They had shared great conversation, laughter, and a bit too much wine, letting the seductive background music mellow the mood. She had known that he was attracted to her, and with every glass of wine, she had warmed more to the way he looked at her, and stroked her hair. She even felt a certain comfort when his finger had softly brushed her cheek. It had been his attempt to kiss her that had caused her to abruptly snap back to reality.

"What are you doing?" she had demanded, raising her voice and pushing him away from her. As if in a single motion, she had leapt off the couch, into her coat, and out the door.

Driving away, she had felt so bad. She had known exactly what he was doing, and that she should have stopped him well before he had tried to kiss her.

"You know, Ken, we never really discussed what happened between us the last evening I was here drinking wine with you." She waited for his response. He seemed reluctant to reply, and instead rose from his chair and walked to the kitchen, where he busied himself preparing some food on a plate. "Do we need to discuss that?" she called.

"I was out of line. I apologize," he called back. "That's the other reason I was reluctant to ask for your help. I wasn't sure how you would respond."

Her rational self told her to just leave it there and move on, but her emotional self was conflicted. Through the fog of the wine, she had sent him all the wrong signals. Her rejection of him must have been sudden, and certainly unexpected. She had hurt him, and that had not been her intention.

"I am sorry if my behaviour that night was hurtful. Perhaps now you have a better understanding of why I reacted the way I did," she said. Ken stopped what he was doing and looked at her with puzzlement on his face, so she added, "as in the way that Janis made me uncomfortable earlier."

"I don't get it." Ken appeared genuinely confused. "How is her suggestion that you should speed up Lena's death connected to you rejecting my kiss?"

In that instant, Jessica knew that she should have listened to her rational self and just moved on. "Yeah, you're right, it's not. Look, the important thing is that we are good, right?"

"I am if you are," Ken replied.

Feeling both relieved and a little foolish, Jessica changed the subject. "It is truly extraordinary that Lena was able to walk the distance from Caring Hands to the farm. I am thinking that I might write a paper on Lena's last days for *The Lancet* medical journal. Unless you have an objection."

"It's not up to me," replied Ken. "Her son, Asher, is her executor, and calls all the shots on her behalf. If I were you, I would submit an article and use a pseudonym."

Jessica started to construct the outline of her paper in her head. It was truly remarkable that Lena not only had had the physical strength to walk to the farm but, despite her medical condition, planned her escape from Caring Hands and known exactly where she was walking.

"Her walk was quite remarkable. It just shows how little medical science knows. Given that she is suffering from fvFTD and a brain tumour, I can't think of a doctor who would have said it was possible."

Ken returned from the kitchen with sliced cheese, liver pâté, tapenade, and crackers, arranged on a plate.

"Here we go," he said, "something to soak up that wine."

Jessica was grateful for his efforts, having skipped dinner to get her rounds finished as quickly as possible. "I am curious; how does it feel to have her here? From what you have told me, her leaving was very hurtful."

"That's true," he said. "Now she is lost in the Persian world of Gilgamesh."

Gilgamesh. The name was vaguely familiar to Jessica. *Probably something I heard in one of those artsy first- or second-year courses at university.*

"As a science major, I didn't pay much attention to what was going on in Persia," she said with a chuckle.

"Persian history, art, and culture were Lena's life's work. In her current condition, she seems to have stepped right into the poem. Fitting, maybe. Perhaps more grist for that paper you want to write." Ken paused and took a sip of whiskey. "That's what she was going on about when we found her in the orchard. Gilgamesh's quest for immortality." Ken paused, looking down at the floor.

"Did he find it?"

"Yeah, in a manner of speaking, he did. He sought out an old sage—Lena would say, historically, it was Noah—as in the guy with the ark—who told him of a bush that, if consumed, would strip away old age and renew life. Sadly, it was stolen by a snake and taken from him forever."

"A snake stole the bush of immortality." Jessica wanted to laugh, but didn't. She wasn't sure how Ken might react to such a contemptuous response.

"Yes. Lena researched the poem's origins and became captivated by references within the poem that seemed to have provided a basis for the books of the Old Testament, which were written a thousand years later."

"Wow, that's interesting." Jessica failed in her efforts to mask her agnosticism. She heard Ken chuckle softly as he refilled her glass with wine.

"Is it?" he asked. "A few minutes ago, you had never heard of the poem, and you are a well-educated woman. Very few people have heard of Gilgamesh, and only a subfraction of those who have care. Yet the proposition contained therein consumed Lena's life. She wrote five books on Persian history, governance, and culture, all of which drew from the discovery of this epic poem, chiselled on stone tablets."

"I didn't mean to sound dismissive. I am a scientist, so I deal in fact, and as a doctor who treats the dying, I can tell you that immortality is neither a real nor a desirable outcome. I am sure that Lena's work was important."

"From an academic perspective, I suppose, but only to a few people. Things got a lot more interesting when Lena's writing started to turn political. She used her historical research to challenge the legitimacy of the dogma pushed down the throats of the Iranian people by the current authoritarian government. Of course, those who took notice were not adoring fans. A high-ranking mufti pronounced a fatwa against her that resulted in two attempts on her life when she was touring with her book." Ken took another drink.

"Oh, my Lord. I had no idea." Jessica was stunned by what Ken had just told her—and by how casually he had said it. For a moment, she tried—but failed—to imagine herself in such a situation. "That's horrifying. Lena must have been terrified."

Ken responded with a slight nod of his head.

"Lena certainly had a full and accomplished life," she said, and her mind drifted, for some unexplained reason, to the Jamaican immigrant patient, Charlie, that she had attended to earlier that day.

Jessica was well acquainted with grief, a complicated companion who came dressed in many different disguises, and Ken's darkening mood had less to do with the unrequited passion of academics or Iranian hit squads and everything to do with the loss of a woman he deeply loved. It seemed to her that, despite grieving their divorce, some part of Ken must have held onto Lena. His loss this time would be final.

Oddly, she found herself feeling envious of him, and as Ken poured himself another scotch and topped up her wine glass, she realized that the anger she felt for Charlie's lonely death was misplaced. It wasn't anger at a society that would permit the poor man to die alone without consequence, except, perhaps, for the relief of his overworked nursing staff; it was anger at herself.

She had made only safe choices during her life, unlike Lena, who, despite whatever internal fears she had had, must have appeared fearless to the outside world. She looked at Ken. His pain over a lost love was obvious, but the soft, enduring pain she carried was from her fear of loving and letting others love her.

"Ken, it's not only OK to grieve; it's essential for your *own* health," said Jessica. She pushed down thoughts about her own situation. It was her way of coping. She noticed how he had folded into his chair. "I know that you know it's not what Lena wrote that's important; it's what she meant to you."

"She meant the world to me," Ken muttered, as if talking to himself. "She has no idea who I am, of course, so it's not like she is saying, 'OK, so I kicked you in the nuts and left you, but now that I need you to care for me,

I'm back.' More fool me, I guess. I can't help but feel responsible for the way things turned out."

"You think you drove her away from you?" Jessica leaned forward and, reaching out her hand, placed it on Ken's knee. "Lena became seriously ill, Ken. Her type of dementia takes years to manifest itself, and chances are that, coupled with the hormonal changes brought on by menopause, Lena went through a pretty profound change mentally. And that's before you factor in a brain tumour. You shouldn't take ownership of her stuff."

"You deal in facts, Jessica; well, consider these facts and tell me I am not the common denominator. At sixteen, my mother left me. My efforts to fit in and to date girls were rejected throughout my high school years. Eventually, I found it was easier to stay to myself and avoid the hurt and disappointment of rejection." Ken took a deep breath. "I was 'too intense,' 'too cerebral,' 'too'… well, you choose the adjective. Then, during my postgraduate work at Oxford, I met Lena." Ken paused, taking a sip of whiskey. "She was not only the most beautiful woman I had met, but brilliant, well-read, sophisticated, and unpretentious. Lena understood me, Jessica, and not only liked me, but said I was a kindred spirit, her soulmate."

Jessica liked that Ken was opening up to her. That is exactly what he needed to do. So she sat quietly, nodding her encouragement for Ken to continue.

"She asked to meet me one evening in the cloister at Oxford. She was so graceful, she almost floated down the covered walkway, stopping me beneath the tall archway that led out to the quadrangle. That's where she told me that she thought she was falling in love with me. I couldn't believe what I was hearing. First of all, she was still married, and we came from two very different backgrounds. Lena was raised in a strict Muslim family, and I am a cradle Catholic. But none of that stopped us from falling madly in love with each other."

"That's a nice story, Ken," Jessica said after a short pause. "You have loved and been loved very deeply—not everybody can say that."

"Lena is a free radical, Jessica, and I think, perhaps, I am, too. It's that unpaired electron that made us similar, not soulmates. Like most free radials, we were capable of an independent existence, which, as academics, we achieved through separate travel to give guest lectures and conduct our research. We were apart for much of our marriage, but we also shared the characteristics of all free radicals: we were highly reactive and unstable."

"Wow," Jessica laughed, "and girls found you too cerebral? Go figure."

"Lena was fearless. She challenged what she believed was a gross distortion of Islamic law. She was passionate about Persian history and culture, and wrote extensively about the great Persian civilization and its demise at the hands of power-hungry zealots, authoritarian regimes, and war. Her historical perspective provided a context for my own work in demography and the consequences of unchecked growth in human populations. We never published together, but together; we became a power couple in academic circles."

"And yet you ended up in a relatively obscure, remote coastal community, farming sheep," said Jessica. She decked a cracker with cheese and popped it into her mouth.

"My colleagues warned me not to publish my last book. It turns out they were right. It was highly controversial and widely condemned within the academic and global diplomatic communities. But I knew better, and had the book published anyway, because even though my findings were not politically correct and didn't suit the desired political narrative, what I wrote was supported by hard, indisputable data."

"I don't get it. If you published factual data, why care what some critics might say?" Jessica asked.

"If there is only one lesson I am permitted to take from life, Jessica, it's to choose wisely those with whom you share the truth. I published well-researched and documented findings on recurring patterns in global populations, and then developed a predictive algorithm based on that research. It was the latter that attracted persistent, defamatory, and toxic commentary." Ken stopped for a moment and sipped his whiskey, pulling himself upright in his chair, as though back in a lecture hall, facing his students. "People are quick to condemn the crimes of past generations, but don't want to hear that the very same patterns of behaviour that authored those crimes still exist. They are simply repackaged and rebranded, but they are ubiquitous in modern society. They are fundamental to the human condition."

"That doesn't sound so controversial."

"Perhaps not to you, but the captains of industry, and those who they finance within state capitals, didn't like what I had to say—nor did they like the fact that it was very difficult to refute. It was easier to demonize and defame the author than challenge the findings. So, I became an academic pariah, and with the fatwa on Lena, we moved to this life of relative obscurity."

"So, what exactly did this algorithm predict?" Jessica asked, both intrigued by what she had just heard and a bit taken back at what seemed to be a pretty pessimistic outlook.

"To properly answer that, it would take a very long conversation. But in short, the algorithm predicted unprecedented global migration and the rise of what I termed 'identity politics,' which would undermine true democracies, replacing them with manufactured democracies and autocracies." Ken paused. "That was the human side of the equation. On the environmental side, our refusal to link population growth with climate change would see a drastic decline in water resources and food production, making both primary weapons during times of war."

"Holy crap," Jessica blurted out, putting a hand to her mouth, shocked by her own response. "Sorry, but … holy crap!"

"Sounds dreadful, for sure. But my work was predicated on finite outcomes. The algorithm also demonstrated how the worst could be avoided if public policy was amended to accommodate a limit-to-growth strategy and an end to the worship of distorted and manipulated science." Ken drained the last of his whiskey, and Jessica caught just the hint of a smile.

"Are you having me on?" she asked.

"No," he replied. "But the horrified expression on your face is priceless. In your business, palliative care, you don't have to concern yourself with outcomes, because you know what the outcome is for every patient. So, what you concern yourself with is how to make the journey toward that final destination as comfortable as possible. In the larger case of humanity, what is shocking is that we can change outcomes, but despite being armed with the predictive capability to direct us toward change, we choose to ignore the direction."

"So, the farm became your hideout?" asked Jessica.

"More like our sanctuary—or at least mine." replied Ken.

"But Lena came with you to the farm—until she became sick, right? You can't blame yourself for her sickness."

"She tried to play the role of farmer, but Lena wasn't born to be a shepherd. She came from a family in Iran that had people take care of menial tasks. As she saw the world, her role was to be a prophet, not a pauper. Despite the risks, it didn't take long for her to miss the attention that came with her high academic status and the publicity that surrounded her writing. Eventually, the reality of life with me, an aging man on a small farm, set in. I became the wrong accessory for the image she chose to portray, and so she walked away."

Jessica tried to process Ken's emotions in light of the information she had just learned about his life. She started to rethink the decision to let Lena stay with him, not for her sake but for his. "No more wine for me, thanks," she said, stopping him from pouring the remaining wine into her now-empty glass. "I'm driving, and will have a full day tomorrow." She hoped that would be a sufficient hint for him, as she was quite certain, given his darkening mood, that more whiskey was not a good idea.

Ken replaced the wine bottle on the small side table, and stared silently into the empty whiskey glass that he held in his hand, before speaking into it. "The night I tried to kiss you reminded me of my efforts to have girlfriends in my teens and early twenties. Flawed—just not one of the cool kids."

Jessica found herself annoyed by his comment, but thought carefully about her response. "It's not like you to bathe yourself in self-pity, Ken," she said. "You're grieving, and that's understandable, but be careful not to go down a rabbit hole. I am here to help if I can."

"Thanks," he said.

She knew from his doubting look that he hadn't forgotten his last comment, and her anger flared internally. She didn't tolerate self-indulgence well, especially when lacquered with self-pity, and she was damned sure that her name was not going on his pitiful list of women who had spurned him.

"Ken," she said, leaning forward and studying his eyes. "That night, you weren't out of line; I was. I rejected your advance because I am a lesbian."

His startled expression showed her clearly that this was an unexpected revelation. "I should have made that clear and not left you to think that I might be interested in you sexually."

"Oh," he replied, and that single word revealed everything that Jessica needed to know. She couldn't help but smile at his expression. "A lesbian? I did not see that coming. How did I miss it?"

"I don't advertise it. In truth, I have become good at hiding it," she replied. "My father was not only a renowned surgeon in Aberdeen, but was also a strict Presbyterian who firmly subscribed to the Westminster Larger Catechism, interpreting the prohibition of adultery spelled out in the seventh commandment to include sodomy and unnatural lusts. I could quote you every scripture that condemns the heinous sin of sodom if you asked me to, but please don't."

"Wow—I wouldn't have guessed it."

"Clearly." Jessica chuckled. "That's obvious from your reaction. I grew up thinking my constant craving was wicked, unnatural, and actually sinful. The thing is, Ken, there is a part of me that still does; that's how powerful my father's influence was on me as a child."

"I never knew my father, so I can't say I understand how that goes. I don't know what to say. I am sure it was—still is—very difficult for you. I'm sorry.

"Thanks," replied Jessica, feeling the need to unburden herself from the turmoil she had felt when Janis had called her out. She wondered if she could trust Ken with the conversation.

"So *that's* why Janis was so interested in you," said Ken, and Jessica felt a slight blush.

"Yes," she replied, deciding there was no point trying to hide the truth. "That's why when you apologized for Janis making me uncomfortable, I thought she had talked to you about the conversation we had when I dropped her at the barn. You're right—she can be pretty blunt. She knew I was a lesbian, and told me so. Thought my hiding it *backwards*."

"That's Janis. No filter at all," said Ken. "How did you respond? Or would you rather not say?"

"That's just it, Ken. I can't say I'm not attracted to her, but even now, as a fully grown, menopausal woman, that gut-wrenching, schoolgirlish fear still exists. I can't explain it."

"Be careful. Janis is a wonderful person and a great friend, but I doubt she has a delicate touch when it comes to this sort of thing. Not to tell tales out of school, but her father was an orthodox rabbi in New York, and to hear her tell the story, was only marginally more tolerable than her Jewish mother, who started to set her up with prospective husbands as soon as she had her first bleed."

Jessica recoiled at Ken's statement. "That's horrible," she said.

"I am quite sure that I am way out of bounds," said Ken, "because it's her story to tell if she wants to. But as a friend of both of you, my advice is to walk slowly into whatever might come of you meeting Janis."

"She does seem to be a bit of an enigma. Are you saying I should steer clear?" asked Jessica.

"Not at all; it's not my place to provide advice, really. Just know that beneath that rough exterior is a very fragile soul. You both share more than you might think," said Ken.

"How so?"

"When her father discovered she was in a lesbian relationship in New York, he disowned her, and forbade her mother from having any contact with her. She and her lover pledged a life together as far away from New York as possible and still on the North American continent. They bought plane tickets, but her lover was a no-show at the airport. Janis chose to come anyway, and as far as I know, she hasn't heard from either her lover or her parents since."

"Wow, I guess we all have our stuff," said Jessica. "She seems to be a real character."

"She is, and one well worth getting to know—as long as you set your boundaries and don't take her rough exterior too seriously. You won't find a better friend, if she chooses to be one—but that, Jessica, will be her choice."

15.

The whirl of the coffee grinder broke the silence as Ken followed his nightly routine, grinding coffee beans to fill the basket in the automated brewing machine, which he had filled with water and set for a very early morning.

Jessica coming out to him was like shattering a thin ice wall that had existed between them. It had provided Ken with an explanation for so much of who this remarkable woman really was. It opened the door to a free conversation about all manner of things, which had gone late into the night.

Ken had told her about Julius Omondi wanting him to grant an interview to one of his students, so when Ken received the email alert on his phone from rehema.tanui@ouce.ox.au.uk, she had encouraged him to open it.

Reading the email, he saw that Julius Omondi's student had wasted no time. She was asking for an interview the following day.

"That will be five in the morning," said Jessica. "I had better go and let you get some sleep. I will check on Lena and then head out."

They had gone together to make sure that Lena was sedated and alright.

"Don't be alarmed if she appears a bit comatose," Jessica told him. "I have heavily sedated her, and introduced pain management into her drip. The combination should enable her to sleep until I get back in the morning, but don't hesitate to call me if anything concerning should happen."

Ken had walked Jessica safely to her car before returning to the house to complete his nightly routine and prepare himself for bed. He felt anxious about his morning call. He had boxed away all the anger, hurt, and most of all, disappointment that the events surrounding his work at Oxford had brought him. He wasn't at all sure he wanted to open that box.

When the topic of the Cairo conference came up in conversation with his former colleague Julius, the familiars—pain, remorse, and betrayal—resurfaced. The sooner he did the interview with Julius's student, the sooner he might be able to shove those emotions back into the box.

Ken texted his agreement to her request, set the alarm on his phone for 4:30 in the morning, climbed into bed, and turned off the light.

The bright, full moon bathed the deck outside in a silver light. Toby had taken up his station outside the French doors, his giant head leaning up against the glass. On summer nights, Ken would pull down the screen, leaving the doors wide open to let in the sweet fragrance of Jasmine from the tall bush that grew outside.

He laid his head against the soft down pillows. The gentle night breeze hissed through the screens of the open bedroom windows, washing his face with fresh, fragrant air, willing his exhausted eyes to close.

"Heavenly Father, may I approach?" he whispered in quiet prayer. "I come to you through your Son, Jesus Christ, to give thanks for this day, for all that you have done for me during this day, and ask for your forgiveness where I have failed you."

It was a nightly ritual that he had practised for as long as he could remember. But on this night, he felt a particularly close connection. "Father, I don't know why you have led her to my door, but I feel certain that she has been strengthened and guided by your hand. I know her time with me is short. Please give me the wisdom and strength to help her in her final hours on this Earth, and I humbly ask, with all my heart, that you look favourably upon her when she makes her final journey. Amen."

His whisper became a mumble, his mind fading into a calm sea of darkness upon which he was carried through fleeting images of days past toward a safe space; a happy place through which he would enter sleep.

Ken directed his mind to the tall masts of *Forever Free* rising off the teak decking, the sails safely secured, into a cloudless, blue sky. Willing his mind aboard, he felt the gentle motion of the sailboat afloat at anchor upon the clear, emerald water of Tentandy Bay.

One Weekend in May

Lena, legs stretched out on the teak deck and her naked torso resting against the mainmast, put down the book she had been reading and got to her feet, causing sparkling silver beads of perspiration to run down the contours of her perfectly tanned body. When she had taken the few steps to the gunwale, she turned and looked at Ken, who shifted beneath the bedsheets, his mind replaying how gracefully she had dived into the cool, welcoming water.

A relentless southeasterly wind had forced them to tack most of the morning, slowing their forward progress and giving the boat a pounding from the rising sea. They decided to change course and sail toward the islands of Hidden Sound, a place they had not sailed before—and one that, on the charts at least, didn't show much promise of a safe anchorage. At least, they had agreed, they would be in the lee of the gale force winds.

Lena, through her binoculars, had spotted what she thought might be a bay beyond a very narrow divide in the jagged rockface on the small island. The island appeared on Ken's paper chart as "Tentandy Island," but there was nothing on the chart that resembled a bay. Concerned that they would navigate too close to the rocks and not have sufficient power from their small motor to head back through the wind and the following current, Ken had checked the electronic Gorman navigation system on the boat to get more accurate information.

Neither of the navigational aids had shown a channel into a bay, but Lena had insisted that they approach the island and check it out. Running the motor as slowly as he dared, Ken had relied on the storm jib for stability. It had been a difficult manoeuvre, but as they drew closer to the cliff face, what had at first appeared to be a simple fissure opened to a narrow water passage through the rock wall, and into a sunlit bay beyond.

Ken kept a close eye on the depth sounder, knowing that he needed at least fourteen feet of water to safely clear the keel. It was a dangerous manoeuvre that could very easily have gone wrong, but they passed through the passage and into a tranquil, sun-filled bay. This uncharted bay became their secret place, their Shangri-La—a refuge from storms both metaphoric and real. Lena named it "Tentandy Bay" out of respect for the island that had given them their most private place.

The dream had stirred his loins, as it always did. He drew deep breaths as his mind floated him back to Lena, who had climbed a short ladder out of the water and back onto the boat, her brown, naked body dripping wet. She had left a trail of water along the deck toward his fully aroused body.

The dream had become one of the few places he could find comfort from the clawing sense of loss that engulfed him every time he thought of his past. Over time, his mind had learned to control the mental visuals, as a television remote might slow, replay, or stop a favourite show; her kiss, her tongue at play on the lobe of his ear, her finger's faint stroke along the length of his arousal. And yet the dream had come with a price to be paid—a reminder of how much, in his waking hours, he had come to miss her skin on his, moving with a natural rhythm, in perfect synchronicity with the rocking waves.

A piercing voice pulled him from his vision. Metallic in sound as the lilting voice of the Muezzin who sang over the citywide broadcasting system, calling the faithful to Dhuhr Salah, as he did every day at noon.

The tall, arched entrance to the rotunda of the International Conference Centre in Cairo beckoned him forward.

Youthful blood coursed through him, fueling the great expectations he held for a lively debate at this conference. Over drinks in their hotel lounge the evening prior to his presentation, Julian, along with several other Oxford colleagues, told him that the abstract of his paper published in the conference literature had caused quite a stir.

That is exactly what Ken, with his newly minted PhD, had hoped it would do. He looked forward to the question-and-answer period that was scheduled to follow his presentation. He knew that what he had written in the paper to be presented would be controversial, so when, the night before, in the smoky hotel bar, his Oxford colleagues had warned him about the negative reaction his work might receive, he had not been surprised. His confidence lay within his belief that his research was impeccable—undebatable, really—and he was energized and ready to meet any challenge.

Ken stirred on his bed, not wanting to be taken where this particular dream—more of a nightmare, actually—always took him. Unlike his dream with Lena, he had no control over the replay of the disaster that had taken place at the Cairo conference, and as he had done many times before when his mind pushed him to this place, he tried to will himself awake, but was pulled back. He knew that this dream always had the same unpleasant ending.

As he walked into the gold, silver, and pearl-embossed entry hall of the Cairo conference centre, he was met by a young woman. She wore a cobalt blue hijab that framed a face almost entirely covered by round, tortoiseshell-rimmed glasses, and had a leatherbound case tucked under her arm. She presented herself with confidence and authority, and stopped directly in front of him.

"Welcome, Dr. Graham," she said, and spoke her name so quickly that to Ken's untrained Western ear, he didn't hear it. He looked to see if it was printed on the credentials tag around her neck and noticed, instead, the word STAFF printed in bold, black letters in the space reserved for the names of delegates.

"Where is Dr. Gupta? He is going to introduce me. I had hoped that we might spend a minute first—"

"There has been a change. I will be introducing you. This way, please."

Ken stirred in his bed, the all-too-familiar serpent of bile that always uncoiled within his stomach ready to strike when he was forced to the crime scene where he had been betrayed. "The main auditorium is the other way. I am scheduled to present to the main congregation at one o'clock in the auditorium. Dr. Gupta is to introduce me."

"Yes, of course," she had said, as she picked up the pace. "Please, follow me."

"No, I will not follow you. Please take me to Dr. Gupta." Ken stopped and looked at the streams of people walking in the opposite direction toward the main auditorium, and a moment of panic took hold.

Every time this nightmare replayed, he wanted it to end differently. Perhaps if he turned over in his bed or flipped his pillow over, by resting his head on the other side, there might be a different outcome, and his life would magically rewind the thirty years.

The woman stopped and feigned a nervous smile. "Dr. Graham, as I have told you, there has been a change. I will be introducing you, and the venue for your presentation is this way. Please follow me; it is almost time for your session."

"Who did you say you were?"

"I am an intern within the UN Department of Population and Development. I have been asked to introduce you. Come, it is not far now."

"An intern? I am going to be introduced by an intern?" The serpent swirled within his gut, loosening its coil with nauseous effect.

The intern led him through the door into a small, windowless lecture room. About fifty seats, raked in five rows of ten up a gently sloping floor, reminded him of his early days as a university lecturer. At the front of the room, a single podium awaited him. Sound and audiovisual equipment had been placed on a folding table along the far wall.

A young, neatly dressed Arab man approached, bowed ever so slightly, and handed Ken a thin, black electronic remote. "Your material is loaded and ready for you. Press this button to start your slides—the forward button advances and the back button returns, then press the start button again to shut off the equipment. You will have no worries."

Then he was gone.

The clock on the wall read 12:55. It was an image seared into his brain, recurring each time he faced this unwanted dream. He was looking out at a sparse audience, fewer than twenty people, and not one of his Oxford colleagues was in the room. Bile raced up his throat ahead of the hissing serpent that dragged him into semi-consciousness.

Tossing in his bed, his dream transformed into a memory. A simple, undignified introduction by an intern.

"Good afternoon," The intern said, "Please welcome Dr. Graham." She then not only stepped away from the podium, but walked out of the room.

Ken looked out at an audience of black faces, arms crossed, in defiant body language. This reception was not at all what he had anticipated, and he was barely able to finish his introductory remarks before he was interrupted by a rotund black man sitting in the middle section of seats.

"We know who you are, Dr. Graham, and we know what is in your paper. We are not here to listen to your racist, white, colonial point of view. The days of the empire are over, and we are here to set you straight. Your views are merely echoes of a noxious past that, thankfully, is gone forever. What you write is no longer relevant. It is inconsistent with the views of the overwhelming majority of those attending this conference."

One Weekend in May

"I am sorry," Ken remembered saying. "I don't know you—"

"Your writing comes as no surprise to any of us here, Dr. Graham," the large black man interrupted. "I am sure it is not lost on you that we represent the black faces of Africa. We are the expanding populations that, according to you, will expand within the next twenty years beyond the capacity of nations to feed them. According to your work, we are the people who will suffer the effects of a changing world climate that will bring drought to some, floods to others, and viral disease unmatched in our history." The speaker leaned forward in his seat. "So, we, the black people of Africa, need to limit our numbers while you, the white man, continue to dominate and exploit in every way. Isn't that what your paper is all about? White domination, the continued plundering of our resources, and keeping us in poverty, dependent upon your charity when and if given."

Ken challenged the man. "I am not sure who you are, but that is not what my paper postulates nor is it remotely close to its conclusions and recommendations."

He later learned that his verbal assailant had been Oscar Kobani, Nigerian minister for economic and social development and, ten years later, with the backing of the Nigerian army, the president.

Ken rolled over and tried burying his head in his pillow. This rehash of events served no purpose. They had been conjured up as a response to the pending interview with Rehema. He propped himself up in his bed and glanced at the red numbers on the small clock radio beside the bed. It was 4:30, so he leaned over and switched off the alarm. He was wide awake now.

He couldn't shake the nightmare. Kobani, through his verbal assault, had, quite ironically, reinforced Ken's hypothesis.

"I am here to tell you that your white, racist views will no longer be tolerated now that black people have taken the reins of power—not only in Africa but increasingly in the United Nations organization. By the year 2050, there will be more black people living in Nigeria than the total US population. The majority of people on the planet will be black, and you, white man, will not be permitted to deny black men and their black women their right to determine how many black children they will raise."

It had been the theme of the conference, which, while not referencing race specifically, concluded that population control, with the notable exception of China's one-child policy, was to be left up to individuals. The conference concluded that economic growth and a more equal global distribution of wealth would bring about a reduction in population growth.

Ken, in the quiet evenings on the farm, often thought about how young and naive he had been. He never looked beyond the veracity of his research. It simply didn't occur to him that publishing the truth would challenge a power paradigm that was so well established, and protected by an artfully crafted cyber-barrier of lies.

He wanted the consequential findings of his work to be grist for economic and political debate, and more importantly, a profound change in public policy. He had never even imagined how the reaction to his work would change his life—that by challenging the global political and economic powers, he would make powerful and ruthless enemies.

It had been the political attendees at the Cairo conference that, in closed-session and private meetings over dinner and drinks, determined to re-commit to the recommendations in the 1987 report of the Brundtland Commission, *Our Common Future*, later published by Oxford University Press.

His work directly challenged those findings, presenting instead what he was certain would become obvious, namely, that the practice of "sustainable development," a phrase introduced by the Brundtland Commission, was an oxymoron, a no-effect placebo in the treatment and cure of the world's real problems, an unwillingness to accept that there are defined and real limits to growth.

In fact, it was precisely because his work threatened to unmask the obvious deception within the concept of "sustainable development" that he had been targeted.

After all, there were billions of dollars to be made by both governments and NGOs alike advancing the fallacy that sustained economic growth, enhanced environmental awareness, and the promise of social equality, all good political buzzwords, would result in a livable planet.

Ken swung his legs out of bed, letting his feet slip into slippers as he rose and pulled on his housecoat.

His first concern was Lena, so he shuffled to the hall and into her room. She appeared asleep, which was consistent with what Jessica had led him to expect, but a pungent odour made him aware that her diaper needed to be changed.

Returning with a bowl of warm, soapy water, he gently and efficiently completed the clean and change, but heard, as he did so, a soft groan. Each time Lena groaned, a slight wrinkle appeared on her brow, and he wondered how badly she was in pain, and mentally filed it as something to be raised with Jessica when she arrived.

When he was satisfied that Lena was clean and resting as comfortably as possible, he took a long, hot shower. He chuckled at himself in the full-length mirror as he slipped on his favourite mustard-coloured, short-sleeved shirt and tucked it into his best pair of jeans. "Oh, shut up," he admonished the voice in his head while raking a comb through his steel-grey hair. "There is nothing wrong with trying to look presentable."

16.

Ken was immediately struck by Rehema Tanui's high cheekbones, perfectly symmetrical face, and cheerful, dark brown eyes, bridged by a delicate, straight nose. He was not one to objectify women, but there was no denying that she was one of the most beautiful women he had ever seen, with classically beautiful lips made more sumptuous by her gently tapered jawline and small, rounded chin. Her slight frown made him worry that he had not concealed his reaction when seeing her, and she had found it inappropriate.

She adjusted the computer camera, slightly revealing an unfinished red brick wall behind her and a very sparsely furnished room that, upon second glance, seemed to be a veranda. She had mentioned in her email setting up the meeting that she was still at home in Kenya due to the restrictions on travel caused by a viral pandemic that was ravishing the country.

"Good evening, Dr. Graham," she said, flashing a wide smile. "It is a real pleasure to meet you, even virtually." She adjusted the blue head-tie scarf that matched her high-collared, light blue blouse. "Although for you, it must be a good morning."

"It's a pleasure to meet you, Ms. Tanui. Julius Omondi spoke very highly of your academic and scholastic abilities," Ken said, and he returned the smile. "Yes, it's exactly 5:30 a.m. Where exactly are you?"

"I am out on the veranda at my parent's home in Nyeri. I hope by sitting out here I will still have enough sunlight, as the veranda is one of the few spots where I can get reliable Wi-Fi—and please, it's Rehema—far less formal."

"Sounds good—then it's *Ken* on this end. Julius is a reader for your doctoral thesis, as I understand things."

"Oh, much more than just a reader. We are collaborating on a book, one chapter of which will be submitted to the post-doctoral committee at Oxford."

Well, that's a detail that Julius conveniently left out. Ken just smiled.

"I take it from your reaction that he didn't mention the book?" said Rehema.

"No, he didn't."

"Is that a problem?" she asked, a touch of caution in her voice.

"That will quite likely depend upon what is in the book. I am very curious about your working thesis. I understand that it is linked to my work, which is why you wanted to connect."

"Absolutely, it is." Her enthusiasm was obvious, and Ken shuffled a little, trying to be more comfortable in his chair.

"Forgive me if I no longer share your enthusiasm, Rehema. This line of academic inquiry will win you no friends—and possibly make you powerful enemies." Ken spoke slowly, hoping that his words would settle in. "My advice, for what it's worth, is that you leave this alone."

"Professor Omondi warned me that may be your response. But Dr. Graham, if we want to survive on this planet, we need to change the public policy narrative and start to discuss a change in what has become our normative response to ever-increasing numbers of people on a finite global landmass."

Ken had a silent chuckle at hearing his words preached back to him by this young woman. "Rehema, if you have read all of my work, as Julius told me you have, you know that you don't need to convince me of that. But that train pulled out of the station in 1972. Many very talented scholars sounded the alarm in speeches, academic papers, and even books, as you plan to do. Their warning fell on deaf ears. You must be aware of the reaction I received after taking my paper to Cairo in 1994."

"I have read some of the defamatory comments that were directed toward you, and of course Professor Omondi has discussed some of that negative reaction with me. Nothing your critics said can refute the fact that your words were prophetic. That is especially true of your work on the rise of new tribalism and the entrenchment of the racial divide through race-based legislation. It has all come to pass, and it is past time that your findings be revisited in light of the new global paradigm." Rehema appeared to be searching through some papers beside her computer. "I am curious about your reference to November 1972. Would that be a reference to Donella Meadows's *Limits to Growth* publication commissioned by the Club of Rome?"

"Exactly. It was those early algorithms and graphs that drew me into this field of study. What should have been the first real opportunity for a serious discussion on the connection between exponential economic and population growth fell short, because it failed to factor in the most critical component: the human condition."

"I am not sure that I am fully following you."

Perhaps it was the intensity in Rehema's wide-open eyes, so alive upon the tiny screen, that reignited the passion he had for this subject—a passion that he had buried years ago.

Only one other person really understood and shared in what he had been writing about, and she had walked out on him, leaving him alone, abandoned to a plague of nightmares. Whiskey had been his short-term solution—not the best, but the most immediate.

"You need to leave this alone, especially because …" Ken let his voice fade, as he thought it best to not to finish what he was about to say.

"Especially because … of what?" Rehema seemed genuinely confused.

He silently debated whether or not he should find an excuse to end the conversation. But there was something about this woman that made him trust her.

Surely, this intelligent black woman had to know that Donella Meadows, along with her husband and two others at MIT, all brilliant in their fields, were undone by a condition invisible to them but not to those who would judge their work. The authors and those who had initiated the Club of Rome and who commissioned the work *Limits to Growth* were all white-skinned, and with a couple of notable exceptions, Donella being one, they were men—and men who held positions of power and wealth. He wasn't at all sure he wanted to get into that conversation with this student.

"Dr. Graham—Ken, are you alright?"

"Rehema, I am going to trust you with what I am about to say. You need to examine—really examine—what motivates you to pursue this line of work, because it will be strenuously challenged, and you need to know—really *know*—that you are on solid ground academically, morally, and personally. Look, I really appreciate your support for my work, but there is a reason that we don't hold conferences on population growth anymore. The global leadership does not want it discussed."

"I know that, which is why I am so determined to get it discussed."

She sounded determined.

Ken liked her. Rehema seemed to have a sharp mind and a pureness of character that reminded him of his early days with Lena. But he also knew that by sticking her neck out, she would open herself up to very hurtful and damaging comments from a wide range of sources. Not only would she be pushing a message that would challenge the rich and powerful, but she would be doing so as a beautiful African woman. He was quite sure that, despite the progress in women's emancipation, far too many powerful men of all races still didn't believe a woman can be both beautiful and brilliant—especially a woman of colour.

"Rehema, I think you really need to think through what your next steps should be. *Limits to Growth* failed not because the postulations were wrong, but because those making them were white-skinned and from wealthy nations. The issue became embroiled in a debate about the North/South divide, the haves and have-nots, the colonials versus the colonized. Anticolonial activism is the saveur du jour, so it will be even more difficult to have this message properly discussed." Ken took a sip of coffee.

"I guess what you are telling me now just reinforces what you wrote before: that in order to properly address a global path forward, we need to refocus our study—concentrate less on what we do, and sharpen our lens on who, as humans, we are." She leaned back in her chair with unblinking eyes.

"Yes." Ken sighed.

"You were one of the first to call out the Club of Rome, weren't you?" asked Rehema, continuing before Ken could respond. "I read the transcript of a lecture where you said they would fail because the global majority would lose the message in their condemnation of the messenger." Rehema shuffled through some papers until she found what she was looking for, and she raised a page in front of the camera.

"Dr. Graham, in light of what you have just told me, is this what you mean when you wrote that we should focus on who, as humans, we are? 'Every species has survival as its prime objective, but in doing so, it seeks to survive with those of its own kind first, those with whom it holds a symbiotic relationship second, and those who do not threaten the prime objective last. It will systematically eliminate all species that do not fit within those three parameters, which is why, in our evolution, humans are the only hominids that have survived of all hominids, all of whom once shared the planet at the same time. Not because of climate change, a superior brain, or competition over dwindling resources. We prevailed because we killed them. We practised genocide, and eliminated them because it benefited us to do so.'" She paused, and then held up a second page. "'Now that we have eliminated the external threat, humans have evolved into divided subsets using a variety of criteria—skin colour being the most obvious. This is the rise of new tribalism, where membership in the tribe is determined by criteria that create a 'members-only' exclusivity. With the external threat to our existence eliminated, absent a fundamental change in the human condition, it is only a matter of time before these subsets and the divisions within them turn on each other.'"

"Yes, that's precisely what I meant. Look, I don't mean to be rude, but I don't need a refresher course on my work, Rehema," said Ken. "Perhaps you should tell me how your book will make a positive contribution to this discussion."

"Yes, of course. I plan, with your permission, to use your predictive algorithm to input changes that have occurred since you published. Specifically, I want to focus on how states are trying to address this tribalism through legislation in those that are democracies, and authoritarian and military rule in those that aren't." She paused and looked at Ken, who nodded, hoping that she would elaborate. "Your algorithm predicted heightened conflict and human displacement as nation-states fail under the weight of debt due to domestic demands from desperate populations. You postulated that this would add to the rising tide of tribalism, the collapse of the established rule of law, and, to put it bluntly, result in anarchy. I want to prove it."

Ken felt conflicted. On one hand, he felt excited at the prospect of his work being updated and applied to the current world. On the other hand, the anxiety left from the PTSD he had experienced after being pilloried by his colleagues, the media, and influential people within the international community surged within him.

"What are your thoughts, Dr. Graham?"

"My thoughts? Listen, you seem like someone who has a great mind and a very bright future. Don't throw it away by spending your time researching solutions that no one will be prepared to implement." He leaned back in his chair, hoping that she wouldn't interpret his comment as being too paternalistic or condescending.

"Wow, when you put it that way, it sounds like there are no solutions. So, what are you suggesting? We should just carry on and let be what will be? With respect, I can't accept that," she countered.

"What I am suggesting, Rehema, is that people are more likely to accept answers than solutions. The reason for that is simple enough. Accepting or rejecting an answer generally comes with little or no consequence, but a solution requires action, which always has a consequence. That's why successful politicians learn to provide answers, not solutions."

"That's an interesting way of looking at the issue," she said. "So, reducing global population is an answer to many problems, but the solution is not palatable—or perhaps, some might say, not even possible."

"Exactly," said Ken. "In the years when the issue was discussed at international conferences, it was very much a matter of, 'you go first,'" he laughed. "As a society, we latch on to catchy phrases like 'sustainable development,' which mean different things to different people. We, as a global society, have become the lunar scholar who points his finger toward the moon and then studies his finger."

"I am going to have to think hard about this conversation," said Rehema.

Ken couldn't help but notice her deflated demeanour. "Hey, I don't want you to get me wrong," he said. "I truly admire your commitment to what I firmly believe is not only a valid academic line of inquiry but a route to finding real and lasting solutions to the most pressing problem facing humankind. I just don't want to see a talent such as yourself destroyed."

"I appreciate your concern," she said, and then, with a slight smile, offered, "Anyway, I thought climate change was the most pressing problem facing humankind."

"It is a huge problem, potentially, and another really good example of what we have been discussing," replied Ken, thinking this segue might provide a chance to lighten the conversation a bit and sound more positive. "We have written a great apocalyptic script, with Mother Nature as our protagonist and carbon emissions in the role of villain, with oil production given a supporting role—and yet the global population, who make it all possible, are mere extras on the set, not even offered coffee at the crafty."

"But surely you don't deny that carbon emissions are a huge contributor to global climate change?"

The shocked look on Rehema's face made him laugh. "Don't worry, I am not a climate change denier. I was simply pointing out that the problem lies on the consumption side, not the production side of the equation.

"Well, to play devil's advocate, if we have no choice, then we will consume what is available."

"We always have a choice; we just refuse to take responsibility for the choices we make. We hear that driving a gas-powered car is harmful to the environment, so we switch to driving an electric vehicle without so much as a thought for how the electricity is generated, or what resources are involved in the production of the car, mining for rare earth minerals, or the environmental cost of disposing of the batteries that come with the car. The proper choice is to not drive a car at all, but to take transit."

"Easier if you live in a Western city," said Rehema, and Ken smiled at the wagging of her finger.

"OK, I will give you that—and I do acknowledge that it is largely Western societies that consume more. After all, we go to great lengths and expenses to extend every life. The pharmaceutical and medical industries pump billions of dollars into anti-aging research so that we live longer, to buy their creams and medications."

"Ouch," laughed Rehema. "OK, guilty of using moisturizer."

One Weekend in May

Ken sensed he was climbing on his soapbox and getting preachy, which made him think of Lena, who would raise her eyebrows as a signal when he did so in mixed company. He thought it best to try to wrap up the discussion, so he returned to the topic of her book. "I am curious: if you are writing a book with Professor Omondi at Oxford, why did you return to Kenya during such uncertain times? The country is facing a terrible virus, is it not?"

"It is," she replied. "My mother became quite sick with the virus, and my father needed my help to care for her, so I flew home from London. The British authorities informed me that I had to quarantine in Kenya before I returned to London, where I will have to quarantine again. It's the new normal, I'm told."

"I am sorry to hear it," said Ken. "How is your mother now?"

Rehema paused. "She died."

Ken felt a punch to his gut. "I am so sorry. My condolences. I had no idea you were going through this. I can be quite cavalier about our need to die when speaking in the abstract, but I know it's quite a different matter when it's close to home."

"Thank you," replied Rehema. "I would welcome a second interview—specifically, on the new tribalism aspect of your work."

"Sure," Ken nodded and finished the coffee in his mug.

Rehema opened a red-covered book that Ken recognized as his last publication, *The Pursuit of Immortality and the Death of a Planet.* "Before we end this session, I would like your comment on one more quote, if you don't mind."

Ken nodded.

She flipped to a bookmarked page. "This is perhaps one of your more controversial quotes," she said. "'Seeking immortality is humankind's greatest carnal indulgence. Viewed through a length of mirrored glass, our aging bodies offer up an unwelcome reflection. The offer of immortal youth, which comes to us in lotions, vitamins, supplements, body-enhancing surgeries, and medications, is designed to disrobe and blindfold us from the truth. This intoxicating seduction provides an image that does not stop time, despite the promise of perpetual youth and longevity.'"

"I was in a pretty dark place when I wrote those words," said Ken. He looked at the confusion on Rehema's face. "My wife, Lena, had just left me. I was pretty sure that one of the reasons was that I, an older man, had become the wrong accessory to the more youthful image she presented."

"Oh, I am sorry to learn that. But nevertheless, it struck a chord with me, and I am prepared to accept that what you have written is true. As a young girl, I was obsessed with 'Western style beauty.' I entered and won the Miss Eldoret beauty contest and was the odds-on favourite to win Miss Kenya, which might have taken me all the way to Miss World. But I was a university freshman, and I read your book. It changed my thinking completely."

"I am sorry if, by reading my book, you denied yourself the opportunity that comes with winning Miss World," he said.

"I am not at all sure I would have won the title, but thank you for your concern. I was referencing the physical characteristics required to be considered beautiful. Those characteristics are undeniably 'Western,' and in many cases white. What once might have been considered beautiful within a cultural context will not meet the test on the international stage. Hence, the growth of the cosmetic surgery industry is designed to remove physical characteristics that once made us distinct in terms of our heritage. But that is a discussion for another day."

"Yes, it is for sure. I was simply trying to point out that society, particularly Western society, has surgically removed dignity from aging."

Rehema smiled. "Thank you so much for this interview. I would like to get back to you in a day or so, after I have had time to properly reflect on what we discussed today. Will that be alright with you?"

"Yes, I am happy to help you in any way I can. Just email me, and we will set up a time for the next call. I am deeply sorry about your mother."

17.

Ken watched through the rain-streaked window as Sheena helped Ethan out of the car. The light rain was welcome. The spring, as springs go, had been dry, so the moisture—more of a heavy mist than rain—would keep the fields green with fresh grazing a little longer. Dressed in appropriate rain gear, he saw that Sheena was headed toward the back door of the house, which opened into a mudroom. He opened the door and greeted his daughter and grandson with a smile, a kiss on the cheek, and a hug.

Ethan was out of his coat and had his boots kicked off before he had taken two steps into the house. "Hi Granddad," he greeted, "can I play Lego?"

His grandson was obsessed with Lego, so Ken had purchased a number of sets so that he had something to build each time he visited.

"I think we should visit for a bit first," suggested Sheena, and Ken chuckled at the exhaled pout that came from Ethan.

With coats properly hung and boots tucked away, the three of them walked along the hall toward the kitchen.

"Do you mind if I put on a pot of tea?" asked Sheena, and Ken nodded his approval. "How is Mom?"

Ken heard the trepidation in his daughter's voice, and in his mind, he knew that the question really being asked was *is she dead yet*? "Your mother had a quiet night. Jessica has been very helpful with the required medications, but I think that they may be losing their effectiveness."

"I spoke briefly with Jessica on the phone earlier. She told me about giving her some additional pain relief if she appears uncomfortable during my visit," said Sheena, filling the electric kettle and flipping on the switch.

Toby's steady bark outside caught Ken's attention. "Sounds like there is an issue in the lower field, Ethan. Go put on your coat and boots, and let's go see what that's all about. I promise you can play Lego when we get back."

He didn't need to be asked twice. He ran back to the mudroom, pulled on his boots, and, grabbing hold of his coat, handed it to Ken, who had followed.

"First things first, Ethan," said Ken, noticing that the left boot was on his right foot and the right on his left. "Let's get these on the proper feet."

Once down the narrow flight of stairs that led off the back deck, Ken offered Ethan a ride on his shoulders, an offer quickly accepted. He picked up the pace and strode through the gate and into the field, heading toward the sound of barking.

"Granddad"—Ethan's lilting voice seemed to sing the honorific—"what's a recluse?"

Ken chuckled. This young man was a thinker. He liked that about him, but he never quite knew the direction of his young mind.

"A recluse, Ethan, is a person who chooses to live alone, and generally avoids other people."

"Is that a good thing or a bad thing?" Ethan asked, his hands resting on his grandfather's head, his knee-high rubber boots draped over his shoulders.

"It is neither good nor bad, Ethan. It is what some people choose to do. Often, people don't like being among other people. They live a solitary life," said Ken, using the word solitary slowly. "That means preferring to be on their own."

"Do you like people, Granddad?" Ethan's inquisitive tone and direct line of questioning gave Ken pause to think. He noticed Toby pacing about, barking at four ravens, lunging at them as they took turns hopping forward at something lying in the field.

Ken knew at once that the object the ravens were after was a newborn lamb, so he hoisted Ethan off his shoulders. "Come on, Ethan," he said to his grandson, and they started to jog toward the dog.

"Why are we running?" Ethan's little legs scissored back and forth over the uneven field, his arms pumping, and his tiny fists clenched, punching the air.

Ken didn't respond, but shouted, clapping his hands to scare the four ravens into the air and into the tall cedars, where they perched, watching.

Toby wagged his tail furiously, happy for the assistance but barking his admonishment at Ken for having taken so long to get to the tiny, white lamb that lay in the field, only partially cleaned of afterbirth.

"Oh, he is so cute, and so small," Ethan remarked as he crouched down to examine the shivering newborn.

Ken scanned the sheep in the field, looking for the telltale signs that would be apparent for any ewe that had just given birth. Experience told him that it would be a one-year-old, first-time mom. Ken was annoyed. He knew that the chances of this tiny creature surviving more than twenty-four hours were slim—judging by the size of the lamb, that it was premature. That's why he didn't intentionally breed one-year-olds.

"How come he is so wet, Granddad? Granddad, what is all that gooey stuff? Is he going to be OK?" Ethan's questions came without pause for a reply from Ken, who pulled out a pair of latex surgical gloves that he always carried in the back pocket of his jeans during lambing season, and stretched them over his large fingers, then cleared the sticky mucus away from the lamb's mouth and nose.

"Can I keep him, Granddad? Can he be my sheep?" Ethan asked as Ken continued to do his best to clean off the tiny lamb that spluttered his first, feeble bleat.

"To start with, Ethan, *he* is a *she*. If you listen carefully, you will hear a kind of rattle when she breathes. Do you hear that?"

Ethan leaned forward, tilting his head so his tiny ear was close to the lamb. "Yeah," he said. "What does that mean, Granddad?"

"It means that this poor little thing has fluid in her lungs. That's not a good sign."

"But she's going to be OK, right? I mean, she's only just been born, so she's going to get stronger, right, Granddad?"

Ken didn't believe that glossing over the harsh truth of things made life any easier. It was important for Ethan to learn that life sometimes presented very unpleasant situations, and this was one of them.

"Hey, bud, would you do your granddad a big favour?"

"Sure."

"Do you see the red door to the shearing shed over there?" he asked, pointing toward the addition behind the main barn, and Ethan nodded. "Hanging on a hook behind the door, you will find a dry towel. Would you mind running over to the shed and bringing me that towel?"

Without reply, Ethan was off like a shot, with Toby bounding along beside him.

A clue to which of the ewes in the field had given birth was provided by one of the four ravens. It had flown down from the cedar tree and hopped behind a small, white ewe that was swirling around, head down, trying to butt the bird away. Ken knew that the smell of the afterbirth would have attracted the bird, so he made a mental note of the derelict ewe while he continued to do her job, cleaning her newborn lamb.

Once Ethan had returned with the towel, Ken was able to do a more thorough job of cleaning up the lamb, which he wrapped in the towel and handed to Ethan to carry to the barn while Ken caught and wrestled the mother into compliance. Both went into a lambing pen to see if there was any chance at all that the ewe would accept her lamb.

Ken used a suction tube to try to clear the air passageway, while Ethan looked on. He had tried presenting the baby to the mother, but she immediately pulled away. Pinning the ewe against the wall of the pen with his body, Ken also reached down to the udder, and milked out colostrum from both bags before latching the lamb onto the teat. Her suckle was so weak that she was barely able to pull the thick fluid through the nipple. Ken noticed the soft, opaque hooves, which confirmed that it was premature, and almost certainly not going to survive.

While doing what he could for the newborn animal, he noticed Ethan watching in uncharacteristic silence. It wasn't until the two of them were washing their hands at the sink in the shearing shed that Ethan finally spoke.

"Granddad, what will happen to that lamb? Will it die?"

Ken looked at the furled brow of his grandson, noting his sad eyes. "Yes, I suspect she will die."

"Can't you do anything to help it live?" Ethan asked, pulling more paper towels off the roll than required to dry his hands.

"I have done what I can, Ethan. You saw me use that suction tube to try to clear the fluid from her lungs, but I don't think I was successful. I showed you her hooves; they were barely formed. She was born too early."

"But in church, I hear Father say that every life has value. There is no value in a life if you die right after you are born." Ethan appeared quite upset, sinking his hands into the pockets of his small denim overalls. "Can't God fix her? Maybe He expects you to fix her."

Ken picked up his grandson, who buried his head in his grandfather's broad shoulder. "I think in church, Father is talking about human life, not farm animals. On a farm, we learn that not everything can be fixed, Ethan, and I think God is OK with that. Maybe He even planned it that way. You and I don't know why that lamb was born too early, but there is always a reason. As a farmer, you have to learn to accept and respect that."

"Not just on the farm," replied Ethan, leaning back so that his eyes were level with his grandfather's, his two hands squeezing his cheeks. "Grandma is going to die, and my dad died." Ken carried Ethan out of the shearing shed, with Toby directly behind them, his long, wet tongue hanging from his mouth. "OK, bud, you have to walk from here," he said. Ethan's comment about his father had shocked Ken, and he was unsure how he should respond. Ken had never met Farouk—a name given to him by Sheena when he had asked her about Ethan's father. Farouk and Sheena had had a casual relationship during their final years at university, but as far as Ken was aware, he was very much alive.

Ken remembered the name because of the family drama that had resulted when Sheena, no longer able to hide her pregnancy, had told her mother that she had decided to keep her child and raise him on her own.

Lena had insisted on knowing who the father was, and when Sheena, on the condition that her mother promised she would not contact the man, told her his name was Farouk, Lena, always the historian, fluent in both Persian and Arabic, made a great deal about the fact that the name meant 'knowing right from wrong'—and this man certainly did not!

But that's really all Ken knew, and as he started the walk back to the house, holding the hand of his grandson, he realized that half of the genetics of this boy was a mystery to him. Not that it mattered to Ken. But it might matter to Ethan as he grew older. Certainly, Ken had not heard that Farouk had died.

"Your Grandma is very sick, Ethan. She will be at peace and out of pain when she dies, so you must try to be happy for her," he finally replied.

"What about my dad?" asked Ethan.

"I don't know about that, Ethan; you should ask your mom."

"I don't think Grandma liked me," said Ethan, and Ken felt a slight squeeze on his hand.

"Your Grandma didn't know you long enough to show you how much she loved you," Ken responded, recalling how Lena had left a month after Ethan's first birthday.

"No, but she could have," said Ethan. A comment to which Ken had no response.

Toby, perhaps feeling left out of the conversation, tried to push himself between Ken and Ethan, so Ethan let go of Ken's hand and put his arm around the dog's neck, and the three of them kept walking toward the house.

"Did your mom tell you that your father was dead?" Ken knew he was stepping over a boundary. It really wasn't his business what Sheena might have told his grandson, and yet …

"She said that I should just accept that my dad is dead. Like you said about the lamb dying, accept and respect."

Ken wasn't sure how he should respond.

"Besides, if my dad wasn't dead, why wouldn't he come to see me?" Ethan's pace up the steep slope leading to the gate out of the field slowed. "Granddad, can I go back up on your shoulders?"

Ken crouched down, and Ethan put one leg over each shoulder, holding tightly onto Ken's head.

"Wow," Ken said, straightening up, "you are becoming a big boy; I am not sure how much longer I will be able to do this."

"You will," Ethan assured his grandfather. "You are strong and can do anything."

"I am glad you think so, Ethan."

"Grandad?"

"What now?"

"When I grow up, can we be best friends? Then we can be a recluse together. I would like that."

"I think we are best friends now, Ethan. But why do you think I am a recluse?"

"Mom said. I heard her tell someone on the phone."

"Did she now?" said Ken, walking through the gate and closing it quickly behind him so that Toby would remain in the field with the sheep. That, and the matter of Ethan's father, were two bones to pick with Sheena when the opportunity arose.

Ethan gently patted out a rhythm on his grandfather's head, as he might use a bongo drum, and Ken swayed with the beat as the two made their way back to the house.

18.

Sheena, a fresh cup of tea in hand, gathered her cardigan around her shoulders as she stood on the front deck of the house, watching her son, Ethan, ride on his grandfather's shoulders through the wooden gate into the lush green field.

She chuckled at the sound of her father's voice in her head: "Always leave the gate as you found it." It was a vague but certain memory she held of once riding those same shoulders. She loved that there was such a strong bond between Ethan and her father, while pushing back the flicker of guilt that, when presented with the choice, she had denied Ethan a father figure in his life.

As she watched the two walk down the field, she had to concede that even Toby's distant bark was part of a peaceful melody that emanated from the property—a sanctuary away from her world of noise and deadlines, critics and demands.

A slight shiver caught her by surprise. Perhaps the cool mist that blushed her cheeks was the cause, so she returned inside and closed the door to the deck. It came again, unambiguous this time, intrinsically linked to the hint of fear she felt at the prospect of seeing her mother.

Sheena had felt her visits with her mother at the nursing home become increasingly hurtful, until she reached the point where she stopped going. Her mother not only treated her like a stranger, but her delusions and paranoia resulted in shouted accusations that Sheena was stealing from her or plotting to dethrone her from a fictional throne.

One Weekend in May

She gently placed her teacup on the kitchen counter and picked up a bouquet of lilacs, freshly cut from a tall bloom at the entryway to the farm, that she had arranged in a crystal vase.

Her mother loved lilacs.

As Sheena carried them down the hallway toward the bedroom door, the fragrant blooms, pastel blue, evoked a strong and pleasant memory from when she was a young girl, when she and her mother would walk hand in hand to cut fresh flowers and then arrange them in crystal vases to perfume each room with a splash of colour.

As she reached the closed bedroom door, she paused, uncertain for a moment, then cracked open the door and peeked inside.

Through the narrow crack of the open door, Sheena could see her mother's face, gaunt and still, mouth open. The only sound was wheezy inhalations, causing a gentle rise and fall in the bedding.

"Hello Momma," she whispered, stepping into the room and hoping, in part, not to wake her, for fear of the reception that she might receive. "I have brought you your favourite flowers." She put the vase next to a leather-bound book that she recognized to be her mother's treatise on the epic Persian poem *Gilgamesh*, lying on a mirrored dresser opposite the bed.

Sheena shifted her gaze from her own reflection and looked over her shoulder at what remained of the woman who had held her as a child and rocked her to sleep. Her reflected image transformed into a little girl in her mother's lap, her head upon her bosom, who fell asleep to the steady beat of a loving heart and her mother's soft song.

Thinking it safe, she walked over to the window, drew back the curtains enough to let in the muted, rainy-day light, and opened the window slightly to a gentle stream of fresh, cool air.

Turning away from the window, Sheena realized that she had not been in the room since her father had refurbished it. A collage of framed photographs had been hung on the opposite wall. They were family pictures that depicted her and Asher when young, celebrating birthdays, and summer holidays on *Forever Free*. And, prominently placed, a familiar photograph of her mother with Hercules, her favourite stallion, and Chuckles, Sheena's show-jumping pony.

Sheena found herself smiling.

These pictures dusted off memories long stored away—good memories of a time when the four had been a family: father, mother, daughter, and brother. But, gazing upon this wall of their lives, a deep melancholy swept over her. It had all fallen apart in some way, swept up and tossed away.

Nonetheless, the fact that her father had gone through old pictures, and had them all framed and mounted on the wall seemed oddly out of character.

In the quiet of the room, Sheena heard her mother's breathing change, and, thinking that she may be waking up, she pulled the dresser-chair closer to the bed. But when her mother settled back, eyes still closed, Sheena reached for the book on the dresser, hoping that reading aloud might be a comfort.

The gentle breeze through the open window lifted the fragrance of the delicate lilacs, circulating their perfume around the otherwise stuffy room. Sheena opened the book. It was familiar to her because her mother had read it to her numerous times. She flipped through the chapters, stopping on a later one entitled "Immortality Lost," turned a page, and started to read.

"Then Gilgamesh raised a punting pole and drew the boat to shore. Utnapishtim spoke to Gilgamesh, saying, Gilgamesh, you came here exhausted and worn out. What can I give you so you can return to your land? I will disclose to you a thing that is hidden. Gilgamesh, I will tell you. There is a plant, like a boxthorn, whose thorns will prick your hand like a rose. If your hands reach that plant, you will become a young man again." Sheena paused and studied her mother, who seemed more relaxed, with her mouth closed and her breathing quieter and less laboured, so Sheena read on.

"Hearing this, Gilgamesh opened a gateway to the Apsu and attached heavy stones to his feet. They dragged him down to the Apsu, where they pulled him. He took the plant, though it pricked his hand, and cut the heavy stones from his feet, letting the waves throw him onto its shores. Gilgamesh spoke to Urshanabi, the ferryman, saying: Urshanabi, this plant is a plant against decay by which a man can attain his survival. I will bring it to Uruk Haven and have an old man eat the plant to test it. The plant's name is 'The Old Man Becomes a Young Man.' Then I will eat it and return to the condition of my youth.

"At twenty leagues, they broke for some food; at thirty leagues, they stopped for the night. Seeing a spring and how cool its waters were, Gilgamesh went down and bathed in the water. A snake smelled the fragrance of the plant, silently came up, and carried it off. While going back, it sloughed off its casing. At that point Gilgamesh sat down, weeping, his tears streaming over the side of his nose." Sheena looked up from the book to see her mother in involuntary motion, arms and legs twitching. She gasped at the sight of tears flowing from her mother's closed eyelids, running over sunken cheeks like raindrops down drought-cracked soil. She looked around the room and spotted a box of tissues on the far end of the nightstand. As she rose from her chair, her mother's weak, breathy voice spoke.

"Counsel me, O ferryman Urshanabi. For whom have my arms laboured, Urshanabi? For whom has my heart's blood roiled? I have nothing good to show for my life. The plant is gone. The waters are coursing twenty leagues away. I will never find the gateway again. My life is over, and I have nothing to show for it." Lena's tear-flooded eyes opened wide as her voice trailed off.

Sheena, caught up in her mother's lines, spoke softly, "to show for it? You have me."

Her mother's head turned, her eyes staring. "Who are you? Why are you here?" Her panic-cracked and shrill voice startled Sheena.

"I am Sheena, your daughter, and you are my mother." Sheena sighed as she spoke the words. This was all too familiar, and her heart sank, along with her body, as it dropped into the chair.

"Water, I must have water. Is it possible that the snake has bitten me? My belly is on fire." Lena reached out a bony hand.

Sheena wiped away a tear. She had no idea what her mother was talking about. It didn't really matter, but her request for water was easy enough to understand.

Rising from the chair, Sheena walked over to the jug on a small triangular table snugly fitted into the corner of the room and found a plastic cup with a straw poking through the fitted lid. The cup was empty, but looked clean enough, so she poured some water into it and snapped the lid back on.

"Oh, that tastes so good," said Lena in the faintest of whispers, and Sheena held the cup as her mother sucked another mouthful of water through the straw. Reaching beneath her, she raised her up into the pillows that were piled against the headrest. Hoping to mask the horror she felt when her fingers rubbed against her mother's backbone and ribs, Sheena smiled into the wet, sunken, grey eyes, peering past folds of flesh-devoid skin.

"Who did you say you were?" Lena asked, her eyes blinking in rapid motion.

"I am your daughter, Sheena."

"Is that so?" Lena seemed to be studying Sheena, who, having replaced the cup on the table, returned to sit on the chair facing her mother. "Are you certain of that?"

Sheena exhaled and dropped her head into her hands. She wanted to leave. It was too much to go through, which was why she had stopped visiting. Her mother never retained anything she said in previous visits; it was like being caught up in some perverse rendition of *Groundhog Day*. "I am your daughter," said Sheena, raising her head and bracing herself for the inevitable denial.

She watched her mother stare at the ceiling, and any hope that today might be different drained away. All too often, what she hoped might be a few seconds of her mother's disconnection from the world would turn into hours. Resting her elbow on the arm of her chair, Sheena closed her eyes and pinched the bridge of her nose, trying to stifle her exasperation as one might try to stop a sneeze.

"Tell me ..." Her mother's voice trailed off, then more clearly asked, "Tell me how you came to be my daughter?"

Startled by her mother's request, Sheena felt a surge of excitement course through her. She didn't know what to say in response, but she had an idea. Sheena walked over to the wall, unhooked a picture of them both when they were much younger, and handed it to her mother.

"That's you and me when I was eight years old, taken by the lake at Thiessen Arm. Do you remember?" Sheena leaned forward and gently rested her hand on her mother's arm. "We sailed up there on Dad's boat, *Forever Free*, one summer, remember?" Her pleading fanned the flicker of hope that ignited within her as she watched her mother's thin, twisted fingers trace the images on the photograph.

"I know you," her mother said as she returned the picture, and Sheena's heart leapt when she saw a sliver of a smile and felt her mother pat her hand. "Your beauty is undeniable, your eyes unmatched, but we could not be together."

"We're together now." Sheena's heart was racing, and she fought back tears as she clutched the photograph that would now forever be a part of her collection. "We can't change the past, but we are together now."

"Perhaps it might have ended differently. We shall never know."

Sheena saw her mother grimace with pain as she shifted in the pillows, and, remembering that Jessica had left a cup of blackberry smoothie on the small table, she followed the instructions she had been given. She took two small white pills from the bottle on the table, crushed them together using two teaspoons, then stirred the powder into the smoothie and fed it to her mother.

"Are you no longer angry with me?" her mother asked, swallowing the last of the smoothie.

"No, I am not angry."

"But you were."

"Perhaps after you left me." Sheena took hold of her mother's hand.

"It was best that I left."

Sheena could barely make out the words that came in breathy waves from her mother's dry, cracked lips, in a hiss and a whisper as the drugs started to take effect. "I love you." Face wet with tears, she gently squeezed her mother's hand, and noticed an almost imperceptible nod.

But her mother's words were clear enough: "I know."

***

The dull pain was a constant now, except when the opiate tide withdrew from the shores of the mind, the retreating waves sharpening it like a knife against steel. But soon enough, that would change.

The plant would restore youth, relieve the stiffness in the hands and feet, and remove this dreadful pressure and pain that crowded inside the head—all unwelcome gifts from the bent-over figure of old age. He would administer it only to the wise and elderly, those who thought and believed, as he did, in Uruk.

For the time being, the burning skin would find relief within the cool waters of the spring-fed lake: one foot in, two feet in, and then a wash of coolness as the body bathed.

Feet dangling deep, the scaly form was felt, and the eyes saw the ripple on the water's surface, caused by lateral undulation from a snake that swam around the body and toward the plant left on the shore.

The snake intended to steal the plant—a familiar nightmare vision, immortality so close, stolen! It must not come to pass.

With frantic energy and arms and legs in full motion, the race was on to get to the plant, but the snake was too fast, and reached the plant, curling itself around it and then pulling it along the bank. As it did so, the snake shed its skin, revealing the slick, vibrant colours of its youth.

Stronger now and with renewed energy, the snake slithered beyond reach, returning to the water and submerging with the plant; it was gone forever. It was too much for the heart to bear; the eyes welled up, and the lungs were devoid of air. There would be no escaping death's call.

On the shore, the ferryman had witnessed this epic tragedy. She turned to him. "Counsel me, O ferryman Urshanabi. For whom have my arms laboured, Urshanabi? For whom has my heart's blood roiled? I have nothing good to show for my life. The plant is gone. The waters are coursing twenty leagues away. I will never find the gateway again. My life is over, and I have nothing to show for it."

The ferryman did not reply. Someone else approached, and she was speaking. "To show for it? You have me."

She felt shock and confusion when a voice other than Urshanabi spoke, as well as her inability to bring the blurred face into focus. And while the female voice was vaguely familiar, the reply given to her demand for the stranger's identity and purpose made no sense. Perhaps the snake had bitten her while passing by in the lake, fooling the mind with its poison. That must be it, and the fire that burned in her belly confirmed her suspicion.

She reached out in hopes that the blurred figure of this unknown woman would bring water, and when she did, and held the cup for her to drink, the cold, sweet liquid calmed the rawness of her throat and cooled the embers in her belly that brought so much pain.

"Oh, that tastes so good," she said, concentrating on finding focus and blinking away the tears. "Who did you say you were?"

"I am your daughter, Sheena."

The woman's face was clearer now. Her features, like her voice, were strangely familiar. It had to be a trick, but who would play such a trick?

Her eyes turned toward the heavens for the answer, which was provided. It was a trick that only Ishtar, the goddess of love and war, could conjure to play on Gilgamesh. Ishtar still had feelings for him, despite his rejection of her and the resulting rage that had caused her to send the beast from Heaven to kill him. *She has come back to tempt me by claiming to be my daughter.*

Strangely, this made sense, although it was an unexpected turn, so he demanded that she tell him how she came to be his daughter.

Ishtar turned and took a few steps into the surrounding fog, and in almost the same instance, he returned, to offer an image encased in a golden border. Goddesses could do that, so it came as no surprise. With one finger, he traced the likeness of himself and Ishtar, and knew at once that the image given was to remind him of the time that she had watched him bathe and had come to him with seductive desire in the hopes that he would be her lover.

Ishtar leaned toward him and placed her hand on his arm. Was she trying to convince him that the image was real—a reincarnation of a time well past? Her words were hard to understand, which was the trouble with goddesses; they often spoke in an unfamiliar tongue. His ears did catch the phrase "forever free," and he struggled to remember if that had been her promise for his compliance with her sexual advances. Perhaps it had been, but he knew that forever was only as far as the horizon. His quest was for immortality, and he had had it in his grasp, but let it go.

"I know you." Prolonging Ishtar's disguise by pretending not to know her would only serve to enrage the goddess once again; it would be better to flatter her, and then, as every epic love story ends, they would discover their union, like immortality, was impossible. "Your beauty is undeniable, your eyes unmatched, but we could not be together." He handed the image back to Ishtar.

"We're together now," Ishtar implored as she turned her head and appeared to wipe back tears while clutching the golden-framed image. "We can't change the past, but we are together now."

"Perhaps it might have ended differently. We shall never know." Ishtar vanished from his sight. Perhaps his bluntness had so offended her that it had given her cause to leave. *No matter, she can administer no punishment greater than I have endured through the loss of the plant that would have saved me from the fate that now draws near.*

But then, to his surprise, Ishtar returned into view and offered him a cup of deep red, sweet wine. He wondered if the goddess was no longer angry with him, and asked her if that was so. Happy with her response, he took the wine and swallowed it.

Ishtar took hold of his hand as he felt waves of fatigue flood over him. It must be that he was in shock from his ordeal with the snake, and knew his quest was over. He had failed.

"It was best that I left," he told Ishtar as his mind slipped back to Enkidu, the one true love in his life, a love lost, because the truth was too much for Ishtar to hear. It was a lesson learned: gods and goddesses ruled to expand the excesses of their pleasures, and ordinary women and men were little more than their play toys.

"I love you."

Ishtar's voice seemed filled with sincere emotion and affection for him, and perhaps that was a message for him to hold onto in these last hours of his life. Perhaps there was some redemption from the deep feelings of disillusionment and regret provided by the knowledge that he, at least, had lived a life worthy of the love of a goddess.

He turned and, through the incoming opiate tide that washed over him in pain-relieving waves, smiled at Ishtar. He was quite sure this would be the last time they would be together, and wanted to acknowledge her love for him.

"I know."

19.

It didn't make sense to him that he felt nervous—scared, actually—as he drove up to the farm gate. He had every right to come to the farm and say goodbye to his mother. It certainly wasn't his choice, but during the night he had convinced himself that it was the respectful thing to do.

He climbed back into the rental car, having stopped to close the gate after driving through. For a moment, he just sat in the driver's seat while the car quietly idled. Perhaps he should have called to let Ken know he was coming; that would have been the polite thing to do. But this man had pulled his mother away from his father, destroyed their family, and now seemed to be holding his dying mother hostage. Nope, no phone call was needed.

He drove up the driveway, trying to control the rising anger he felt toward Ken Graham, who dared call himself his stepfather. Over the many years, this anger had become deeply rooted, holding Asher away from this place as an anchor holds a boat from drifting toward a welcoming shore. Over his morning coffee, he had done the math; it had been seven years since he had seen him, and, frankly, he didn't really care if he saw him on this occasion.

Asher had two reasons to be at the farm.

The first was to see his mother for the last time and to pay his respects. He had stopped at a local retail shop and bought some flowers to bring with him. He really had no idea if she would like them; that wasn't the point; it was his gesture of thanks for having been his mother.

The second reason was to give Ken his mother's written instructions for the disposal of her remains; he had written in the instruction: *No service.*

As executor, making the addition was his prerogative; besides, other than Ken and Sheena, he couldn't imagine who would attend. He certainly wouldn't. He loathed funerals, which he saw as an unnecessary expense to indulge the emotions of the living.

As he drove between the white flowering dogwood and green willow with a sorrowful bow over the creamy blue elderberry, Asher reassured himself that this was not going to be a long visit.

He would ask to see his mother, who he was quite sure would not know him, deliver the flowers to her, and tell her how much he loved her. He was almost embarrassed by the self-acknowledgement, so he had actually rehearsed the visit before heading down to reception and checking out of his hotel. He had planned to tell his mother how much he would miss her when she died, but he couldn't quantify exactly how much that might be, and didn't want to lie to her in her final moments.

Rounding the corner of the driveway, he saw Sheena's metallic blue minivan parked along the oval, and his heart sank. *Well, that was a miscalculation. I hope she doesn't have her kid with her.*

Asher didn't know how to react to Ethan. He didn't want to be mean, but he wouldn't accept that they were related, and he bridled when the kid called him "uncle."

He slowed the car down, wondering if it would be possible to avoid seeing Sheena and Ethan. For just a moment, he actually thought of driving around the oval and directly to the airport, but stopped himself and parked his rental car next to the van.

He had a duty to perform. He took his role as executor of his mother's affairs seriously, and the instructions for the disposal of her remains, written on the letter neatly folded and tucked into the envelope in his breast pocket, were to be followed to the letter. So he climbed out of the car, walked up the stairs to the front door of the house, and found the courage to rap the centre-mounted iron doorknocker against the strike plate.

***

"Are you OK?" Ken asked his daughter, who sat on the side of the bed, sobbing, next to her sleeping mother.

"She knew me, Dad," Sheena blubbered. "It was amazing. I actually got to tell her that I loved her. She heard me, she understood, and she told me that she knew that I loved her. I am so relieved that I could tell her that, and that she knew that I did; I miss her, Dad, and all of us as a family."

Ken extended his hand to his daughter, who took it, letting him pull her up and into a hug. He held her tightly. "What did she say to you?" he asked, thinking it unlikely that her mother had recognized her. Though clearly, they seemed to have shared a conversation.

"It was this picture," said Sheena, pulling back from the hug and handing her father the framed picture she had taken from the wall. "Mom studied it, and it must have triggered a memory for her, because she looked at me and told me that she knew me and how beautiful I was, and she asked me if I was still angry with her because she had left. It was very real; she knew I had been angry."

Ken's curiosity took hold. Was it possible that a single photograph could trigger her memory? And if it had, perhaps something similar had happened at the nursing home. That was why she had left and walked to the farm. Maybe she really had been coming home.

"She told me that she couldn't stay here and that it was best that she left, but she didn't say why." Sheena took a breath and looked toward the open bedroom door. "Where's Ethan?"

"Rummaging through his granddad's closet looking for the box of Lego." Ken turned to replace the picture on the hanger on the wall. "That's amazing, sweetheart. I am so happy that you had a connection, and let her know how much you loved her."

Sheena walked over to her father. "Would it be OK if I kept this picture?"

A loud series of knocks on the front door startled them both.

***

Asher's first thoughts were that Ken appeared older—slightly stooped over, with thinner and much greyer hair. But he was still big in stature, providing an imposing figure in the frame of the opened door.

"Asher, I wasn't expecting you, but I am glad that you have come," said Ken. Those were his first face-to-face words with Asher in several years, and he took a step back to allow Asher to enter the house.

"Good morning," he said as he walked into the house, looking away to avoid eye contact with Ken. "I would like to see my mother."

"Asher?" Sheena's voice didn't mask her surprise.

Feeling really awkward, he couldn't help but notice that Sheena looked well; the sheen in her shoulder-length dark brown hair, unblemished skin, and clear dark brown eyes. Thinner than the last time they had been together, his half-sister seemed to be thriving.

"Hi. You're keeping well, I see." The words were more muttered than spoken. "I came to see Mom."

"She is sleeping at the moment. I had to give her a painkiller, which is also a sedative. Sorry, if I had known you were coming—"

"Yeah, well, you didn't, so it's not on you. Besides, she wouldn't know who I am anyway."

"She knew me this morning, Asher," said Sheena softly. "Perhaps a bit later, when she's awake. The flowers are beautiful; would you like me to put them in a vase for you to take to her?"

Asher was suddenly at war with himself as he desperately tried to manage his anger at her comment. Had his mother really been lucid enough to recognize Sheena? She hadn't recognized him on any of his previous visits. His doubt solidified. *She's lying.* Yeah, that was a more likely explanation. *There she goes, putting me down again. Sweetly offering to put my flowers in a vase to take to my mother, who, by the way, was able to recognize her, but wouldn't know who the fuck I was! What a passive-aggressive bitch.*

The rational side of his brain shortened the halter-rope on his anger. High-strung like a thoroughbred stallion, he reigned it in. "Yeah, a vase would be good, thanks"—he handed the flowers to Sheena—"as long as she knows they are from me."

"You can give them to her yourself," Ken assured him, closing the door and extending a hand. "May I take your coat?"

"Oh, no thanks, that's OK." Asher straightened the collar of his jacket, rejecting the offer. "I won't be staying long. I just came to pay my last respects and leave her the flowers. Oh, and to give you this." Asher reached into the breast pocket of his coat and pulled out the envelope.

"What's this?" asked Ken.

"A letter outlining my mother's funeral arrangements, such as they are: a simple cremation, pine box coffin with no service." He handed it to Ken.

"Well, come in, Asher. Your mother is in the guest bedroom at the end of the hall, and you are welcome to stay as long as you like." Ken took the envelope he had been handed and opened it.

Asher took a few awkward steps into the hall. "Like I said, I won't be staying; I have to catch a flight."

It had been years since he had been in this house. Still, he had not been able to erase the thought that being in the house of the man who had cuckolded his father made him disloyal. A more rational part of his brain told him that all this had happened many years ago, and had Sheena not been born, it was possible he might have been able to accept that. But Sheena was a living reminder of the disrespect to his father.

They weren't family.

Asher had thought that his decision to live with his father had made that obvious. It had been an easy choice, but it had come with a high price—one that he had obviously thought was worth paying. All he wanted to do was get this over with, and if that meant making a rare concession to Ken, then so be it.

"After careful consideration, I am prepared to accept that it will appear strange for me to insist my mother be returned to the care home I intend to sue for negligence," he said, looking at the woolen weave in the long amber, gold, and green Persian carpet that covered the hallway floor. "I have told the care home that as long as she has access to proper medical attention, I will consent to her being here."

"Thank you," replied Ken. "I take it then that you are flying out to attend your conference?"

Asher bit his lower lip, willing himself not to rise and respond to Ken poking at the contusion from the punch of guilt he had when he confirmed with the conference organizers that he would arrive in time to present his paper.

Damn!

It was none of Ken's business where he was going. He had offered Ken a concession by agreeing that his mother could remain at the house, so he chose not to respond as he walked down the hallway toward the guest bedroom. *Don't look back and give that bastard the satisfaction.*

20.

Entering the room, he first thought his mother was dead, but a twitch of her index finger, a flutter of her eyelid, and an occasional wheeze from her half-open mouth told him otherwise. He gazed at her pallid face and for a moment, wondered if he was the one afflicted with dementia. He had no recollection of the person lying before him, a frail facsimile of her former self, contracted by age and illness.

The door opened and Sheena entered with the flowers that he had purchased, neatly arranged in a glass vase, which she placed on the table.

"I hope the arranging is OK," she said.

"Sure, they look good, thank you," he replied.

"Asher—"

Asher raised his hand, stopping his half-sister from finishing her sentence. "Don't," he said, turning away from her and noticing the wall of framed photographs. "I would like a moment alone with my mother."

After Sheena had left the room, closing the door behind her, he walked over to the wall and studied the photographs. He was taken aback to see himself as a young boy, his eyes wide and his mouth stretched open with laughter. He was holding the wheel of a sailboat, and Ken was standing next to him in a similar pose.

A few frames over, another photograph showed him at the same age, wedged between Ken and the round belly of his pregnant mother. His mother's arms were around his waist, their cheeks touching, and her headscarf was pulled back by the wind. He was leaning into Ken, his arm

One Weekend in May

over the man's shoulder. He studied their faces. They were all laughing; they looked happy, even exhilarated.

Asher had no memory of having the pictures taken and wondered, given that both Ken and his mother were with him in the second picture, who might have taken them. He stared at the three happy faces. The composition seemed strange to him. When had he been a part of the lives of Ken and his mother? When was the last time he had laughed?

As an almost subconscious act, Asher took out his phone and, adjusting it to avoid any glare or reflection from the glass covering the photographs, took pictures of only those that were of interest to him, not really at all surprised that most were of his mother with Sheena. He put his phone down. He didn't need pictures of Sheena as a baby, then an adolescent, a teenager, and wearing her college cap and gown.

He also skipped over the few with Ken, but one photograph in particular—centred within the collage of photos—caught his eye and made him take up his phone. It was a picture of the four of them—his mother, Ken, Sheena, and himself—taken in front of a blooming rose garden with a stone building in the background.

Ken was standing beside his mother, who was seated on a chair with a preschool-aged Sheena sitting on her lap. He was standing on the opposite side of the chair from Ken, and he could tell from the Eaton school blazer that he was about fourteen, just prior to sitting his O-level exams. Once again, Ken, his mother, and Sheena were smiling, but not him.

Asher looked at his image. There was no smile on this boy's pouting face; his posture slumped. His image was dull, in stark contrast to the beaming light of the others. Asher noticed the adoring look on his mother's face as she smiled down at the baby. He couldn't remember posing for the picture, but what shocked him as he looked at the black-framed picture was that he recognized the rose garden and building. The picture had been taken in the courtyard of his father's building in Tehran.

How could that possibly be correct? When had they been together in Tehran? He had no memory of such a time. But he would never forget the way his mother looked at that little girl, and how her love for the baby had replaced the love she once had for him. That little girl was their progeny;

he wasn't—at least not Ken's—and his mother had abandoned his father, to whom it mattered that he was a boy and heir.

That's why his choice to live with his father had, in reality, been no choice at all. His mind drifted back to the day that he had arrived at Mehrabad International Airport, all his belongings in a big leather suitcase that was so heavy he could barely lift it. Ibrahim, his father's personal secretary, had met him, and to Asher's relief, the driver took care of his suitcase, putting it into the trunk of the black Mercedes.

He had arrived late at night, so traffic was light, and the drive, which would have taken more than an hour on crammed roads during the day, went swiftly. His father's luxury apartment overlooked the Iranian Art Museum Gardens in the prestigious Elahiyeh neighbourhood.

During the drive, Ibrahim had barely spoken, leaving him to look out the window and wonder what his life would be like with his father in Tehran. Had he known the extent of his father's generosity, he would not have wasted the time thinking about it.

Arriving at the five-storey apartment building, Ibrahim had escorted Asher through the lobby and into the posh, gold-inlaid elevator, barking instructions at the driver to use the service elevator further down the hall to bring up his suitcase. Using a key that he took from his breast pocket, Ibrahim had unlocked the elevator panel providing access to the fifth floor, then pushed the small black button marked with the number 5.

The spacious apartment encompassed the entire top floor, and Ibrahim escorted him down a short hallway to the closed door of his father's office, knocked three times, and with a short nod of his head, left him standing alone outside.

As he stood silently beside his dying mother's bed, Asher thought about that August, on his ninth birthday, when he had decided to go and live with his father. He scanned the pictures on the wall. That decision had saved him from all of this, he thought as he looked over the collection of pictures of his mother and sister taken at various ages on horseback, at lakes, or atop a treeless, rocky hilltop where, presumably, they had all hiked to marvel at the expansive view across green treetops, toward an azure sea sparkling in the sun.

What a different life he had led from that of this family! And that was all thanks to his father's unconditional love and support for him, which manifested itself in such a generous expense account that, though it was managed by Ibrahim, had provided for his education.

As he turned back to look at what was left of his mother, he wondered what their lives might have been had she stayed with his father.

His father was such a handsome man, with ice-blue eyes beneath wavy black hair that greyed at the temples. His salt-and-pepper beard was always immaculately groomed above a white shirt collar that was always crisply pressed. As he thought about his father, he couldn't help but notice the contrast a picture of Ken provided. Ken's face appeared creased by the sun; his hair was dishevelled, one side of his collar out, the other under the lapel of a wrinkled jacket. *What could she have possibly seen in this man?*

The thoughts of his late father brought with them the smell of stale tobacco and aging leather book bindings. They were the smells that filled his father's study, and it suddenly struck him that he could not remember a time when he was with his father and not in that room.

He recalled hearing his father, whom he called "Ustadi," meaning *teacher*, yell for him to enter, and when he did, he saw the great man sitting at his large, leather-inlaid desk. The positioning of the desk, centred in front of bay windows, gave it the appearance of a stage. On either side, floor-to-ceiling bookcases were crammed with books of all sizes. Ustadi's attending audience.

His father looked up and smiled at him. "Asher, it's good to see you. I am glad that you have come to your senses." He remembered the words clearly because that is what he had done—come to his senses. Where would he be today if he had not made that decision to accept the love and generosity of this man?

His father reached for a beautifully chased silver cigarette case decorated with birds, animals, and foliage. He flipped it open and took out a cigarette, which he lit before sitting back in the tall leather chair.

"I am sure that you are exhausted from your long journey, my son. So, tonight you will sleep well, for tomorrow you start the rest of your life. With my generosity, if you perform to my expectations, and I have no doubt you will, you will never look back."

His father's words had stayed with him and been a source of encouragement during tough days, and there were so many tough days as a dark-skinned "Arab" boy in a predominantly white English prep school where, at nine years old, he was at least not the youngest boarder.

"There is no need for you to unpack," his father continued. "Good fortune, my son. I have managed to get you into Lockers Park; there you will be prepped for Eaton, and then you will be able to choose your university. You are to leave on a flight to London at 12:30 tomorrow." His father rounded his mouth and puffed out cigarette smoke in perfect rings. "You will, of course, follow in my footsteps and study physics." He drew on his cigarette, and Asher momentarily relived the feeling of shock at what he had just heard. It had barely been a week since he had told his mother of his decision, and he hadn't been back with his father for longer than five minutes.

"I can see that you are overwhelmed by my generosity, boy. Don't be. You are my son. The key that unlocks the door to success is education, and the best education costs money. Fortunately for you, I happen to have a good supply."

"But I came to live with you," he remembered pleading.

"What you meant to say is, 'Thank you, Father'" had been Ustadi's response.

"I am to study physics."

The return of that thought brought a grin to his lips, and he looked down at his mother. His mother had always told him he would be, like her, a historian. But the word *physics*, spoken by his father, was a command, not a suggestion. It had been the first time he had ever heard the word, let alone considered the study of the scientific discipline. He knew that his father had been an influential scholar, but at nine years of age, he had had no idea why.

"Physics is at the heart of all science, and you are free to choose any specialty within the discipline other than nuclear physics, where I stand at the peak. You are to find your own mountain to conquer. I wouldn't want it said that I used influence to get you your success."

Asher had lived up to his father's expectations, graduating with distinction from Edinburgh University. He had completed his doctorate at MIT under the mentorship of Professor Niles Bohr, who found him work as a researcher, and later, a teacher. The university had become his home, and as he stood, feeling awkward and conflicted, at the bedside of his dying mother, he couldn't wait to get back.

His mother started to wheeze, causing a small amount of panic in Asher. It occurred to him that, while comfortable paying his last respects in the abstract of time, as reflected in the family pictures on the wall, he didn't want her to wake up while he was there. Asleep, she was his mother, as he wanted to remember her.

He took his mother's hand and pressed it to his lips. As angry as he was with her for the life she had chosen—one that hadn't included him, that had denied him a family—he had never stopped loving his mother, and he felt that now.

A portrait of his mother when she was in her thirties caught his eye. There was something about the picture that brought her alive to him. Her dark hair framed a smiling face, and her hazel eyes looked so directly into the camera lens that they seemed to follow him in the room.

He thought about taking it. He would be on the other side of the world before Ken realized he had stolen it, if he noticed at all. But that would be stealing, and he couldn't do that. So he placed it gently on the pillow next to his mother, and took a then-and-now photo. It would be a constant reminder of the mother he had always hoped he would have.

Lena stirred in the bed again, her expression signalling pain. He had no idea what he should do, so it was time to go. It was time for him to make peace with himself about leaving before she passed. *There is nothing for you here.* It had been a recurring thought since he had climbed out of bed that morning. *Besides, you have a flight to catch.*

21.

Ken drove the Kubota tractor under the cover of an open shed, and turned off the key. He had used the backhoe attachment to dig a grave, into which he had gently placed the little lamb that had not lived the day.

He hadn't heard Toby's bark at the opening or closing of the gates when Sheena had returned to the farm, nor had he heard the police car over the growl of the diesel tractor as Alice Joe drove the police Ford Bronco up the driveway and parked next to Sheena's car.

He wondered why Sheena had come back, but the sight of the police car caused his heart to sink momentarily. *This can't be good*, he thought, climbing off the tractor. He had not been forthcoming with Alice, and wondered if there had been a decision taken to lay a charge of some sort against him.

When he stepped into the house, Sheena and Alice were in conversation, and the mood seemed light enough. His entrance interrupted their laughter.

"Dad," Sheena greeted, "you have a visitor."

"Nice to see you again, Alice," said Ken, smiling at the officer.

"She is here to follow up on her previous visit," Sheena informed him, raising her brow slightly.

"Yeah," Alice inserted, "to sign off on the paperwork. I have to file an official report, Ken. It seems that's what policing's all about these days, Ken: reports. And what's written in those reports is important; it will determine what comes next. So, do you have a minute?"

Ken looked at Sheena, who was gathering her coat.

"It's time for me to go and get Ethan from his playdate," she said. "I came back because I wanted to have a talk with you, but that can wait. Mom is comfortable; the sedatives seem to be managing the pain, but she is only semi-conscious most of the time. I will see you tomorrow, but please call me if you need me or if there is any change."

"You take the time you need to say goodbye to your family," said Alice. "I am in no rush."

Ken and Sheena found Ethan in Ken's study; he was busy at work building a large Lego dinosaur.

"Wow, that's an awesome dinosaur," Ken remarked as Ethan locked the final pieces together.

"Triceratops," said Ethan. "Thanks for getting me this, Granddad. I don't have a Triceratops."

"Well, you do now," said his mother, "so put everything in the box; it's time for us to go."

"Can I take this home, Granddad?"

"Why not leave it here for next time you visit?" his mother asked, but Ken was quick to reply.

"You take it home, Ethan; I will see if I can find you a pterodactyl to complete your set."

"Great, just what I need. You can barely move in that room as it is, Dad," Sheena said, then pulled her father aside. "Are you in some kind of trouble with the police?"

"I hope not," he replied. "But I didn't tell Alice that your mother was here when she first came by, and there was a silver alert in place, so that may have broken some law, which might result in a charge of some sort. I will chat with Alice. She seems pretty reasonable."

"OK, well, we are all packed up and set to go, so we will let ourselves out through the deck doors from your bedroom. You go and take care of the police, and text me when everything is handled, OK?"

Ken took the kiss on his cheek from Sheena and a big hug from Ethan, and saw the two out the door. He then walked down the hall into the living room, where Alice sat upright on the couch, legs together, seated at attention, her dark blue RCMP pants cuffing the polished black boots, her police-issued electronic notepad resting on her lap.

"Your daughter seems nice, Ken," she said.

"Yes, she's a great kid," said Ken, sitting in the chair opposite. "Listen, about earlier—"

"Be careful what you say," she interrupted. "It will become the official record of what has happened here. I will start by reading you what I have written, and you can tell me if I have it right, OK?"

Alice didn't wait for him to reply, but started to read from the notepad. "At approximately 10:15 a.m., constable Alice Joe arrived at the farm owned by Ken Graham. She first looked for Mr. Graham at the barn, but he wasn't there. Constable Joe found a brown leather suitcase that matched the description of the suitcase that had been in the possession of Ms. Lena Murshid when she had left the Caring Hands hospice facility. Constable Joe drove her vehicle up to the house, and Mr. Graham came out to meet her. Constable Joe informed Mr. Graham that she was looking for Ms. Murshid, who was the subject of a silver alert. Mr. Graham informed the constable that Ms. Murshid had arrived at his farm earlier that morning in a weak and vulnerable state, and that he had taken her up to his house to attend to her and stabilize her condition. He informed Constable Joe that he was unaware that a silver alert had been issued, but that he intended to notify the Caring Hands hospice that she was safe and resting comfortably in his home, and make arrangements for her return to the hospice. Constable Joe gave the brown suitcase to Mr. Graham and informed him that she would advise the authorities and terminate the alert." She took a breath and then asked him, "Pretty cut-and-dried, hey, Ken? Did I get it right? Anything you would like me to add?"

Ken looked into Alice's unblinking, dark brown eyes, which concealed what she was thinking. *She would make quite a poker player. That account is not exactly as I remember. Is this some kind of honesty test?*

"It's your report, Constable," he said, ending an awkward pause.

Alice nodded her agreement and turned off her notepad, tucking it back into the narrow leather carrying case.

"Thank you," he said, and then, noticing she didn't immediately get up from the chair, he asked, "Can I get you anything—tea or coffee?"

"You got any Diet Pepsi?" she asked. Her request surprised him. He generally didn't buy it, but as it happened, he actually did have a couple of cans of Diet Pepsi that Janis had brought over one evening a few weeks ago. According to Janis, it was a healthier choice with her rum than regular cola.

"I need to go take a look at Ms. Murshid," said Alice. "I can't close the file unless I can say I actually saw that the subject was not compromised in any way. Is that OK for me to do while you fix me that Pepsi?"

Ken showed Alice to the spare bedroom, where Lena lay motionless in bed, plugged into her intravenous feed. He then walked back to the kitchen, took a can of Diet Pepsi from the fridge, and emptied it into a tall glass before returning to the living room.

The swish of the pant material between Alice's ample thighs sounded her return down the hall and into the living room. Her Kevlar vest, belt with attachments, and the protruding butt of her handgun accentuated her already short and stocky form.

"Everything OK?" Ken asked, handing Alice the glass of Diet Pepsi.

"Thanks, yeah—but not so good for her, eh?" she replied, and took a long drink from the glass.

"If you don't mind me asking, what made you want to be a cop?" asked Ken.

"Gotta be something, right? I can't just sit on the couch and watch TV all day, although some do. Not me, though. I want to do something to help those who need it."

"Why not a doctor, nurse, or even social worker?" asked Ken. "Any one of those jobs lets you help people without potentially putting yourself in harm's way."

"It costs a lot of money to become a doctor or a nurse, Ken, but the government will pay for me to train to be a police officer—especially if I agree to work on reserve. Besides, given the choice, white people won't choose an Indian for their doctor or nurse. As for being a social worker, that's the biggest part of my job as a police officer. The difference is that a police officer has the authority to stop antisocial behaviour; social workers just pick up the broken pieces; they don't prevent the breaking."

"And as a cop, do you think you can prevent the breaking?" Ken wasn't quite sure what Alice meant, but he tried to keep the conversation alive while she finished her drink.

"I try to, but being a cop isn't as easy as I thought it would be. Most of the time, the rules get in the way."

"Rules?"

"Yeah, just like this report. It seems that half my time as a cop is spent filling out paperwork. The more active you are as a cop, the more reports you have to write."

"It's important to have a record of how things went down," replied Ken. He felt nervous, not wanting to revisit the distorted narrative of his own actions that Alice was about to put into the official record.

"Indians have become good at telling stories, Ken. Nobody paints the picture of righteous indignation quite like us Indigenous folk. God knows it's been generations in the making, and white people feel so guilty for the cruel actions of your ancestors that you are prepared to believe pretty much whatever we tell you about ours." She tilted the pop can against her lips and swallowed a mouthful of Diet Pepsi.

"You're right, there is a collective guilt for past actions—" Ken started to say, but was interrupted by Alice.

"Sure, there is, but the past is a collective inheritance, Ken. We all share it, and carry the stories our elders passed along to us. Some of them were good storytellers on both sides, so we go to the official record of how things went down, as you put it. To the official reports. The thing is, if we don't like what we read, if the reports don't reflect what our elders have told us, well then, we change them."

Alice paused, took a deep breath, then continued.

"It's a lot different today. Today, it's all about power for the people, truth for power, and demanding new rules. But by what authority is that power given, and whose truth is it that we are to follow?" Alice shook her head, and Ken was pretty sure that this conversation had nothing whatsoever to do with Lena's walk to the farm. "When you work on-reserve, Ken, you never quite know whose rules you're dealing with—your staff sergeant's, the elected chief and council, or the hereditary chief."

"I can see that might make things quite complicated," Ken responded, as Alice finished her Pepsi and walked to the kitchen, placing her empty glass in the sink.

"Yeah, but why should it?" she said, returning to the chair where she had left her notepad. "If you molest your kid, beat your wife, or kill your girlfriend, what difference does it make to the victim who your ancestors were?"

Ken tried to hide his shock at her blunt and troubling reply. He didn't really have much firsthand information about conditions on the reserve, but he had done extensive reading on the impact that child confiscation and imposed residential school attendance had had on many within the Indigenous community. He wasn't sure if that's what Alice was referring to, so he couched his words carefully.

"I am sure you agree, Alice, that what took place in the past has left generational trauma that has caused, and can explain the kind of behaviour you mentioned," he said, and for the first time he saw her emotion—it was anger.

"It might explain it, but should a kid molester, wife beater, or murderer get sidetracked from justice because they're Indigenous?" Her anger was unmistakable, and Ken held back the follow-up comment he was about to make, thinking it wiser not to say anything. Alice continued to speak. "You really want to know why I became a cop, Ken? It's so I can lock up those perverts who think it's OK to rape little girls and beat up moms who try to stop them. I wanted to be the person the abused could come to for help. And, as an Indigenous cop, I have some legitimacy when I call out those who believe that their family history is excuse enough for their behaviour. I choose to challenge those who protect the guilty by diverting them away from the justice system because the perp is addicted to drugs, alcohol, or both."

"But addiction that results from past trauma is very real, and not exclusive to any group in society," Ken said softly, feeling increasingly uncomfortable with the conversation. "Surely, you will acknowledge that."

"Yeah, it's real. So is the trauma that comes from lying awake at night, hearing the clumsy, stumbling, drunken approach of your mother's latest hook-up coming for you, knowing you are powerless to stop him from violating you, and knowing that there is nobody who will believe you, let alone do anything about it. Well, there is somebody now, Ken."

"I am so sorry, Alice." Ken was at a complete loss as to what else he could say. He had no idea about her personal circumstances, but felt sure that he had just learned about them.

Alice held up her notepad. "The truth is not always as it is told or as it is written. Truth is polymorphous, Ken. What we choose to present is determined by what we are trying to achieve when the choice is made. Thanks for the Pepsi; I will see you around." With that, Alice tucked her notepad under her arm and walked out through the door.

22.

Asher studied the photograph on his laptop, trying to tune out the two squabbling children who had arrived in the small cafe with a portly woman he assumed was their mother. Much to his annoyance, they had chosen to sit at the table beside him.

After leaving the farm, Asher had driven directly to the small regional Brockhurst airport. It consisted of one main building that looked like a renovated airport hangar, sufficient for the one commercial carrier with only four flights a day to the city.

Like everything else in this Godforsaken town, he had thought, as he drove around the open car parking lot looking for the marked rental car stalls, *they certainly didn't spend any money on the design of this place.*

At the service counter, Asher had checked his luggage, produced his ticket and passport, and, despite the two-hour wait before boarding, felt a wave of relief when presented with his through-flight tickets to Copenhagen. He couldn't get out of town fast enough.

Still, he had a couple of hours to kill, so he had gone over to a small craft services centre that was advertised as the "Cloud Café," to see what might be available.

He had passed on the unappetizing food displayed in the chilled, glass case, despite the recommendation from the young man behind the counter that if the food was heated in the microwave oven, it would taste pretty good.

Instead, Asher had settled for a black coffee, and chosen a small table as far from the counter as possible, where he had set up his laptop. He had wanted to download the photo he had taken of the picture of his mother, Ken, Sheena, and himself in the rose garden at his father's building in Tehran.

It can't be in Tehran. But where else would it be? He had no memory of the picture being taken; in fact, he had no memory of his mother, Ken, or Sheena ever being in Tehran. Seeing it had caused deeply unsettling feelings that he had not been able to shake since leaving the farm.

He had just downloaded the image from his phone to the laptop in order to look at it more closely when the mother and her two children arrived to sit and fight over hotdogs next to him.

Despite the annoying distraction, he expanded the photograph on his laptop screen so that he could study the details in the picture. He had to concede that it looked like the rose garden outside his father's building—albeit an older planting. When he expanded the picture, he saw the sign in the background, printed in Farsi. *There is no doubt about it. I have walked past that sign many times.*

He moved the image on the screen with his index finger until the picture of him as a boy was centred. It was then that he saw the gold cap of his Parker fountain pen and the trademark arrow clip holding it in place in the breast pocket of his Eaton jacket. *No fucking way.* It seemed a lifetime ago since that gold-inlaid pen, the last gift from his father, had been his most prized possession.

He had treasured that pen, especially during the hours spent learning to write in Farsi, working on the wide and fine scripts the variable nib made possible. It had been years since he had even thought about the pen, which, in that moment, acted like a key that unlocked a trunk full of memories long put away.

He worked his finger on the built-in mouse to pull the image back to its original format. The sound of the fighting children faded into the ambient sound, until he heard nothing at all, as he became fully absorbed in the reluctant opening of the dusty trunk. Apprehension, fear, and sadness were the first to make their escape.

He was back in his father's office, standing before the large walnut desk, beaming with pride as his father studied his school report card. He had topped his form scholastically on his term-end exams, scoring the highest mark in the school's history in mathematics.

He knew how pleased his father would be at his accomplishment and also knew that his marks would trump the form master's comments about him not mixing well with the other boys and only providing a minimal contribution to team sports—most notably, rugby and football.

The master had mentioned, however, that he had proven to be a better-than-average spin bowler in cricket, and excellent with the foil, making his decision not to join the school fencing team a disappointment to all involved.

It was then that his father opened a desk drawer, took out the royal blue felt box that contained the gold pen, and gave it to him as a gift to celebrate—perhaps reward him for—his achievements. It was the last time that he and his father would be together, though he had had no way of knowing that would be the case.

The gold Parker pen had come to symbolize so much in his mind. The pen, like his father, was the gold standard of excellence, and it, too, a year after his father's death, had been stolen from him.

The squabble at the table next to him had escalated into an all-out war between the siblings, who no longer limited themselves to verbal attacks, but had started a full-on fight that had caused several other adults to come to the assistance of the mother, who seemed incapable of managing the children.

In the chaos of the conflict at the next table, Asher failed to notice a familiar figure approaching.

***

Sheena had considered leaving Ethan with his grandfather, but thought a playdate with a friend might be a better option for both her son and her father. Her dad, after all, had enough on his plate without her adding Ethan to his day. So she made a call to a friend who lived a few doors away from her, and was delighted at the welcome given her request to drop Ethan by to play with her two kids.

She had checked the flight schedule online and confirmed that the next flight to the city didn't leave for several hours. With little else for him to do, she hoped that Asher had gone directly to the airport.

As she turned onto the airport road, the first hint of apprehension came over her. Asher was such an angry person, and had no qualms with showing his contempt for her and her father. But when she had seen him leave the room of their dying mother, she had seen a broken man alone in an increasingly uncaring world.

It was in that moment that a thought hit her like a bolt of lightning, and she couldn't put it away. Asher, whether or not he liked or admitted it, was her family. They shared a mother, and with her death, Asher would have no living parent; in fact, she would be his only living relative.

The rain had stopped, and the narrow road now steamed with the warmth of sunlight. Sheena had her eyes focused ahead, but her mind concentrated on the speech she had rehearsed and decided to deliver to Asher.

It was a speech about family, about the fact that the two of them were connected by their mother, regardless of his misplaced anger toward her father. It would be the last chance that she had to reach out to Asher and try to establish some level of relationship with him.

Any concern that Asher might not drive directly to the airport evaporated when she recognized his rental car parked in the Budget stall.

She parked her car and sat for a moment, to think through how she might approach him. This could be her last meeting with her brother, and she was determined to speak her mind, but she would have to get him to listen and not walk away. He needed to know that his anger toward her father was unfounded. *No*, she thought, and she tapped the palm of her hand against the steering wheel. *She* needed him to know the truth about his father, if he didn't already know it—and if he did, he needed to accept it.

She looked through the windshield and over the hood. The view evoked the memory of the hours spent together in the car after her mother had insisted they travel together across the country. It would be a road trip, her mother had told her. Besides, her mother felt it was her duty to deliver Sheena safely to Dalhousie University in Halifax.

The memory of that time together had been packed away for quite some time, but she had unpacked it in the last few days to remember the time when she and her mother were very close. They had shared their secrets, their fears, and their passions.

It was on that trip that her mother shared the story about how the relationship between her parents had happened. She had also learned a great deal about Asher's father, his work in Iran, and what had happened to him. Before she had told her, though, they had made a pinky promise to never speak of it again.

As she sat in her car looking toward the terminal building, she was convinced that her half-brother didn't know the truth about why his mother had left his father. In fact, she wondered if he really knew his father at all.

Quite unexpectedly, her mind drifted back to the spring break during her last year at Dalhousie, and to her relationship with Farouk. She could still see him as clearly, as if he were standing outside the car, tall, with the wavy black hair that framed his handsome, confident face. Farouk was the poster boy for success; she knew he would have completed his MBA and taken a law degree. She had no doubt that he would succeed at whatever venture he chose, and would be a wealthy man just like his father—though, despite his passion for the cause, she doubted he would ever return to Palestine.

There had been days when she had felt guilty for the way she had ended her relationship with Farouk—no remorse, but guilt just the same. She had never doubted they shared a love for each other, and there had been a time when she even considered a life with him. But after their no-strings-attached lovers' weekend in Boston, something deep within her changed.

She couldn't explain Ethan's conception. She had taken the appropriate precautions and certainly had not planned a pregnancy. Her real—though hidden—motivation for that trip across the border had been to see Asher.

It hadn't been an easy task to convince Farouk to go, because he had been concerned that he would be profiled at the border and that if the border police checked his record, they would find his arrest at a pro-Palestinian rally in New York two years earlier.

But Sheena had been very persuasive, and the promise of a weekend with her in a fancy hotel in Boston was all she needed to convince him to take the risk. Looking back on the trip, Sheena had to admit that she had been naïve. Despite her mixed heritage, she blended in with the faces of the white middle class, and couldn't really relate to Farouk's concerns. Besides, she was far more interested in her studies in marine biology than she was in global politics.

She glanced at the digital car clock; she still had a bit more than an hour before they would call Asher's flight. She really needed to do this, but her stomach was tied in knots. *Why does this always happen?*

She had had the same feeling on the short journey from Boston to Cambridge, but on that occasion, Farouk had been there to back her up and calm her after she confided her fears to him. "Whatever his reaction, Sheena, that's on him, not you." He had told her. "Your intentions are pure enough; if he can't see that, then it is he who is blind, not you."

Her motivation to see Asher, who had been newly accepted into the PhD program and granted a teaching assistant position at MIT, had been as strong then as the motivation she felt in this moment. On that occasion, she had been on a mission and, in addition, wanted to personally offer condolences to Asher for the very recent loss of his father. Now, he was about to lose his mother—*their* mother.

She took a deep breath. *Come on, you can do this.* She got out of the car and walked across the road and through the automatic doors, which silently slid open as she approached.

There were only two places that he could be: sitting in the rows of seats in the waiting lounge or in the Cloud Café. Not seeing him in the former, she made her way to the café and saw him sitting at a small table toward the back. He looked impatient with a group of people who seemed to be trying to resolve a conflict at the table next to him.

Most people who arrived early for a flight chose the small café as the place of choice to wait to be called through security, and this day seemed to be no different, with only two of the small tables unoccupied.

Asher appeared distracted by the turmoil at the neighbouring table, and for a moment he seemed not to notice her arrival.

"Hi," she said, and Asher glanced up. Then, a look of shock registered on his face.

"Hello," he replied. "What are you doing here?"

"Asher, I want to talk to you. Perhaps we can take a short walk outside, where it is less noisy and more private."

Asher appeared to consider the request for a moment, his eyes glancing between her and the two unruly kids.

"Walk where? And what is there to talk about?"

"There's a bench we can sit on outside. It's in a small park on the other side of the bus loop. Like, maybe a three-minute walk." She said it with a smile.

"And what is it that you want to talk about?" he asked.

"Asher, our mother is dying. You are leaving. Whether we admit it or not, our lives are changing. I really want to talk to you before you get on that plane and fly out of my life for good." The dampness that formed in her eyes caught her by surprise, and she was quick to sweep it away.

She didn't want to cry, and had not even considered that she might, but the wave of emotion that swept over her seemed to mellow her half-brother, who closed his laptop and tucked it into the case, and, rising from his chair, hooked the strap over his shoulder.

"Sure," he said, "lead the way."

23.

They walked outside into the late afternoon sun, which had warmed a gentle breeze that rustled the claret-coloured blossoms of a huge Robinia tree. Sheena and Asher walked in silence until they arrived at a long, narrow bench, shaded, at the base of the tree.

He had been surprised to see her standing at his table in the terminal building, and his first thought had been to demand that she go away. But when she said *our mother is dying* and suggested that would bring a change to their lives, it had struck a chord.

He understood, after all, that she was not responsible for the actions of her father, and somehow, seeing how much distress their mother's death was causing Sheena made him curb the impulse to tell her to just fuck off.

"Asher, I don't want this to be the last time we ever speak to each other," Sheena said when they were seated on the bench. "The undeniable truth is that we share the same mother; her blood flows in my veins just as much as it does in yours. We are family."

He bridled at the word. It was as instinctive a reaction as blinking away a dust particle from his eye. Her father had taken his mother away from his family; how dare she suggest that he was part of that?

"I want no part of your family. I would have thought that was clear to you by now."

"I am not asking you to embrace my father, though I think that you have judged him unfairly. I am asking you to embrace the part of me that is our mother. Asher, my father will die someday, you and I will be all that is left of the union of your father and our mother, and my father and our mother. We are linked by blood. Doesn't that mean *anything* to you?"

Asher thought for a moment. *This is all so easy for her. My mother loved me before she came along.* He hated that he was so jealous of Sheena. "When you were born, our mother no longer had time or love for me," he said. "So, now that she's dying, you want me to be your family."

"Asher, that's simply not true," replied Sheena, and Asher reined in his growing anger. "Our mother loved you. She always spoke of you and how proud she was of your academic accomplishments. She never stopped caring about you, and went to great length to make sure that you were safe."

Her last comment straightened Asher's back. "What do you mean you made sure I was safe? Safe from what?"

"Do you remember that spring when I came down from Dalhousie with Farouk to visit you at MIT? You had just started your PhD and had a teaching assistant position there."

"Vaguely," he replied, though he remembered that meeting very clearly.

"Your father had just died."

"I remember. What about it?"

"I came down to tell you how sorry I was that your dad had died, and to make sure that you were going to be OK."

Asher thought it best to hide his distaste for her remark. How dare she suggest that her uninvited visit to MIT was to somehow look after his welfare. She had been a senior in university, and hanging all over some Arab boyfriend—a Palestinian, if he remembered correctly, and he was pretty sure he did. She had brought this guy down with her because she thought that just because he was from the Middle East, somehow, that would buy points with him. It was absurd.

"Seriously, you want me to believe that you came to MIT to look after me? I don't think so. If I remember correctly, you were pretty hot and heavy with that Farouk character. I am pretty sure I was a second thought—or a convenient alibi to use with Mom for your weekend sleazefest."

Sheena looked down at the ground, and Asher noticed her bite softly on her top lip. Still, her demeanour suggested that she wouldn't take the bait and get hooked into an argument over her moral conduct.

"Thanks for that, Asher. I am sorry if that's your opinion of me. Mom suggested that I should take advantage of spring break to go down to Boston, and then detour to Cambridge."

"Why would she do that?" Asher was growing impatient with the conversation, and flipped open his phone to see the time. A call for him to go through security couldn't come soon enough. "Coincidentally, I bumped into Farouk at the airport in Toronto, waiting for my connecting flight to Vancouver on my way here. I can't say I recognized him, but he recognized me, and told me that he and his wife and two small kids are moving out here."

"What?!"

Sheena's shocked face delighted Asher.

"Yeah, it seems he has done pretty well for himself and become a partner in a big national law firm. I congratulated him, and told him that since he was going west, he would have the opportunity to meet his son. I must say he seemed pretty shocked—almost as though you hadn't told him about Ethan."

"Asher! Why did you tell him that? You had no business telling him anything. Besides, how do you know that Ethan is his son?"

"Are you seriously going to tell me that he isn't?" He was revelling in Sheena's anger and panic.

"You are such an asshole!" Her anger was palpable, and he couldn't help but smile.

"Well, don't blame me for the result of your weekend fuckfest with Farouk. It seems to me that the man deserves to know the truth. Besides, it sounds like he is making at least a mid-level six-figure salary—maybe you can ding him for child support." Asher said it with a feigned smile.

"God, you are an ass! I really don't know why I bother with you."

"I don't know why you are so angry with me. You're the one who got pregnant; you're the one who kept it a secret from his father. You even went so far as to turn down a high-profile research job just to get as far away from him as possible. Instead, you took a crappy high school teaching job in this shithole. You can't tell me the money wouldn't come in handy. And don't try to tell me that your trip to Boston was Mom's idea." Asher stood up from the bench. He had had enough of Sheena.

"It was."

"Seriously? Mom was so concerned about me that she asked you to come down to Cambridge and check up on me to see if I was doing alright—give me a break!" Asher reached for his laptop bag and pulled the strap over his shoulder.

"Not to check up on you, but to meet with Professor Bohr."

Sheena might just as well have slapped him in the face—the shock of hearing Bohr's name come out of her mouth completely caught him off guard.

"What did you say?" He had heard her perfectly well, but he wanted to hear it again, and he put his laptop back on the bench.

"Mom asked me to meet with Niles Bohr."

"Why?"

"Niles Bohr had been a colleague of Mom and my father at Oxford, and when things became dangerous, your father asked Mom to help get you into the United States. So, she contacted Niles to see if he would take you on as a PhD student at MIT, as your status at Edinburgh had been compromised. I was delivering a thank you and a small gift from Mom for his help."

Asher was gobsmacked. "What the hell are you talking about?"

"When I was accepted into Dalhousie, Mom insisted that we travel together from the West Coast to take me to the university. She said it was a mother's duty, and she always felt guilty that she didn't have the chance to do the same for you. Anyway, we rented a car and drove to Halifax. It was a long trip, with plenty of time and opportunity for Mom to unveil family secrets that she thought I should know."

Asher was listening intently, wondering exactly where this conversation was going.

"Apparently, a couple of years before you entered Edinburgh University, your dad asked that we all meet in Tehran, and arranged for you to fly there during a reading break from school. According to Mom, he was reluctant to make the request, because he was concerned for our safety."

"This isn't making any sense, Sheena." Asher was growing angry. "My father was a high-ranking academic and very well respected in every quarter. If this is an attempt at posthumous slander, I won't hear it."

"It really isn't. I am telling you exactly what Mom confided in me, and I gave her my word that I would keep it to myself—which I have done until now. It's just 'cause you are so angry with my dad, Mom, and me, and think the absolute worst of us, that I need you to know the truth. And when you do, if you still want nothing to do with me … well, so be it, I guess."

Asher really didn't want to hear anything more, and yet, for some reason, he felt compelled to let Sheena finish. "I don't need to hear a long story, Sheena—and anyway, I don't have much time."

"OK, OK. We went to Tehran—my dad, our mom, and me—and you met us there. It was supposed to be reconciliation—reunion or something—I don't really know, but the real reason was to get your trust money out of the country."

"What are you fucking talking about?" Asher was furious. "My trust is administered by Ibrahim, and has been since the very beginning."

"I am afraid not, Asher. Since that visit we made to Tehran, your trust has been administered by my dad." Sheena raised her voice and pushed forward, despite Asher's fury. "That's because your father specifically asked that my father get your money safely out of the country."

Asher was beside himself. This was an outrageous story that had to be a lie from start to finish. It was a set-up—maybe to get access to the balance of funds in his trust? But that made no sense, because if Ken had access to the money, he would have taken it. No, this was simply a way for Sheena to discredit his father. "Why did I agree to listen to your bullshit?"

"It's not bullshit, it's the truth."

"If my dad wanted the money out of Iran, why wouldn't he transfer it out himself? This makes no sense at all."

"He couldn't send money out of the country, and he was not permitted to leave the country himself. That's why he asked us to come to Tehran. He knew on some level, I guess, that it would be the last time he would see Mom and you."

"What? Why?"

"Your dad had been instrumental in the development of the Iranian nuclear energy program, but as one of the top nuclear physicists in the world, the revolutionary government wanted him to dedicate his talents toward nuclear weapons, which he was reluctant to do. So, according to what Mom told me, the government made life difficult for him by freezing his bank accounts and keeping him under a sort of house arrest. He was only permitted to travel from his apartment to the university and the nuclear development centre." Sheena paused for a moment, and Asher sat, stunned by what he was hearing, so much so that the roar of the arriving aircraft that was his ticket out made him jump.

"I better finish; you don't have much more time," Sheena continued. "Your dad apparently arranged to have his most trusted aid, this guy Ibrahim, pay off the manager of the bank and slowly withdraw all of the trust funds, which he hid in the safe in his apartment, until he could package it up and arrange to transport the money out."

"The morning that we arrived in Tehran, your dad caught Ibrahim stealing money from the safe and fired him on the spot. We spent the day together, but that night your dad arranged for a car and driver to take my dad, along with bags full of your trust money, to the Turkish border. Your father paid a senior officer he knew in the Turkish military to meet my dad and get him, with your trust money, safely over the border.

"Ibrahim, it turns out, wasn't smart enough to know that your dad couldn't turn him over to the authorities without disclosing the illegal withdrawal of funds. Anyway, according to what Mom told me, Ibrahim ran to the authorities and, to save his own skin, told them that your dad was spying for the Americans. We were long gone by the time the authorities came for your dad the next day."

"So, that's the origin of that picture of us in the rose garden in Tehran?" Asher was beyond shock; he felt sick to his stomach.

"Yes."

"Why wasn't my dad in the picture?" he asked in a hushed tone.

"Because he was behind the camera. Mom has told me that he sent us the picture, along with a letter, later that same year. Mom said that he must have smuggled the letter out somehow, because your dad wrote that he was in a program of political re-education and not to believe anything that was attributed to him within the press, or by the government."

Asher was crushed by this news. How was it possible that he had been so self-absorbed that he had had no knowledge of what had happened to his father?

"How is it that I didn't know any of this? Why wasn't I told?"

"You were pretty much focused on what was important to you. My dad made sure your trust money kept coming, and you have been a very angry soul. You have been very hard to talk to, and when we have tried, you haven't wanted to listen," Sheena said. "Come on, you had better get through security. May I walk you there?"

"Yeah, I would like that."

He felt Sheena's hand on his shoulder. The burden he had been carrying somehow felt lighter, and he knew it had nothing to do with his laptop bag, which Sheena had picked up in her other hand. They walked together into the terminal building and to the active security door.

"Thank you, sister," he said, taking his laptop from her and hoping that his moist eyes and sheepishness were not taken as a sign of his emotional weakness. He felt totally broken inside, and shocked by his impulse to give her a hug.

Too soon.

He turned and walked through the door.

24.

Ken sat at the oak desk in his study and turned on his computer. The apprehension he had felt before his first Zoom meeting with Rehema had now been replaced by excitement. A big part of him didn't want to admit to the feeling, having promised himself that he would not be drawn back into his work.

He was flattered that this young PhD student had taken such a keen interest in his work, and his last conversation with Rehema had played over and over in his mind, rekindling the deeply held convictions that, for the better part of his life, had defined him.

He typed the meeting code and password into the appropriate boxes on the Zoom login page, and upon pushing enter, the tiny green light on the camera perched on his desk flicked on.

The face that popped up in the box on his screen looked tired, and if he hadn't recognized the familiar photographs and wall in the background, he would have thought he was looking at someone else—an older man with dishevelled, grey hair, and flaccid skin hanging beneath his chin. It was a reminder of why he didn't have mirrors in his house.

Rehema was the conference convener, and she had not yet joined the meeting, so it provided Ken the opportunity to run a comb through his hair. He then placed the small camera on top of the computer tower to provide a more elevated and flattering angle.

"Hello, Dr. Graham." Rehema's white teeth flashed against her ebony skin as her face flashed onto Ken's screen.

"Hi, Rehema, and it's Ken." He had noticed the red brick background of her father's porch had been replaced by a tall, woven tapestry as her background. "How are you? Are you still at your parents' home?" he asked, smiling at Rehema, who was adjusting the camera on her end.

"I am very well, thanks. I am still in Nyeri, but today I am at the Kenyatta University campus. An old friend and former colleague has been gracious enough to offer me the use of her office. I will have a much better connection here."

"How is your father holding up after the loss of your mother?" Ken asked with a bit of reservation, not wanting to ask an inappropriate question.

"He is doing the best that he can under the circumstances, thanks. My brother has taken a leave from work and will stay with him for a week or so. That will help greatly. Thank you for asking."

Ken nodded, feeling a bit relieved. "Shall we get started then?"

"Thank you. May I start by asking you to elaborate on what I believe is the general thesis of *Human Boundaries Beyond Political Borders*? If I am reading this correctly, almost fifteen years ago, you predicted an unprecedented global migration, where people would move with such frequency and in such numbers that their arrival at national borders would exceed the ability of governments to stop their entry into the country." Rehema paused for a moment, looking up and out toward Ken. "Well, you were spot on there."

"It was an easy prediction based on the algorithm I was using."

"But then you go on to assert that this will, and I am reading here from your book, 'result in the transference of nationalist authority into a new tribalism that will transform jurisprudence.' I am not sure I fully understand what you are saying here."

"Governments, regardless of their form, legislate based upon a nationalist agenda that creates laws that are general in their application and designed and enforced to protect the interests of the nation."

Ken paused. As excited as he felt toward this subject, he could not forget the harsh personal attacks that he had received as he toured university campuses talking about his book. The evidence was undeniable. Changing populations within nations were eroding the ability of governments—especially democratic systems of government—to establish a rule of law that applied equally to all those who lived within their borders.

Ken smiled toward the little camera on his computer. "Governments of virtually all stripes hold citizenship ceremonies for immigrants who choose to become citizens of the country. Many have courses that teach those immigrants about the core values, the laws, and the social contract that are applied to those citizens." He looked at Rehema, who was back to typing in her notebook.

"In virtually all countries where significantly large migrant populations are arriving, either as refugees, legal immigrants, or through illegal entry, the percentage of those taking citizenship tests is declining. Put another way, the percentage of non-citizen resident populations is increasing." He wondered if he should have been better prepared and had the census statistics available to prove his point.

"So, are you saying that these non-citizens are changing the way governments have to govern?" Rehema asked.

"Countries that have a constitution—and most do—reference their constitution as the foundation upon which laws are based. It is a foundation that—in most cases—provides for basic individual rights and freedoms and certain guarantees for citizens of those states. New candidates for citizenship are taught it, and consent to living by it when granted citizenship. But there are unprecedented numbers of people on the move not by choice, but by necessity. They risk their lives and the lives of their children to get into a country for survival, not because they believe in the values and the rule of law that have evolved in the countries in which they seek asylum."

"But surely you aren't saying that immigrants are a threat to peace, order, and good government? That's been the charge against you," Rehema said, looking up from her notepad.

"No, I am not suggesting that at all." Ken appreciated the question. That had certainly been one of many erroneous statements made against him on a wide range of public platforms.

"What I identified in my early research and what my predictive algorithm confirmed was that 'citizenship,' as an identifier, has become less important than race, gender, and other 'tribal'—as I called them—identities." He paused and waited for Rehema to look up from her typing.

"The significance of this change has been the degree to which these identities have influenced government policy. The result has been legislation that is written specifically to address the concerns of those 'tribal collectives'—again, my words. This has created a challenge to the foundational principles of most constitutions—namely, that every citizen is equal."

"Because … ?"

"Because where every individual can become a citizen, citizens can't become a different race or gender, which creates an exclusivity and potential inequality in the law."

"Is that the transformation of jurisprudence? This change in identifiers?"

"Yes." Ken was pretty sure that Rehema knew exactly what he was postulating, because they had had that discussion during their first Zoom call.

Anxiety started to creep into his mind as he wondered why she was so keen to have him elaborate in such detail. He shifted a bit in his seat, trying to tackle the uncomfortable feeling that had overtaken him. He had been set up by too many people in the past who had requested interviews, claiming to be neutral or unbiased, only to write a scathing interpretation of what he had told them.

"Look, Rehema, I advised you when we last spoke that this was likely not a productive avenue for you to pursue. People would rather not hear what I have to tell them, and I am not sure that it will do you much good to take this on."

"Well, I believe that the patient should not blame the doctor for an accurate diagnosis. I have read your work extensively, Ken, and I know it is not an opinion but rather evidence from documented research and algorithmic testing. The predictions that you made twenty years ago are coming true today. That's undeniable, and there is every reason to believe that this transformation in governance is happening," said Rehema. "That change is at the heart of what I plan to write in my book. What will all this mean in terms of social change, and possibly world order?"

"That's the million-dollar question," he said. "The answer will only be found through a proper analysis of the predictions of my past studies, and using that data to postulate what is most likely to result from the changes that have occurred." Ken paused, and the two sat silently, looking at each other through their computer screens.

"So," Rehema said, with a broad smile. "Do you want to write it with me?"

Her question startled him. *Do I want to write a book with her?* Rehema was right; what had been a prediction twenty years ago had become a reality today. The algorithm had worked, and with the input of current data, it would produce a comparable predictive analysis.

He put his hand over his mouth as if to physically prevent the smile of excitement he felt at this prospect.

"One more week and I will be finished with my quarantine here, then I will fly back to Oxford, where I will have to quarantine for another two weeks. So, Ken, what do you say? I have a spare bedroom in my flat, and there's an empty desk in the office beside me at Oxford. Do you want to join me?"

25.

Saturday's light rain had freshened the air. Overnight, the sky had cleared to greet the rising sun that lit a clear blue sky.

Jessica called Ken before her scheduled 8 a.m. rounds from her car after she had parked at the centre. She had been relieved to hear that Lena was still resting comfortably, though she had no reason to think that wouldn't be the case, provided Ken had no problem changing her IV drip.

The cocktail of drugs in the IV that she had prepared for Lena would hopefully help provide a painless, albeit slow transition from life to death. She cared for Ken, whom she felt had accepted a considerable burden by taking Lena in. She hadn't told Ken that she had prepared one final IV bag that would accelerate Lena's journey, but simply promised him that she would drop by in the early afternoon.

She would have offered to head to the farm as soon as she had completed her rounds at the centre, which had been her original intention, but just as she had parked at the center and was about to call Ken, Janis's number lit up on her screen.

"Hi there—or should I say good morning?" Janis's voice came clearly over the car's Bluetooth.

"Good morning," Jessica replied, feeling a slight touch of excitement.

"Any chance you'd be into Sunday brunch at my place?" Janis asked. "Nothing too fancy; we can do light, with muffins, or full-on eggs, sausage, and bacon. Your choice."

Jessica's first impulse was to say no. *Just thank Janis for the invitation, then decline her offer.* She had a perfect excuse. She was busy with morning rounds. *Besides, there is Ken and Lena that need your attention—and besides, look at what you are wearing. Definitely not suitable to wear to brunch with Janis.* There would be no time to return home and change.

She glanced down at her ankle-high boots beneath the shapely, snug-fitting blue jeans. That part of the wardrobe was acceptable, but she wasn't too sure about the flower-patterned, form-fitting sleeveless top. Her assessment took only a few seconds, and she was alarmed by the thought that she might override her reactive self and actually consider accepting the invitation.

"Hello? Are you still there?" asked Janis.

"Ah, yes, I am here. Sorry, I am just heading to do my morning rounds at the centre," she replied. She was filled with the emotions of a high school girl being asked out on a first date, which, considering she was pushing sixty years of age, seemed pretty stupid. But stupid or not, those emotions took hold, and she heard herself say, "Sure, thank you; that sounds lovely," and immediately regretted having said it.

Once she arrived at the centre, she went to her office and took advantage of the full-length mirror that hung on the inside of her closet door, to better assess her outfit.

There was a time, she thought, when the skin below her triceps had been a little firmer, but the sleeveless flower top was form-fitting and low-cut enough that she was prepared to bank on both to be a sufficient distraction.

She thought it would have to do, feeling a little weird that she was letting how she appeared actually matter. She pulled her white medical coat over her clothes, took her electronic notepad in hand, and started her rounds, trying to keep her mind focused on the needs of her patients instead of questioning why on earth she had accepted Janis's invitation.

By the time she had finished seeing all but the last patient, she had resolved to call Janis back as soon as she was free, and to apologize. She would tell her that something had come up, and that she would be unable to come after all.

Having made the decision to make the call, she felt much better—relieved, in fact. She exchanged the file of the last patient with the attending nurse and read the name on the tab. It was Charlie Brown.

Jessica was so focused on reading the notes in the file that when she walked into the long hallway, she bumped into the nurse with whom she had done rounds the previous day.

"I am so sorry," said Jessica. "What brings you in on a Sunday?"

"Well, we have had a bit of a miracle," replied the nurse. "I came in just to lend a hand. I take it that you haven't been to Charlie's room yet."

"What miracle? He's the last patient on my rounds—I'm headed there now."

Jessica watched the tall, slim nurse walk her way down the hall, and with a wave, call back to her, "You'll see."

Jessica hurried down the hall, trying to read the file at the same time. There was nothing substantively new in the file, but she did note that the morning medications had not been checked off. Charlie Brown had terminal cancer, and under normal protocols, she would have been informed when she arrived at the centre if he had passed during the night.

The door to his room was ajar, so she pushed it open—and looked at an empty bed. Next to the bed, sitting in the wide green leather chair with his back to the door, was a familiar figure, with grey curly hair and black skin, contrasted against a starched white shirt beneath a collared jacket.

Jessica was dumbfounded, but there before her eyes sat Charlie, fully dressed and—his senior years notwithstanding—looking fit enough.

"Charlie?"

The man turned to look at her, and she took a step backward and gasped. She was looking into the healthy face of the man that she knew to be Charlie. It was impossible.

"Laurence," responded the man. "I am Charlie's twin brother. You must be Doctor Gunn."

"Jessica Gunn, yes." She tried not to stare at the man, who had the same eyes and the same nose. "Are you Charlie's identical twin?"

Laurence chuckled and shook his head. "Not identical, but we did look a lot alike—and not just because we were both black." His chuckle turned into a nervous laugh.

Jessica felt awkward. That is not what she had meant—this man looked like a healthy version of her patient, Charlie.

"Charlie passed about an hour ago," the attending nurse said. "Mr. Brown asked that we not tell you immediately, as he wanted an opportunity to speak with you. I hope that is alright."

"Don't be angry with the nurses," said Laurence. "I asked them to make sure we could meet. They came for my brother about ten minutes ago, but I thank the Lord my God that I found him in time to see him, speak with him, and put his mind at peace on a few things." Laurence paused and seemed for a moment to lose himself in thought. "He finally got to kick the ball, and scored a fifty-yard field goal."

"You had been looking for Charlie?" she asked.

"Tarone—his name was Tarone Brown—and yes, I have been looking for him for the better part of a year now." With a wide, meaty black hand, Laurence wiped away a tear that had rolled down his full cheeks.

"Tarone told me how wonderful you were to him. More than a doctor, more like a friend. I really want to thank you for all the love and care you gave him. God knows you were one of the few people on this planet who did."

"How did he get the name Charlie?" asked Jessica. "That's the name he gave when he was admitted."

"He gave it to himself. You know, like the kid in the comic strip. He was Charlie Brown, the loveable loser, always a day late and a dollar short. It wasn't really true, but over the years he convinced himself, to the point that he came to believe it."

The reference to the comic meant nothing to Jessica, as she had only heard somewhat vague references to Charles Schulz. She was, however, surprised to learn that Charlie, or Tarone, had had such an appreciation for her.

She treated all her patients with compassion, and hadn't really singled him out except for the fact that unlike most of her patients, who were often anxious to share the memories of their lives, both good and bad, Charlie had been a very private man, very alone in the world, so much so that she had been surprised when the duty nurse had mentioned the previous day that she thought he might have a brother in Jamaica. Charlie never mentioned a brother or any connection he had with Jamaica.

"I am very sorry that I have not kept you informed, but until yesterday, I had no information about any family—and even then, it was not confirmed," she said to Laurence.

"That sounds about right. Tarone would not mention that he had family. He went a long way to hide from all that goes on in Jamaica, coming all the way to this backwoods place."

"What was he hiding from?" asked Jessica. She had often sensed that Charlie had secrets, but had not felt it her place to pry.

"That's a long story for another day," said Laurence. "Like I said, I thank God that he led me to Tarone, so that I could set things straight with him."

"You had a falling out with your brother?" asked Jessica.

Laurence just shook his head and stared down at the floor. "You know, it's a hell of a thing to have your best life stolen from you."

"I don't understand."

"And I guess if I'm honest, neither do I. God moves in mysterious ways. Isn't that the old cliché?"

"I think that people blame God for a lot of things that He isn't guilty of doing," said Jessica, hoping that she might help Laurence, but not really understanding the root of the issue. "So, you were able to set things straight with Tarone?"

"Yeah, I was. You see, Tarone, like God, wasn't guilty of doing things he had been accused of, like raping and killing a fourteen-year-old girl in Jamaica. He always said he was innocent; he even told anybody who would listen that he knew who had done it—Llanzo Jackson.

"He might as well have been singin' in the wind for all the good it did him. The police released his name as the perp they liked for the crime, and that was that. Hate spewed out on social media, his face was all over the papers, and vigilante gangs thought that if they were the ones to catch him and string him up, it would be good for their image—help them get new recruits, you understand what I mean? So, he ran." Laurence looked up and around the room, trying to keep his tears from spilling. "He ran to this place, and spent his life looking over his shoulder for something he didn't do."

One Weekend in May

"That is a truly horrible story, Laurence; I am so sorry to hear it. I feal so bad for Charlie. I cannot imagine living a huge part of my life hiding from a lie." Jessica felt a strange twinge, but pushed it aside.

"So, I got to tell him firsthand that the guy who he suspected, Llanzo Jackson, was the real killer. He gave a deathbed confession, and the DNA tests they did confirmed it was him, not Tarone, who had raped and killed that little girl. It seems my brother had been the loveable, honest guy he had always claimed to be."

Jessica felt physically ill. "I am truly sorry you lost so much time with your brother, Laurence. Is there anything that I can do to help you at this time?"

"God is in my corner, Doc. He made sure you ministered to Tarone, and he made sure I found him in time to speak to him, to hold him, and to let him know I had never stopped believing in him or loving him." Laurence took a breath and swallowed hard as two more tears escaped. "But there is something that you could help me with."

"Of course, I am happy to help in any way I can. What would you have me do?"

"Help me to get him home."

Jessica hadn't seen that request coming. "Get him home to Jamaica?" she asked, hoping that wasn't what he had meant, but feeling pretty sure that it was.

"Yes. He needs to be buried with his family," said Laurence. "I have some money, so I am not asking for that; it's just that I don't know the rules or even where to begin with something like this."

"I don't know the rules either," said Jessica, "but I am quite sure there is a way that I can help to make that happen." She had absolutely no idea how to fly a dead body and a living relative all the way to Jamaica. She would start with the duty staff in the morgue, thinking they would have faced this issue before.

"I really appreciate that, Doc."

Jessica smiled and shook his hand. "One last question: what did you mean by Charlie finally getting to kick the ball?"

"There's not much to it, really," said Laurence. "Tarone was born about twenty minutes after me, and he always felt that he didn't quite measure

156

up. I was better in school, in sports, and with the girls. I think, in a way, he blamed me. In his head, I was Lucy with that football. Always talking him into things, like Lucy offered to hold the ball for Charlie Brown, but pulled it away every time he tried to kick it."

Right. Jessica had seen the cartoon, with the fat little bald-headed kid landing on his buttocks after the dark-haired girl holding the ball pulled it away at the last minute. "I get it. Giving him the news that he would finally be believed was his kick of the ball" Jessica said while trying to imagine the weight that would come off a person's shoulders, especially in their final hours, knowing they had been exonerated after a lifetime of being presumed guilty. "How did Charlie react to your news? There must have been a part of him that felt nothing but rage for the man who had sat silent all those years and let him take the blame."

"He looked at me and said, 'I told you so.'" Laurence's face lit up into a broad, toothy grin. "And I told him that I never doubted him, and how sorry I was that he had to spend his life hiding from a lie."

"I can't imagine how he felt," she said. The conversation was deeply unsettling.

"Well, I can only tell you his final words on it when he took my hand and squeezed it," Laurence continued, looking into Jessica's eyes. "Tarone said, 'Brother, I knew I was innocent, and God did, too. If you think hiding from a lie is hard, imagine how hard it has to be to spend your life hiding from the truth.'"

Laurence's words hit her like she had put her finger in a light socket. She felt dizzy, and knew that she needed to end the conversation.

Jessica looked at her watch. "Laurence, it has been a real pleasure to meet you. I wish only that the circumstances surrounding our meeting had been different. Please make sure that the duty nurse here has your contact information, and I will make sure that the appropriate authorities are in contact with you about what is necessary to get your brother home.

26.

Janis Lieberman carried the folding three-step ladder from the narrow cupboard in the pantry into the kitchen. She placed the ladder in front of her fridge, and climbed up so she could reach the cupboards. She was on the hunt for the waffle iron.

There was no denying her spirits had been lifted by Jessica's acceptance of her brunch invitation, and she hummed "The Long and Winding Road" as she shuffled the few appliances that were in the cupboard until she saw what she was looking for.

I'm not sure if you are a waffle kind of gal, Jess. She carried the appliance down the few steps and placed it on the counter. *But if you are, then I've got you covered.*

"Many times I've been alone, and many times I've cried. Anyway, you'll never know, the many ways I've tried." She sang the lyrics aloud as she folded up the stepladder and replaced it in the cupboard. Hosting Jessica would provide a much-needed distraction from the heartbreaking news she had been confronted with when she had returned home from Ken's farm.

She took a wet cloth and wiped the counter of the island in the centre of the small farmhouse kitchen as her mind drifted back to her conversation with Jessica in her car before she had dropped her off to finish the chores at Ken's barn.

Janis had felt an attraction when she met Jessica at the barn, but she knew enough and was respectful enough to let that feeling play out. The offer to give her a ride to the barn and their shared jibe at Ken all seemed to be further confirmation of her suspicion about her new friend. But, in the quiet of her home, Janis had to concede that it was a bold move to confront Jessica about her sexuality.

Bottom line, it's not your business, Janis, and calling her backward—not cool. Janis prepped the automatic coffee maker, and pretended the beans where those uncool words getting ground into a fine powder.

She knew that Ken didn't have a clue, and despite the considerable age difference between him and Jessica, Janis was sure that Ken had developed feelings for her. What had she called him? *A loveable putz—yep, that was it, and it sums up Ken to a T.* And, of course, if Jessica wanted to stay closeted, that would be her choice. But Janis felt a certain excitement at the prospect that would not be the case.

What Janis felt a lot less certain about was what to do with the news that she had received when driving home to find Brahm de Jong, the oldest of the five de Jong children who had inherited their parents' farm. It had been his mother who had who had leased the property to her.

Janis had parked her truck in the high-roofed, open garage and walked to the house to find Brahm sitting in one of the two whicker chairs on her porch.

"I didn't expect you, Brahm," she had said. "Everything OK?"

"I wanted to come over and tell you in person, Janis—and please know this is not my choice, but I am outvoted. The family has decided to list the property for sale."

It was a gut punch, and she collapsed in the chair beside him.

"Seriously? What the fuck, Brahm? What about our deal? Why are you listing the place? I am managing things, paying all the bills, and maintaining them for you guys. I don't get it." Her words spilled out of her mouth, and she doubled forward in the chair.

"Your deal died with my mother, Janis, and I think you know that. Besides, it's not my choice. I tried to get the others to change their minds, but with the current market conditions, this property is worth millions of dollars. They want the money." Brahm rose and started toward the steps.

"When are you listing it, and how much are you asking?" Janis had asked.

"Next week," replied Brahm. "The realtors say that we should list it at five million. It will likely sell in the high fours. Of course, it will take a bit of time to sell at that price, and you are certainly welcome to stay until whoever buys it takes possession—unless, of course, you want to buy it."

"Fuck off, Brahm! You know damned well I don't have that kind of money."

"I am really sorry, Janis. I know how much this place has meant to you."

And that's the thing about it. She pulled two bowls out of a drawer in the kitchen island and placed them on the counter. *The only fucking reason this property is worth that much money is because of all the fucking work I've put into it over the last ten years.*

"If you are prepared to put in the time and money to improve the house and property, you can live here as long as you want." That's what Brahm's mother, Maud, had told her when they had discussed her taking on the property. "None of my children want this place," she had told her after Frankie's funeral. "They won't work it the way their father and I have. So if you want to farm it, I will sign a lease that lets you have it."

At the time, Janis recalled, she had had no clue how to run a farm, nor did she have the skill set to do the work that needed to be done to improve the aging house, barn, and leaning fences. But taking on the farm had been the opportunity she needed to pull her mind away from the hurt and betrayal she felt toward her family and that lying bitch she had thought would be her life partner.

Janis set her oven at 400 Fahrenheit, then took a bag of oat bran and some whole wheat flour out of a deep drawer and put them next to the two bowls. Baking was a skill—like carpentry, plumbing, electrical wiring, and farming—that she had taught herself during the remaking of her life. And damn it, she had become good at all of them.

She took an egg out of the carton in the fridge, cracked it into a glass measuring cup, and whipped it up before mixing it into a cup of milk. *Why is life so fucking unfair?* She poured the mixture into one of the bowls, along with three tablespoons of yogurt, a half-cup of maple syrup, and a quarter-cup of buttermilk.

It was my hard work that fixed up the barn and repaired the fencing. She had learned how to prune and maintain the orchards, how to run a tractor, to test and evaluate the soil. *I doubled the fucking hay yield, you dumb prick. I invested my money.* She stirred the mixture in the bowl so vigorously, some spilled over the edge. *How dare you tell me you know what this farm means to me. You have no fucking clue.*

Janis sniffed back the bead of moisture that had threatened to run from her nose and wiped the tears that welled in her eyes. *Shit, how many tablespoons of baking powder have I put in with the flour?* She added a teaspoon and a half of ground cinnamon, a pinch of salt, and some frozen blueberries. *That's going to have to do.*

As Janis mixed the dry and wet ingredients together and spooned the mixture into the muffin pans, the oven pinged. *Well, here goes. I hope I got this right.* She put the filled pans into the preheated oven. Blueberry oat bran muffins were her favourite, and she hoped Jessica would enjoy them.

Just when I thought things were taking a real turn for the better.

The familiar ringtone from her phone, which she had left on the kitchen counter, snapped her away from her thoughts of having to move. Her heart sank; she knew it was too good to be true. *That's going to be Jessica cancelling brunch.*

She walked over to the phone and unclipped the leather cover. Her blood froze in her veins when she saw the number displayed on the screen: (929) 524-1636.

Janis let the phone ring twice more and stared at the number that she knew by heart, considering whether to answer or decline the call. On the fifth ring, she answered.

"Hello," she said.

"Janis, is that you?" the tremulous, somewhat hoarse voice burst from the phone.

"Yes," replied Janis. Hearing the voice left her feeling faint.

"This is your mudda."

27.

Sheena stepped forward and kneeled at the communion rail, and Ethan stood at attention beside her. The sixth Sunday of Easter Mass was ending. Sheena had received the Eucharist from the priest, who had placed his hand on her son's head before she rose, took Ethan's hand, and walked back to their pew.

"Aren't we going to light a candle for Grandma?" Ethan whispered in her ear, barely audible over the choir, as they kneeled together at their pew.

"Shhh … say your prayers. When Mass has ended, we will light a candle." She squeezed his hand and gave him a quick wink.

Despite her mother never taking up the Catholic faith, Sheena was quite certain that they both worshipped the same merciful God, and as she kneeled, she reflected on the last reading given during Mass, Revelation 21.10–22. *And he carried me away in the spirit to a great and high mountain, and shewed me that great city … .* So, she prayed that the soul of her mother would find peace, and that God would look favourably upon her when she passed.

When the Mass ended, she took Ethan by the hand and walked to the gold-embossed votive stand on the right side of the ornate altar.

"Which candle do I light?" asked Ethan, his voice still a whisper, as she handed him the lit lighting stick.

"Light the candle that you think Grandma would like the best. And don't forget to say a prayer," she replied, lighting a thin stick of her own and choosing a candle to light while she again prayed for the soul of her mother.

"Can I go and find Liam now?" asked Ethan as he snuffed out the lighting stick in the small container of sand at the edge of the wooden stand.

"Hold up. I will come with you, and we will find Liam and his parents together," Sheena said, handing her son a small backpack that she had tucked under the pew. "Don't lose this, please; it has your soccer uniform and boots in it."

Liam's parents weren't hard to find. The foyer was filled with parishioners who had lined up to dip their fingers in holy water, cross themselves, and greet the priest who stood at the exit doors. Liam had already unzipped and pulled off the coat that he had worn over his bright red soccer jersey with the number 9 in bold white on his back.

Ethan let go of her hand and ran to meet Liam. He said something she could not hear to his parents before the two boys bolted through the large, wooded doors, down the concrete steps that led to the parking lot.

Sheena waited for her turn to shake the hand of the Priest, who leaned in and quietly whispered his personal condolences.

"Thank you for mentioning her during Mass and asking the congregation to pray for her eternal repose. That meant a great deal to me," she said, offering the priest a brief smile. "I like to think that even though she was not a Catholic, our prayers for her will be heard."

"I didn't know your mother well," said the priest, "but what I did know of her led me to believe that she was a woman of great conviction and faith. I am quite sure that God will look favourably upon her during her last hours on this earth, and her spiritual resurrection." Even as he spoke the last word, he had turned to the next parishioner and placed his hand upon the head of the small baby she was holding.

It all seemed a bit too rehearsed and lacking in sincerity, but she quickly rationalized his manner, acknowledging that he must face hundreds of parishioners who have lost or are in the process of losing a loved one. What else was he supposed to say? Still, she felt a bit of rancour. After all, this was *her* mother.

Liam's mother was waiting for her outside. "Good morning, Aisling," said Sheena. "Thank you for taking Ethan to soccer. I saw that Liam wasted no time getting into the striker's role," she said, referencing Liam's number 9 soccer shirt.

"He insisted on wearing it to church," Aisling replied with a laugh. "Don't you worry; Ethan is in good hands now. Iain has gone to the car to settle the pair of them—and trust me, Dad rules."

"Well, please pass on my thanks to Iain also," said Sheena. "I am just going to scoot over to the farm to make sure my dad is managing alright, then I will come and get Ethan from the after-game ice cream at Dairy Queen.

"I am so sorry for what you're going through," said Aisling. "I've been where you are, and it's not easy, but these kids of ours help us to move on—that's for sure. Frankly, we don't have a choice in the matter."

Sheena smiled and lipped a silent *thank you* to Aisling, whose comment had made her feel a little better, and as she walked along the sidewalk, lined by blooming pink wild roses, her spirits were lifted. Arriving at her car, she climbed in behind the steering wheel and reached for her cell phone, which she had left plugged in to charge.

She thought she should give Dad a call and let him know she was going to drive to the farm.

"Hey there, good morning," she said when her father answered her call. "How are things out there this morning?"

"Hi, sweetheart." Ken's calm voice reassured her. "Your mom had a peaceful night. But she is very close to the end."

"Are you managing alright?" she asked.

"I am doing OK, thanks. Jessica arrived a few minutes ago. She has been incredibly helpful." Her father sounded exhausted, the overtones of sadness unmistakeable.

An unfamiliar feeling came over her. It was not that she had not known this day would come—quite the contrary. There had been days when she was leaving the care home that she had wished it would come sooner. But now, after her mother had finally recognized her and told her that she loved her, what soaked her mind was the flood of memories: fun times, laughter, boat rides, horse shows, and those intimate moments squished together in her favourite chair while she was being read a bedtime story.

Tears welled in her eyes until her grief, which she had tried so hard to hide, burst into the light of the morning sun. She held the phone away so her father would not hear her sobbing, and put her hand over her mouth to stifle her cry.

"Sheena, are you still there?" Her father's voice in microscratch on the tiny phone speaker pushed her to compose herself.

"I just left the church, Dad, and will head over there now." She spoke the words in monotone to mask the trembling aftershock from the first emotional quake that had so overwhelmed her. "Should I stop and pick up some donuts for you to have with your morning coffee? Honey crullers—I know they are your favourites."

"I'm good, but thanks for the thought. See you when you get here."

***

Jessica closed the bedroom door behind her and walked down the hall and into the kitchen, where Ken stood looking out the bay window just beyond the sink, then sat on a bar stool at the kitchen island.

He seemed deep in thought. A melancholy expression lined his sun-marked face.

"You OK?" she finally asked.

"I was looking at the wisteria," he replied, and she walked over to join him at the window.

"It's beautiful," she said, looking at the multitude of light purple blossoms that hung from within the green leaves of a wild cherry tree.

"It has grown all the way to the very top. Must be at least thirty feet high," he said.

"Very unusual, but really quite magnificent," replied Jessica, marvelling at how the vine-like stem of the wisteria was so hidden within the foliage of the cherry tree.

"Lena and I bought the plant the very first summer we moved on to the farm. We were still living in the tiny cabin down by the barn at the time. When we selected the building site for the house and completed the house plans, I knew that this window would be here, so I planted the wisteria at the base of the cherry tree, hoping that one day, Lena and I would be looking out this window and enjoying its beauty. Mission accomplished, wisteria. It only took ten years." Ken paused, then said "But Lena didn't stay around long enough to see the show."

"People don't usually plan their lives around a garden plant, Ken. No matter how stunning it may be for the short few days or weeks that it blooms."

"Not anymore, they don't," replied Ken, walking over to the coffee maker on the island. "Can I pour you a cup of coffee?"

"No thanks," she replied, anxious to be on her way, but not wanting to leave Ken in a vulnerable state. "I can't stay too long, but I have made arrangements for later this afternoon."

"Arrangements?"

She looked carefully at him. Understandably, he appeared tired, but it was the emotional stress that seemed to engulf him that Jessica was more concerned about. "Yes, Ken. Lena will not regain consciousness now. She will slowly drift into a very deep sleep until her heart stops. I will only be gone for a couple of hours, then I will return. You don't need to worry or do anything more. The coroner's office is expecting my call, and when I call them, they will send a vehicle for Lena."

Ken didn't appear to have heard a word that she had said to him. "We ferociously hold on to false assumptions all our lives. We convince ourselves that they give us predictability, even certainty, with respect to outcomes," he said.

"Um, OK if you say so." She really had no idea what he was talking about.

"There is only one predictable outcome that follows our birth, Jessica, and that's our inevitable death. The thrill of life is not knowing the when, why, or the how of it. Gilgamesh couldn't escape that finality, despite having been led to the bush of immortality and holding it in his hands." Ken poured himself a mug full of coffee.

"Did you hear what I said about Lena?" asked Jessica, trying to pull him back to the situation at hand. "What does any of that have to do with her?"

"It has everything to do with her," he replied. "And yes, I heard everything you just told me. You will be back in a few hours, and Lena will fall into a deep sleep and eventually die. The coroner will send a vehicle to pick up her body. Did I miss anything?"

"Ken, are you sure you're OK?"

"I am really sad. It's hard for me to watch Lena die. But I get it; we are all going to die. It's not only a predictable outcome, but an essential one. Now that the when, why, and how of it are known, all I am left with is to reflect on the choices she made and the reasons that she made them. Death is the last piece of the puzzle that was Lena Murshid.

"I think I may be ready."

"Ready for what?" Ken's little speech had concerned her. Grief can be a powerful emotion. and she wasn't at all sure what he meant.

"The PhD student—Rehema—the one I mentioned was going to call this morning, asked me if I would like to go to Oxford and to reengage in my work and co-author a book on the issues of global population, changing governance, and human survival. I am seriously considering it, much to my surprise," he said.

"Seriously?" Ken's comment caught her by surprise. This seemed completely out of character, at least from the little that she knew of him. "I thought that you were completely turned off by all the crap you took the last time you put your head above the foxhole."

"I didn't say I wasn't nervous at the prospect of stepping back into academia," he replied. "But something over this weekend has rekindled that fire. Rehema seems like a brilliant student, and as she said to me during our last meeting, you don't condemn the doctor because you don't like the diagnosis. She's been a bit of a wake-up call."

"Wow" was all that Jessica could say, while her mind wondered if this was simply his mind's way of deflecting the grief he obviously felt over Lena's death. "What about the farm? What happens to that?"

"Well, there is that," he said, tossing out the dregs of coffee from his now-empty cup. "I haven't really thought that bit through. I would really hate to sell it, though the market is hot for rural farm property at the moment. Lots of people want to escape from the cities and find sanctuary on rural acreages. The thing is, I would never be able to replace it."

"I have to say I am really surprised, Ken, but really excited at the opportunity for you. Heading off to England may do you a world of good. Listen, I really have to run," she said, gathering up her coat and starting toward the door. "I will be back in a couple of hours, I promise. Just keep an eye on Lena. But as I said, the dye is cast."

28.

Sheena saw Jessica's vehicle approaching, so she pulled over beside the tall lilac bush at the entry to the farm, and opened the gate so she could drive past.

As Jessica pulled up, she lowered the driver's side window. "Good morning, Sheena," she said with a smile.

Sheena returned the salutation and waved as she slowly drove past and onto the narrow road that led toward the highway. She was happy that Jessica had been such a good friend to her father and given her mother such good care.

Mindful that Toby was likely out and about, she drove through the gate and closed it behind her before continuing up to the house. Oddly, she felt very nervous as she parked, got out of her car, and walked toward the steps that led up to the large deck and the front door to her father's house.

If she was completely honest with herself, her nervousness stemmed from not knowing what she should do or say in these circumstances. Her mother was dying; that much was certain, but the dementia and tumour had already stolen her away. In many ways, she had already come to terms with her loss.

The real source of her nervous discomfort, she admitted to herself as she walked up the steps to the front door, was not knowing what to do or say to her father. He had always been such a powerful and positive force in her life, but ever since his divorce from her mother, and especially in the last twenty-four hours, she had seen a very different man.

When her parents' marriage had ended, her father—who had never been shy about sharing his opinions, especially on matters of international politics—had seemed to withdraw into the shadows. It was as though something inside him had broken.

Sheena reached for the box of six honey crullers that she had picked up before driving to the farm. She knew that her father had only said he didn't want them to save her the trouble of picking them up. She was quite certain that he would enjoy them.

When she reached the front door, she tapped a couple of times before entering the house, where she found her father sitting in his familiar leather chair, reading what appeared to be a manuscript for one of his books.

"Hi there," she said, removing her coat and hanging it in the free-standing wardrobe next to the door. Ethan and I missed you in church, but we totally understand why you couldn't come. What's the latest?"

"The latest is that I am happy to see you. Where is Ethan?"

"With Aislin and Iain O'Sullivan, they have taken him to the soccer match," she replied. "Ethan and Liam are on the same team. I don't like to miss his games, but I thought it important that I come over and be with you."

Her father put down the manuscript he was reading and rose from his chair, surprising her with a bear hug. He was not usually that tactile.

"That's very sweet of you," he said, releasing her from his hug. "Truthfully, there really is nothing more you can do. Don't go in—just hold onto the happy memory of your visit with her yesterday. These last few hours will not be pleasant—though, as far as I can tell, your mother is free from discomfort. Should I put on the water for tea?"

Her father's slow movement was impossible for her not to notice, as was the slight curve of his spine and roundness of his shoulders. "I'll do it," she said. "You sit and be comfortable. I brought you some honey crullers anyway, so you can join me for a cup of tea and a cruller. What are you reading?"

"*Artificial Intelligence and the Rise of Totalitarian Science*," he said, returning to his chair and putting the manuscript on the small table beside him. "It is still unpublished. I will stick with coffee, thanks."

"Mind if I help myself, then?" She called back to him from the kitchen island, where she plugged in a small electric kettle.

"Help yourself."

Sheena pulled open the thin drawer on the kitchen counter that contained a variety of teas, and selected a spiced green tea. She dropped the tea bag into the porcelain teapot and filled it with boiling water. She hadn't seen her father pay any attention to his books or academic writing in a long time, and the title he had just mentioned was unfamiliar to her.

She took two plates from the cupboard and put a honey cruller on each before grabbing the carafe and filling his coffee mug.

"There you go," she said, placing one of the plates on the small table next to his chair. "Your favourite—enjoy!"

She took a big bite out of her donut and dropped herself into the loveseat facing her dad, who smiled, nodded, and raised his mug.

"Is this something new that you have written?" she asked. "I don't recall that title."

"The writing isn't new, but I couldn't find a publisher brave enough to print and distribute it," replied Ken.

"Lots of really good writers get turned down, Dad; you know that."

For a moment, the two sat in silence, and she sipped her tea and ate her donut, noticing that her father seemed distracted. He hadn't touched his coffee, let alone the donut. She knew him well enough to know that this was not a normal reaction or mood. But given the circumstances, it was not really unexpected. She knew how much he loved her mother, so no wonder her death was proving to be very traumatic. What she needed to do was take the conversation somewhere else.

"What made you read it again now?" she asked, thinking that he had done so as a distraction.

"To refresh my mind," he said.

"That's great," she said, sipping on her tea. "Something new for me to read."

Sheena was a bit surprised when her father's face lit up with laughter. "You aren't going to read it. You haven't read any of the books that I have written—which is OK. I am not offended by that, nor am I trying to be critical of you."

"Well, I have heard you and Mom talk about all of them many times. I loved to listen to you two discuss your work," she said, feeling slightly hurt, but also embarrassed and a little ashamed. Immediately, she realized that she had taken the conversation back to her dying mother. "OK, so tell me what's this one is about."

"It is about what is going to happen when we let AI decide what's best for us."

"Like the movie ... what was it called? You know the one, where the machines are killing all the humans."

"Not exactly; that was science fiction. What I am writing about is a scientific fact. We are creating components that use algorithms that are so sophisticated that it is beyond our mental capacity to fully comprehend them, so we become dependent upon even more complex AI systems to do the programming for us," he said. "There will be very real and very serious consequences when that day arrives, and it's not far off."

She had no idea what anything her father had just said meant. Her takeaway was that it didn't sound very good, but rather like a pretty pessimistic outlook on the future. Come to think about it, that was the feeling that she had often felt when, as a young person growing up, she had overheard conversations between her parents along similar lines. *More doomsday shit I would rather not think about.*

"OK, so what prompted you to read it again now?" she asked, thinking it a more rhetorical question and not really wanting to get into too detailed a discussion on the matter.

"Because I am considering going back to Oxford to co-author a book that will include some of this material," he said in such a matter-of-fact manner that she wondered if she had really heard what she thought she had heard him say.

"What?!"

"There is a PhD student at Oxford who is working under Julius Omondi—you might remember him—and she is heavily engaged in a review of my work. She has asked me to co-author a book with her, and I am seriously considering doing so."

Sheena didn't know what to say. This revelation was so far from what she thought might be possible for her father that she wondered if he was losing his grip on reality like her mother had. "Dad, you can't be serious."

"Why not?"

"How long have you known this student? In fact, what do you know about this student?"

"I just met her on a Zoom call yesterday, and we spoke again this morning. Her name is Rehema Tanui; she is from Kenya and is a junior fellow at Oxford University working under Julius, who is now an eminence grise. She seems quite brilliant, but what's most appealing is her passion for and understanding of my work."

"This is a joke, right, Dad?" An unexpected and unexplainable sense of panic started to overtake her. How was it possible that her mother was about to die, and as soon as she was gone, her father would be leaving the country to return to Oxford? This was madness. He was too old to be tripping off with some post-graduate student at Oxford. *Besides, what about the farm, Toby, and the sheep? What about Ethan—and most of all, what about me?* And that was the nub of it all. She suddenly felt that she might soon be all alone.

"I am not joking," he said, smiling back at her. "You think that I am becoming a recluse here on the farm. Well, this will have me step back into the events of the world."

"Where did you get the idea that I think you are becoming a recluse?" His reference to her description of him as a recluse shocked her. True, she had frequently said just that to many of her friends—but never to anyone he knew, and certainly not within his earshot.

"Out of the mouths of babes," he said with a chuckle. "Ethan was really curious to know more about a recluse, leading me to deduce that the only likely place he might have heard the term was from his mother. He thought it best to let her think it was a deduction rather than toss Ethan under the bus. If I am wrong, I apologize in advance for laying that at your feet."

"Well, you are pretty isolated out here, and you have become a bit agoraphobic. But I don't remember using the term recluse." She tried to erase every memory of her use of the term as she said the words, but she went with the lie, hoping to save face. "You're not a young man anymore, Dad;

this amount of travel and upheaval could prove really hard on you. Not only that—what about the farm? Besides, you have always said that you would never go back to academic life, not after the way you were treated."

"When did I say that I would never go back to academic life?" he asked with a broad smile on his face.

"I don't remember exactly when, but I have heard you talk many times about how badly you and Mom were treated in the press, on social media, and even in academic circles."

"Well, all that's true, but I have not said that I would never go back to academic life; that is your deduction based upon your assumptions. You simply assume that because of all of the negatives, I won't go back. It's a prevarication, Sheena, and Rehema's comments earlier today clearly illustrated that my work has been subject to many prevarications, which have compounded over the years due to my silence."

"Dad, stop. Please stop. You are grieving Mom's death. You are not thinking clearly. You can't possibly head off to Oxford; you love it here on the farm. It's your sanctuary. You have said so many times." She was so upset that she failed to hear the scolding tone in her voice, which was only compounded by her father's bemused look at her. He could be so damned patronizing.

"Sheena, listen to yourself. I thought that you would be happy that I have someone interested in my work and who values my input even at my advanced age, to the extent that she has asked me to join her at Oxford to set out the parameters for our collaboration on a new book. I do love this farm, yes; it is my sanctuary. And yes, I am grieving for your mother, and have been quietly doing so since she decided to leave our marriage. But none of those things mean that I cannot go to Oxford and work with Rehema on a new book."

Sheena held out her phone, on which she had Googled the name Rehema Tanui, Oxford University. A photograph of a stunningly beautiful woman appeared above a biography that included a list of publications and the classes that she taught in the field of demography.

"This Rehema Tanui?" she asked, turning her phone toward her father so he, too, could see the photograph. "No wonder you want to head off to Oxford with her. But Dad, how old is this woman—and how old are you?"

As soon as she had said the words, she saw the all-too-familiar darkening of his eyes as the anger that she had come to fear as a child came over her father's face. "Joking, Dad—just trying to lighten the mood," she added, hoping to recover from her previous comment.

"Sheena, you really are way out of line. You weren't joking at all, and it speaks volumes about what you really think of me if you believe that I would head to Oxford University to chase after a woman."

"I said I was joking, Dad."

"Right—and my reaction to your comment has nothing to do with you trying to make it all a joke. You think you know a great deal about me, Sheena—and I am sure you have valid opinions, good or bad, about me as your father. But you don't know much about Ken Graham, scholar and author."

Her father took a deep breath and picked up his manuscript. "When I told you what this book was about, you didn't understand anything that I said. I could see in your face that you didn't, and you didn't ask me to clarify anything that I had said. Why? Because you don't really care what it's about. My book is irrelevant to you, just as my years of study are irrelevant to you. I understand why. It's because my work has never interfered with my role as your father."

He stopped speaking, giving Sheena an opening. "Dad, that's not true." She felt bad. She could see how visibly hurt her father was by her thoughtless remark.

"It is true, Sheena, and on one level, it's to be expected," he said, leaning forward in his chair. "You have defined my role as your father, by making it clear where your boundaries are in terms of what you will and will not accept from me. I appreciate that, and I have tried to respect that. But be honest with yourself, Sheena; you don't know me—only your version of me. Hell, you don't even know what donut I prefer. When did I ever tell you that a honey cruller was my favourite donut? Never, not ever."

Shocked and hurt by his remark, she pushed back. "But you always have honey crullers; they have always been your favourites."

Her father leaned back in his chair and chuckled, shaking his head. "Nope, that preference is all yours; you have told me so. You introduced me to honey crullers, and I don't mind one with a cup of coffee. You decided they were my favourites. Look, it's nice to share something in common, and I try not to hurt your feelings, so I have never corrected you. But for the record, donuts aren't important to me." Her father stopped, and appeared really frustrated by the conversation. "That's what I mean by false assumptions. We all do it. We all go through life believing things to be true that aren't."

Who cared about a silly donut anyway? He was making her feel like she was six years old again. OK, so she had always brought them, saying they were his favourites, knowing that, in truth, she liked them best. So what? What bothered her more was her father telling her that she didn't know him as a man outside of his paternal role—when she really thought about that, she had to admit that was true.

She had spent hours with her mother talking about all manner of things, and she had shared a wonderful road trip with her when heading off to university. As a young girl, then, despite some volatile teenage years, and as a woman, she had cried in her mother's arms, confiding her innermost secrets. And on the brighter and happier days, she had listened intently to the stories her mother had told her of her own time at Oxford and of the work she was doing in Persian history. She had read books that her mother had recommended, and she had read all of the books that her mother had written.

Sheena looked at the man who sat opposite her; perhaps for the first time, she really looked at him, seeing beyond his paternal aura. He was right; she really didn't know much about him. Certainly nothing about his work, beyond what she had gleaned overhearing the conversations he had had with her mother.

It really had all come down to a honey cruller. In momentary silence, her mind flipped through the pages of her life with her father, seeing each page carrying a similar assumptive watermark. In her mind, she closed the book, each page with a gilded edge of remorse, because for the first time in her life, she saw Ken Graham, the man, not her father.

She finally broke the silence. "I will admit that I don't understand what you have written in that book. Even if I read it cover to cover, I might still not fully understand. But I have never said you or your work are irrelevant."

"Look, I get it. You were always much closer to your mother than you were to me. I am quite sure that I have been responsible, in the main, for how our relationship has evolved. Since your mother left, you have done the obligatory, checking in and inviting me to dinner, and I have responded in kind with you and Ethan. I have never wanted to interfere with the choices you have made and continue to make in your life."

"I know that, and I appreciate it," replied Sheena.

"You shouldn't ever assume that my distancing myself from your choices means that I don't love you or that I don't love Ethan. I am incredibly proud of how you have managed, as a single mom, to raise him." Her dad's voice had softened, but she knew him too well to not expect the *but* that she was sure would follow.

"Now that I am getting old, you have decided to see me in the role of your aging father, who has chosen to hermit himself on a farm with a dog and a bunch of sheep. It's not a choice that you would embrace, which is why you and Ethan don't live with me on the farm property. In fact, I suspect that somewhere in that brain of yours, you have reached the conclusion that I am, or very soon will be, too old to live here alone. You said as much when we spoke on the phone yesterday."

She could sense where the conversation was going, and she didn't have the emotional strength to deal with it. "Dad, I don't want to fight—especially today."

Sheena did think that he was getting too old for the farm, and it was true; she had told him so on many occasions. It was immediately obvious to her that her father was going to ask her how she could use his love and life on the farm as a reason not to go to Oxford when, out of the other side of her mouth, she was telling him he was too old to live on the farm. He was very good at that kind of verbal entrapment, and she really didn't need it today.

"I care about you. You're my dad, who I love a great deal, and you are Ethan's grandfather, who he also loves, so you will just have to excuse me if I show concern. Fathers and grandfathers are an important part of a daughter's or grandson's life. OK? Can we call a truce?"

"I didn't think we were fighting—and I love you both as well, so a truce is now in effect." He smiled at her. "I completely agree with you; fathers and grandfathers are important figures in the lives of their children and grandchildren." Her father looked directly at her, and she knew the *but* was about to fall like the proverbial second shoe. "I wasn't aware that Farouk was dead."

"What?!" She sat up in the loveseat. His remark completely took her by surprise. "Farouk isn't dead—far from it. Why would you think he's dead?"

"Because Ethan told me that's what you told him; that his father is dead."

Sheena could feel the crimson blush rise up her neck, coming to rest upon the soft roundness of her cheeks. She was flushed with embarrassment, and yet awash with anger. "With respect, Dad, I really think that is none of your business."

"So there is a qualifier when it comes to the importance of fathers and grandfathers—is that it?" He leaned forward again, this time looking directly into her eyes. "Ethan has a right to know if his father is alive, and who and where he is. It *is* my business; I am his grandfather, and we are family, and that includes, whether you like it or not, Farouk."

"It's not that simple, Dad." The familiar feeling of being scolded returned—this time as a sixteen-year-old, as if she had stayed late with a boy and missed curfew. Her father could be so intense when angry, and while he had never raised a hand against her, he didn't need to. All it took was one look at his angry eyebrows dancing above his fiery eyes.

"You surely haven't forgotten what we went through with your mother and Asher, trying to keep him close while respecting his decision to reject me in favour of Salman. Families are never easy, Sheena. I think you should consider contacting him."

"There's no need for that, thanks to Asher!" she replied, angry at having to discuss the topic at all. "I still can't believe that he would do such a thing, but then that's Asher for you."

"How does this involve Asher?"

"Apparently, Farouk has been made a partner at Osman, Thompson, and Sandhu, LLP; I checked it online. He will head up the practice here in the western office. Farouk and Asher were on the same flight to Vancouver, if you can believe that coincidence, so Asher told him about Ethan." Sheena's anger simmered as she thought back to the email that she had received from Farouk that morning. "Not only did he tell him about Ethan—he also gave him my email and mailing address."

"Asher told you this?"

"Asher gloated over it when we met at the airport yesterday," she replied.

"You met with Asher at the airport?"

Sheena would have preferred not to have told her father about her meeting Asher or the fact that she had disclosed the truth about his trust fund, but all that seemed too late now.

"Yes, he needed to know the truth about his father and how you and mom have managed his trust and made it possible for him to succeed. I hope you aren't angry with me. I know that Mom didn't want him to know."

"She was pretty insistent, that's for sure—but that all seems like water under the bridge now, doesn't it?" said Ken. "No, I am not angry with you. What do you plan to do about Farouk?"

"Predictably, I got an email from him this morning. He sounds pretty angry with me for not telling him about Ethan. But on a more positive note, he was hoping that I would be receptive to a meeting to discuss an introduction."

Sheena said it with some reluctance. She really did not want to discuss Farouk's possible return to her life, and she certainly didn't want to include her father in a discussion about Farouk being a part of her son's life. She knew what his position would be; he had just made that pretty clear.

"Did you respond?" her father asked.

"Not yet," Sheena said. "I need some time to think about it before I get back to him."

"Well, I think your first concern is Ethan. The sooner that you tell him that his father is alive and may be working only a few hours away, the better." Sheena bristled at her father's words. This was not his business. *You think I don't know I have to talk to Ethan? I don't need you telling me that. So much for respecting my boundaries!*

"What were you saying a minute ago about respecting my boundaries?" She shot an angry glance his way.

"Hey"—he raised a hand as if to stop her advance—"I understand that this raises potential complications. But you have to deal with the fact that you lied to Ethan."

Being told that she had lied was a trigger that went a long way back in her relationship with her father, so she used every ounce of resolve to keep her temper in check. "Dad, mom is lying in the other room, dying. Can we please discuss this another day?"

"Sure, you're right; that was insensitive of me," her father said, getting out of his chair and carrying the cup filled with cold coffee to the kitchen counter. "It's enough to manage the loss of your mother. I'm sorry to have upset you. This can all wait for another day, and I will always be here to help if you like—but it's your call."

"He is married with two children of his own. According to his email, he has told his wife, and she will be supportive. It's just that until now, it's only been Ethan and me," said Sheena. "I am afraid that will change."

"It has never been only Ethan and you, Sheena. Farouk has always been a part of that equation, and you have simply tried to factor him out."

Sheena felt a wave of fatigue sweep over her. The events of the weekend were proving too much for her. She wanted to go and get Ethan, go home, and rest. She needed time to think.

She got up from the loveseat, walked over to her father, and gave him a hug, thankful that he was so receptive to it, and feeling strangely comforted and safe in his embrace. They didn't hug much, she thought, tightening her squeeze. Perhaps they should do it more.

"So, you are going to be OK then, Dad?"

"I am going to be fine," her father replied, releasing her from his embrace.

She walked to the wardrobe and reached in for her coat, deciding not to put it on because the weight of the crushing sadness made her wonder if she could lift her arms to do so.

Her father opened and held the door for her, and she slowly walked over to him, rose on tiptoes, then leaned in and gave him a kiss on the cheek.

"I love you, Dad."

"I love you, too."

29.

Jessica had decided to go to the farm after discussing the return of Charlie's body to Jamaica with the coroner. That meeting had proved opportune to also arrange for the coroner to pick up Lena's remains from the farm later in the day. And that arrangement would provide, should she need one, a valid reason to escape from her visit with Janis.

She understood the quiet practice of physician-assisted death when the patient is at the very end of their lives, and she was thankful that the laws governing the medical practice had provided the latitude necessary for her to make that call with Lena.

Without her intervention, it would be impossible to determine exactly when Lena's body would fully shut down. And despite the pain relief the drugs provide, she had witnessed firsthand the suffering that happens when organs fail.

Her mind was filled with a variety of disorganized thoughts as she drove away from the farm. She was at peace with her decision, taken with Ken's consent, to change out Lena's IV bag and hook up the more powerful cocktail that she had prepared. Strictly speaking, Ken had told her she would require Asher's consent, but both agreed that he had offloaded that final responsibility before he had left for his conference.

None of what she had to do that morning was new to Jessica, but it never became easier. The only issue that caused her to pause was that she didn't have an accurate figure for Lena's body weight, so she relied upon her years of experience to formulate a satisfactory dose to ease her into death and not traumatize her in her final hours.

What Jessica was far less certain about was the wisdom of going over to Janis's for brunch.

Before she had gone to Charlie's room, she had decided not to go. She would call Janis and use the best excuse she had—namely, having to manage Ken and attend to Lena—and ask for a raincheck. But her meeting with Laurence and hearing Charlie's story had changed her mind. Yet, she didn't fully understand why.

She knew there was no direct parallel between Tarone's life and hers, but it wasn't lost on her that both had lived the life of a runaway. Tarone had fled to hide from being prosecuted for who he was not, and Jessica had fled to shield herself from who she was.

Jessica had topped her classes in medical school, and she had had her pick of residencies in any of the major medical centres in any major city in the world. And it is not that she hadn't tried to walk that road. But the guilt that had been instilled in her by her father seemed inescapable. And at close to sixty years of age, she was driving down a remote country road for a rendezvous, trying, finally, to break free and live her truth.

Reaching the main highway, she took a left turn and headed east toward Kettle Bay, following the directions that Janis had texted her earlier in the morning. As she drove, she argued with the voice in her head as to which character she should be cast as in the playscript, *The Life of Charlie*.

Maybe you fit the role of Llanzo Jackson?

Well, that's bullshit! I didn't commit a violent crime against and innocent girl!

Seriously? Look at yourself in that rearview mirror, Jessica, and tell me that you didn't commit a crime against an innocent girl.

The thought hit her so hard, the car swerved.

Jessica turned on the car's sound system, cranked up the volume, and pushed her foot down on the accelerator, hoping that Florence + The Machine belting out "Breaking Down" at high volume might drown out that inconvenient voice in her head. Or that the added speed might outrun it.

Jessica took note of the highway sign indicating that Sturt Road was only a few hundred metres ahead. She had wondered if the name had been a typo in Janis's text, but obviously not. She slowed the car down and signalled to turn, then lowered the volume of the fab four rocking out "Real Love" as she continued to sing along. "Don't need to be alone, no need to be alone …"

Sturt Road was a narrow, winding road that led up a fairly steep incline before dropping into a wide-open valley of fenced fields on either side. Janis had typed that the entrance to her farm was on the left-hand side of the road, about a ten-minute drive from the highway, and that she should look for the large, round wooden sign with time-faded writing: "Rustige Werlanden Boerderij."

Jessica pulled up the text on her phone, which rested in the holder on the car's dashboard, and read her instructions as she drove slowly along the road, keeping an eye out for the round sign. The closer she got to ten minutes from the time she left the highway, the more anxious and nervous she became—which on one level seemed irrational, but which, on a different and much deeper level, tested her resolve not to turn around.

Janis hadn't exaggerated the time-faded writing on the sign. The faint lettering and the tall grass that had grown around the sign made it hard to read. In any event, she had no idea what the sign said. *It's just Dutch to me,* she thought.

She had no doubt that she was in the right place, and took a deep breath as she turned down the narrow driveway. The dirt road, canopied by tall green willows, forked, so she took the route marked "house" rather than the alternative: "barn."

The house, a small, shiplap-sided square building with a green tin roof and a single gable, featured a surrounding porch. This place had seen better days. It wasn't what she had expected when she thought of Janis living on a farm—but then again, she acknowledged as she turned off the engine, she hadn't really known what to expect.

As she stepped out of the car, she heard Janis say, "Hi there! Glad you made it," and looked up to see her host standing barefoot on the porch, her baggy grey cotton cut-off shorts half-hidden by an oversized black t-shirt depicting the iconic logo of the Rolling Stones 1978 tour, their name encircling a wide, fat red tongue extending from juicy red lips, beneath white teeth.

Jessica watched as Janis hopped down the few stairs off the porch to greet her. *Interesting choice of outfit.*

"Shalom," said Janis, smiling at her, and Jessica followed her up the few stairs, across the porch, and into a surprisingly modern, recently renovated interior.

"Wow—"

"Book by its cover, right? Yeah, I am pretty proud of the work I have done inside this old box. It's not fancy, but it's cozy."

"It's really nice." Jessica was genuinely impressed with the modern flooring, impressive Italian tile on the kitchen backsplash and wall, and the open concept. She was quite sure that was not the way the interior of the house would have appeared when first built.

"So, what's your poison?" asked Janis.

"My poison?" Jessica wasn't sure what Janis meant.

"Coffee or tea? What can I get you? Coffee is made, but I can put on water for tea, no problem."

Jessica couldn't shake the discomfort that she felt. Her stomach was churning so fast that she worried that she might not keep either coffee or tea down, but she didn't want to appear impolite.

"You know, I am good for right now; I have had one hell of a morning. Is it OK if I pass for the moment? Perhaps a coffee in a bit," she said.

"Hey, no pressure; take a seat. Do you want to talk about it?" said Janis, gesturing for Jessica to take the larger of the two plush chairs in the sitting room.

"It's just work," said Jessica. "I had a patient die this morning, which is pretty much my normal day, except that his brother had travelled all the way from Jamaica to find him. Something about the guy's life story really bothered me. Then, of course, there's the situation with Lena out at Ken's. I work hard at keeping my feelings out of my work, but for some reason, this morning, it all seems to have been too personal."

"I'm sorry, Jess. Can I call you Jess? I don't know how you do what you do."

"I don't cross lines; that's how I manage," said Jessica. "Jess is fine." She liked that Janis called her Jess. No one else had shortened her name that way—it wasn't Jessie, which she hated. Both her mother and father had used that abbreviation. The obvious contradiction about not crossing lines resonated as the words came out of her mouth. Sitting in Janis's house was a pretty big line that she normally would not have crossed.

"But today you crossed the line, is that it?" asked Janis, taking a seat on a pillowed wooden rocker directly across from her.

"Something like that, yes."

"Well, if it's any consolation, I have had a fuck-awful twenty-four hours myself," said Janis, getting up and heading to the kitchen. "I know exactly what we need." She stopped and turned toward Jessica. "Listen, I don't really know you, and, well … swearing started to be a bit of my shtick when I was younger. Now, it's just a bad habit. I don't mean to offend."

"I grew up in Aberdeen and have been a woman trying to strive in a practice historically reserved for men. Don't worry about it. I am sure that I can match you if it comes to that," replied Jessica with a laugh.

"Well, I've never been to Aberdeen, so I wouldn't know," said Janis, opening a cupboard in the kitchen. "I think that we should start brunch with a tall Baileys." She took out two tall liquor glasses and filled them with the light brown, creamed Irish whiskey.

"That sounds great," replied Jessica, watching her silvery, curly-haired host stretch on her tiptoes to reach the bottle of Baileys. She accepted the drink and raised the glass toward Janis, who immediately said, "*L'chaim.*"

"You have already been over to Ken's, I guess," said Janis, returning to the rocker and taking a sip of Baileys.

Jessica nodded. She wasn't really sure how much she should share with Janis. After all, Lena was a patient, and Ken also deserved privacy. So she thought better about answering.

Janis nodded back. "I got it—enough said. But Ken's going to be alright?"

"I think so," she replied. "But I have to say that for the guy who Lena divorced, he seems to have gone out of his way for her. I think there is a part of him that is still in love with her."

"You think?" asked Janis with a snort. "Ken is a great guy, don't get me wrong—he has been really good to me. But when it comes to Lena … well … I can't explain it. He turns into a real schmuck. They were amazing together when I first dragged my sorry ass here from New York. He's the one who introduced me to the owner of this farm. If not for Kenny, I wouldn't be living in this little piece of paradise." She chuckled and took another drink of Baileys. "But toward the end of their relationship, well, let's just say that woman did him no favours. It was hard to watch."

"He showed me that last manuscript he wrote," she continued. "To be truthful, I really didn't understand what it was all about—something to do with artificial intelligence and science. Anyway, whatever he wrote was sent out for peer review, and brought down wrath from the gods of science. It was the proverbial last straw, and it all but destroyed him. So, what did Lena do when he was trashed? She fucked him over big time, demanded a divorce, and just walked out of his life. He was a mess, Jessica, I can tell you."

The depth of passion in Janis's voice was evidence of how much she cared for Ken, and it prompted Jessica to wonder why. Obviously, Ken had been instrumental in helping Janis adjust to being part of the community, which must have been a huge adjustment for her, having left the bustle of New York and landed literally at the end of the highway in tiny Brockhurst. *Welcome to Brockhurst. No one just drives through.*

"So, what was your relationship with Ken, if you don't mind me asking?"

"I am one hundred percent on the girls' team, if that's what you're asking," replied Janis, and Jessica felt a tinge of embarrassment, because that was, at least in part, what she was asking.

"Obviously," she replied, trying to mask her other intention. "How did you come to meet him?"

"I met him through Lena," she replied.

"Oh, OK." Jessica hadn't expected that answer, which she felt was incomplete, but not wanting to sound like an inquisitor, she let the conversation lapse for a moment.

"Lena was a very attractive, very intelligent woman," Janis said after a moment of silence between them. "She was also a brilliant historian and writer, and was ready to take on the fight for the rights of women in Iran despite the fatwa that had been taken out against her. I greatly admired her, and when she came to give a speech and do a book signing in New York, I went to hear and meet her."

One Weekend in May

"You met Lena in New York?" Jessica was surprised by the revelation. She had never considered that Janis might have met Lena before coming to Brockhurst.

Janis slowly nodded her head in acknowledgement. "Lena is the reason that I came to Brockhurst. I mean, as charming as this little back eddy is, I didn't go searching for it on a map when I decided to leave New York."

"So, you and Lena …" Jessica's surprise had switched to astonishment.

"I wish! You're *meshuggeneh*."

Jessica had no idea what she had just been called. "I'm what?"

"Crazy," Janis replied. "It's all water under the bridge now. You would be crazy if you thought that I could actually muff-dive with Lena. Not that I wouldn't have if she had been up for it."

"OK, got it," said Jessica, trying not to show her discomfort with Janis's blunt conversation.

"Don't look so shocked. I was seriously attracted to her, but there were other complications beyond the fact that she was Muslim, straight, and married. I was in a relationship at the time, and had to deal with my own situation in New York."

"Your father, the Rabbi, mother, and fiancée," Jessica said, realizing at once that she had betrayed Ken's confidence—and hoping, in vain as it quickly turned out, that Janis would not call her on it.

"Fucking Kenny. He told you that. Am I right?" said Janis, shaking her head. "Wow, he can be such a schnegger."

"I am not sure what that means, but in Ken's defence, I asked him about you, and he just gave me the Coles Notes."

"Did he?" said Janis, laughing. "Good old Kenny—you can always count on him to be your fluffer.

"The truth? When I was a kid, around nine or ten maybe, I knew I was different from the other kids—and I also knew that I had to hide it from my mother and especially my father. I was lucky to be the oldest, with two younger sisters and a younger brother. As the oldest, I could go missing for hours and no one would notice. My guess is that my mother was relieved to have me out of the house. I would take the L train into Manhattan after school and spend hours in the Argosy bookstore on East 59th Street in Midtown. It was my place to hide." Janis paused for a moment, then got up and went to the kitchen, where she put two freshly baked muffins on each of two plates, and poured two cups of coffee, while continuing to speak.

"One day, I came across a book by an author named Werner Keller. The title of the book was *The Bible as History*. That book changed my life." Janis put a plate with a muffin on the table beside Jessica, along with a cup of black coffee. "How do you take it? Cream, sugar? More Baileys?"

"Black is perfect, thanks," said Jessica, getting a glimpse, for the first time, of the girl who had become the woman now serving her coffee. "Actually, how about Baileys in the coffee?"

Janis obliged, and then continued. "That book not only ignited a passion for history, but it also unmasked layers of half-truths and misinterpretations—and even a few outright lies—that had come out of the mouth of my father, the Rabbi."

"You mean his religious teaching?" asked Jessica.

"That's exactly what I mean. And keep in mind that, at that age, my father was my source of truth."

She reached for the handle of a shallow drawer on the side table next to the wooden rocker and pulled it open. "Any idea what this is?" she asked, and Jessica took the small object that Janis handed her.

Jessica had not seen anything quite like the small, toy-like gadget that she had given her. If she was to guess, she would have said it was a crude, four-sided spinning top with a different letter on each face. "A spinning top," she guessed.

"Yes, exactly, it is a dreidel," confirmed Janis. "Throughout my childhood, the dreidel was brought out during Hannukah, and my brother, my two sisters, and I were taught the significance of the dreidel as it relates to Hannukah. The letters on the four sides, *n, g, h,* and *s,* we were told, were the first letter of an abbreviation from the original Hebrew, *nes gadol haya sham*, which, roughly translated, means 'a great miracle happened here.'"

"You have lost me," said Jessica. She felt embarrassed that she knew nothing about Hannukah except that it happened roughly around the same time on the calendar as Christmas. Her father had been rigid in his view that Christian teachings were completely incompatible with Jewish theology, and that she should leave it alone.

"The point I am trying to make here is that what we as kids were told about the dreidel simply wasn't true. As kids, we were taught that it was a symbol of the resistance movement who fought against assimilation by the Greeks."

Jessica found this side of Janis fascinating. She had no idea that this rough-and-tumble, foul-mouthed woman, who seemed to have the broadest range of skills imaginable, had been a bookworm as a kid and, apparently, a student of history.

"Basically, the dreidel is used in a gambling game. Every Hannukah, we played with chocolate coins. You put your stake in the middle, and depending upon which of the four possible letters lands face up after each spin, you either have to do nothing, put in the same stake again, take half the stake on the table, or take the whole pot."

Janis paused briefly.

"My father, also my fucking Rabbi, told me that during the time when the Seleucid authorities outlawed studying the Torah, around 164 BCE, groups of Jews who were resisting assimilation and planning an insurrection against the Greeks and Hellenized Jews would take a dreidel with them when they met, so if they were seen, it would appear that they were just a bunch of Jews at a gambling game. Hence, it had today become a treasured symbol of the pureness of the true Jewish people."

"And I'm guessing that you discovered it wasn't true?" Jessica asked, then drank a mouthful of Baileys-infused coffee.

"Werner's book was full of photographs of archaeological objects that provided a positive link to passages of scripture. But what fascinated me was how those discoveries also provided an insight into translations that had been either inadvertently or deliberately falsified. I found his work fascinating, and I was hooked.

"I was only a train ride away from one of the top archaeology departments in the world, so I applied to Columbia to study Middle Eastern history. It was during that time that I came across Lena's work."

"Wait. So you were a PhD student?"

"Yeah, in Middle Eastern history. I know, right? Look at the old fart now. It's pretty hard to believe I was a candidate to be Dr. Lieberman."

"Did you finish and get your degree?"

"My life kind of imploded right around the time I was scheduled to defend my thesis. I had taken more years than is normal to finish, and that had pissed off a lot of the professors. I kind of became the perennial student, and was given some first- and second-year courses to teach. The good news was that it gave me enough money to live on; the bad news, it slowed my desire to finish my doctorate."

"I would never have guessed when we first met at Ken's barn that you had been a PhD student in Middle Eastern history," said Jessica, hoping that she had not offended Janis.

"Ken missed that part when giving you his Coles Notes on Janis Lieberman's failed relationships with her Rabbi father, mother, and fiancée, did he?"

"Janis, please don't," said Jessica. "He was really respectful of you, and made it clear that your story is yours to tell." Returning to the conversation, she asked, "And the dreidels?"

"I studied the historical significance of the spinning top, trying to give credibility to my father's teachings. He, after all, was the pillar of knowledge about the Jewish faith and history. This was the man who had made it clear that the scripture did not accept anything but binary gender identity, and the union between a man and a woman. It was taught to me with the same conviction and authority as the lesson about the dreidel."

She stopped talking, and for a moment, the only sound in the room was the hum of the fridge motor.

"No dreidels have ever been found as part of any excavated artifacts. In truth, the idea of the dreidel as a symbol of resistance, while a good story to tell young, impressionable Jews, is complete fiction. The most credible historical fact about this little toy is that the Jews most likely borrowed the dreidel from their Christian neighbours in the mid-eighteenth century."

Janis's cynical tone had returned, and Jessica fully understood why. The thought of the parallel with her relationship with her strict presbyterian father remained all too present in her mind, given her conversation with Ken the previous evening.

"You know," said Janis, leaning back and rocking a bit. "I think what attracted me to Lena when I first met her in New York was her tenacious efforts to get to the truth of things. She was never afraid to call out folklore when it was presented as fact."

"You said that Lena was the reason you came here, to Brockhurst?"

Janis nodded, then asked, "Are you hungry? I haven't put much of a brunch together so far. I took out the waffle iron …"

"No, thank you. I should have mentioned that I am not a big breakfast-eater. I rarely have time for much more than a coffee on the run." Jessica paused, and thought she saw the shadow of an unpleasant thought sweep across Janis's face. "I am really sorry for what you went through as a kid. I can relate, believe me," she said, finishing her muffin. "These are delicious, by the way."

For a moment, Jessica let silence prevail, thinking that Janis might want to take their conversation in a different direction—but there it was again, the flicker of a shadow of a distracting thought—and Jessica's mind flashed back to Janis's comment about having had a bad twenty-four hours. Clearly, something was on her mind, but mindful of the boundaries that she would demand for herself, she thought better not to pry. Perhaps it was time for her to activate her escape plan.

"The coffee and muffin were great, and I have enjoyed getting to know you a bit better and to see where you live," said Jessica. "Perhaps we should leave it there for today."

"Please don't go," said Janis, leaning forward and running her fingers through her tightly curled hair. "I am sorry, I am being a putz. I am distracted, that's all. I'm trying to figure a few things out. Sorry, I should be a better host."

"Care to share?" asked Jessica with a smile. "Sometimes, two heads are better than one."

"A lie told by two sailors to a barmaid." Janis laughed at her rude joke, and must have seen the shock on Jessica's face. "Sorry—bad Janis—no more inappropriate jokes, I promise. It's just that yesterday, I was in control of my life, and thought I could see the horizon. Today … ? I haven't a fucking clue what I am going to do or where I am going to be."

The shock from the statement pushed Jessica back into her seat, surprised by the wave of emotion that was flooding over Janis. It was completely unexpected, and seemed out of character for this tough, no-nonsense woman. And yet, the tears that welled in Janis's eyes put a lie to the façade, and Jessica felt an unreserved compassion.

"Janis, I am so sorry. Please let me help you. What has happened?"

Janis blew out a deep breath through pursed lips and, with her forefinger and thumb, rubbed the moisture from her eyes. "Yesterday, when I came home from Ken's, Brahm de Jong was here. He is one of the five de Jong kids who inherited this place from their parents. They have decided to sell the farm and plan to list it as early as next week."

"What? I thought you owned this place."

"Jess, I don't own fuck all—not here, not New York, not anywhere. I have tossed my life away chasing after promises that have evaporated like sheep's piss off a hot rock."

Jessica walked over to the rocker and kneeled down. "Hey, I am not one to put much stock in a cliché, but it's always darkest before the light."

"Dawn."

"What?"

"Dawn, you mensch. It's always the darkest before the dawn." Janis chuckled, looking into Jessica's eyes, and with two fingers, she moved strands of auburn hair off Jessica's face. "If you're going to rely on a cliché, then at least get it right."

A slight shiver ran down to Jessica's toes as Janis's fingers touched her forehead and slid her hair off her face, tucking it gently behind her ear. It was the first time that Jessica could remember such unreserved excitement in reaction to being touched, and it made her very nervous. She stood up and walked back to her chair. "Thank you for the correction. Should I ask what a mensch is?"

"Nope, Google it in the dictionary of Jewish slang. It's homework." Janis laughed. "But, seriously, thank you."

"What you said about chasing promises—do you want to talk to me about that?" asked Jessica.

"Look, I don't want to sit here kvetching about my life," said Janis. "I made my choices, and I own them. It's just that you only get one turn at the plate, so you have to have a game plan. You have to decide what pitch you can get the barrel of your bat to, then be patient; don't go chasing sliders."

"Baseball? Just guessing." Jessica was unable to relate at all to what Janis had just said.

"God, you are so fucking adorable! Yes, baseball. The point is that I had a plan. I was engaged to a woman, Sarah, with whom I thought I shared a common dream. We tried to keep our relationship discrete, but people, being who they are, ratted me out to my mother, who dutifully told my father, who, in order to maintain the image he had so meticulously cultivated within his congregation, disowned me."

Janis took a breath, and wiped a tardy tear from her cheek.

"Lena told me about Brockhurst, a small, backwater farming community in a country where gay marriage was legal. Lena convinced me and my fiancée that this place was nothing short of paradise. Her husband knew of a farm that was becoming available, with an almost certain prospect for a very long-term lease arrangement, no money down."

Janis paused again, as though reliving the conversation in her head.

"It would be a sanctuary for Sarah and me, just as her farm was a sanctuary for Lena and the man she adored, her husband, Ken. It was, she told me, their forever place. She painted a picture of a safe, secure, place surrounded by people who would care for and love us. I fell for it—hook, line, and sinker—and thought that Sarah had also."

"So," said Jessica, slowly putting the pieces together in her mind, and thinking it safe to speak her thoughts out loud. "Sarah leaves you at the airport, Lena divorces Ken, shattering their forever place, and now, you get told that the property you thought you had on a long-term lease is up for sale. Wow—I get it."

"Oh, and this morning, my mother, who has not spoken to me for years, phoned. My father has had a stroke. She says his dying wish is for me to fly to New York to see him before he passes." Janis said it with a long sigh.

"Oh my God, Janis!" Jessica was on her feet again and at the side of the rocker. "I am so very sorry."

"Yeah, well, he can go ahead and fucking die, the miserable old man."

"You have to go to see him, Janis. He is your father. If he has asked you to come, it's because he wants to see you. He is likely to try to get things off his chest, or say things that have been left unsaid." Jessica thought of how much had been left unresolved with her own father, and how much guilt she carried around because so much had been left unsaid between them.

"He's been building a stairway to heaven all his life," said Janis, "and unfortunately, I am a few missing treads on his riser. He just wants to see me so that he can plug them in and finish the job."

"And you would deny him that, why?" Jessica responded sharply. "What on earth is in it for you to deny your dying father peace in his last hours?"

"He has denied me a certain peace my entire life," replied Janis.

"Do you believe in God?" asked Jessica, walking away from the rocker to perch on the broad windowsill of the wide picture window through which the mid-morning sun shone.

"What the fuck kind of question is that?" asked Janis. "Have you not been listening to what I have told you?"

"It's a simple enough question," replied Jessica, "and yes, I get that you have taken a great deal of interest trying to prove, or disprove, the Word as it appears in the Bible."

"I wouldn't take such offence at the distortion of His word and teaching if I didn't believe, would I?" retorted Janis.

"I don't know—you still haven't answered my question."

"Yes, OK, I believe in God. I just don't support the institutions that purport to bring forth his word. There is more human than host in most of what goes on in the churches, mosques, and synagogues of the world."

"Then," asked Jessica, folding her arms across her chest. "What do you think God would want you to do?"

"For fuck's sake, Jessica, this is a major guilt trip you are laying on me," replied Janis, jumping out of the rocker.

"Go to New York and see your father, and then comfort your mother. I promise you, it will haunt you the rest of your life if you don't. Many were never given the chance to set things right. Don't lose this chance." Jessica was firm, but spoke softly as she watched Janis pace around the room.

"So, what's your story then?" asked Janis, and Jessica muted her smile at the obvious effort to change the subject. "How did you end up in this back eddy where time seems to move backwards?"

"Nothing as dramatic or potentially glamorous as finding my forever place in paradise," replied Jessica. She picked up her coffee cup and walked to where the bottle of Baileys sat on the table. "I was working in a major hospital in London, and was sick of being passed over for promotion and having to constantly yield to the dicks who called themselves doctors. May I?" she asked, unscrewing the cap of Baileys. "Will you join?"

"No, I am good—help yourself. I have a bottle of fifteen-year-old Irish Single Malt which I plan to take over to Ken's early this evening, assuming that Lena will be taken care of by then." said, Janis and she walked toward a small pantry. "I think that I will save myself for a proper drowning with Ken—and you, if you'll come."

"She will," replied Jessica, referring to the plan she had made with the coroner earlier in the day. "I have arranged for the coroner to send transportation at one o'clock. That will give Ken time to grieve with her for a short while. It seems the best way to get full closure." Jessica looked at the large wall clock, noting that the day was already approaching noon.

"I hope that you will be there. There are no people in this whole fucking world who know how to celebrate the passing of a life better than the Irish." said Janis, coming out of the pantry with a bottle that she planted on the table. "The only people who come close to the Irish are the Chinese, and that's not because they know how to drink, but because there are so fucking many of them on the planet, they have had a lot of practice. I know, I know—my bad—that was probably racist. Then again, a reformed Irish alcoholic might say my first comment was racist."

"A reformed Irish alcoholic?" Jessica laughed as she returned to her chair with her mug of Baileys. "They're called Englishmen. The Irish ship all non-drinkers off the island." Jessica had let her full Scottish brogue flow with her last comment, and the two laughed at her silly joke.

"So, you came here to escape doctor dicks in the City of London. Did I hear that right?"

"Yeah, that kinda sums it up," Jessica replied. "The chief surgeon of the hospital thought he was God's gift to women, and thought it his right, if not his duty, to fuck every woman in the place. I was one notch on his belt that he couldn't make, and my punishment was to be banished to the palliative section of the psych ward. It was the final straw for me. I saw this job advertised online, applied, and voila—here I am."

"And you met Ken when you were treating Lena." Janis stated it more as a fact than a question, and Jessica nodded. "Ken is a really special kind of guy," Janis continued. "I have read some of his work, and he has a really different—and yet very compelling—insight into the way the world is evolving."

"Not a very popular one, apparently," added Jessica.

"He's not wrong, though; at least, the bit I read about how we, as humans, are driven by a prime directive, and how that will cause the rise of identity politics. The world is changing, and not all of it in a good way. Fuck, Jessica, lesbians like you and me have become mainstream—not cool at all. It's no wonder my old man had a stroke. His ninety-year-old ass was probably introduced to a 'she' with a beard and a dick." Janis laughed hard.

"I am really surprised that he is considering returning to Oxford to work on another book," said Jessica, recalling her earlier conversation with Ken.

"What? Are you shitting me?" The surprise on Janis's face startled Jessica.

"No, not at all. Apparently, there is some postgraduate student at Oxford who really wants him to go over there and work with her as a co-author on her book. He told me that he was seriously considering it," replied Jessica, sipping her Baileys with one eye on the wall clock.

For a moment, Janis sat silent, and Jessica wondered what it was that she had said that had caused the pause in the conversation. "Are you OK?" she asked.

"So, he said he is considering pulling up stakes and going back to Oxford?" The panic in Janis's voice was unmistakeable, and Jessica realized the source—clearly, it was the thought that Ken might leave Brockhurst.

"I didn't get the idea that he was pulling up stakes; in fact, I think that the one thing that might hold him back from taking the challenge is not knowing what to do with Toby and the farm."

Janis looked at Jessica, and Jessica heard her thoughts.

"Maybe," she said. "I mean, it would be a win-win."

"At least until I get sorted out—I mean, he would be likely gone a few months at least, right?" said Janis.

"Yes, for sure, and we both know that whatever he decides and for whatever reason, that farm is Ken's sanctuary," added Jessica. "He won't want to give it up."

"And he is no spring chicken anymore, right? It might be good for him to have some company in the house," said Janis. "Maybe even a palliative care nurse. We can talk to him tonight."

"Let's not get too far ahead of ourselves," laughed Jessica. "Listen to us, planning Ken's future and the future of his farm—he won't know what hit him.

"Well, I am faced with the reality of having to relocate,—that much I know for sure—and this might be an opportunity, at least in the short term," said Janis. "What about you, now that you are out?"

"Out to you and Ken, I guess. But let's face it, Janis, it's late in life for me to be joining the rainbow parade; I have spent a lifetime watching from the sidewalk."

"Bullshit," said Janis. "I call bullshit on that, Jessica. You have always been part of the rainbow parade; the only difference is that you are being honest about it. Now, when you see your reflection when you walk past that store window, you'll see Jessica Gunn, not some anonymous figure hiding behind an expressionless mask."

"It's all a bit daunting, if I am to be perfectly honest," she said. "Especially when it comes to intimacy. I am not sure how—or even if—I can go there."

"Well, it's been said that I am a pretty good teacher," said Janis with a smile. "Thing is—and I mean this in the most sincere and polite way possible—you have to get past fucking before you get to intimacy, and lots get off the train at the first stop and never make the destination."

"I am not interested in the first stop. I have had to fake it with enough dicks in my life, pretending to be straight and be part of the crowd by puffing up the egos of male conquistadors. That's why I came here—to get away from all that."

"Fair comment," said Janis.

"So, what's next for you, then?" asked Jessica.

"I suppose I had better buy myself a roundtrip ticket to New York. You gave me a ticket to the five-star guilt trip, like it or not."

"I have never been to New York," said Jessica, having anticipated that would be Janis's answer.

"Looking for a tour guide?" asked Janis. "I work cheap."

Jessica just smiled.

30.

Ken followed his daughter onto the deck and watched as she walked down the stairs, climbed into her car, waved goodbye, and drove away down the long, narrow driveway.

For a moment, he just stood still, silent in contemplation, while around him, American robins, yellow-rumped warblers, and song sparrows formed an unseen choir, hidden within the cedar, maple, and firs.

There wouldn't be a coffin spray or vases filled with carefully arranged, long-stemmed flowers. But her passing would not be without a floral salute. The perennial wild of the rock garden saw to that: fragrant red and white roses, tall above purple daisies that kept time with the beat of the breeze, which carried the sweet fragrance of mock orange and purple lavender.

Ken thought back to seeing Lena at the farm gate. Gilgamesh, she had claimed to be, and he recalled that it all came about after helping his ewe birth her lamb. It seemed like a distant memory.

There are times in one's life when fate's fingers flick us in the ear and awaken us from our self-imposed slumber to face providence, confront our fears, and recognize that life as it comes, not as we might long for it to be, triumphs.

This weekend had been such a time.

The cottony clouds dissolved in whisps of condensation, allowing the sun to light up the floral show and give warmth to the birdsong choir that filled the air, perfectly on cue. Ken took a long inhale of scented air, marvelling at the colour and hopeful melody that provided service for a life that was coming to an end.

Toby sat watching at the gate that opened to the field of grazing lambs and bleating mother ewes. *Nothing much gets past you, does it?* Ken felt quite certain that the dog was aware that his boss was hurting, and that something significant was taking place.

Only on a rare occasion would Ken let his dog through the gate—and this qualified—so he walked to the gate, and the tail of the big dog started to wag.

Toby seemed thrilled with the prospect of time on the deck with his boss, so when the gate was opened for him, he obediently followed Ken up the steps to the big wicker chair shaded by the timbered arch above him.

Ken stroked the furry head that had plopped on his lap, and let his mind drift, as though watching a well-edited silent movie of the life he had had with Lena. There had been so many good times, and such passion in their work and in their play. But only the scenes of laughter, romance, and family made the cut—everything else had been left on the cutting-room floor.

But in the real world, his mind knew the script for all three acts of the play, a tragedy in which he would stand alone to take the final bow. A lifelong play with a deuteragonist who had given him such joy and such compassion, but—in the final act—so much pain.

Through it all, the good and the bad, they always had had each other's back, no matter what, and he found himself chuckling aloud, wiping his moist eyes, at the scene of Lena, amongst a group of stone-faced friends, laughing at her own jokes. He was always in step and laughed along, never leaving her to laugh alone.

A meaty paw landed on his knee, and he realized that he had stopped grooming his companion, who, with blinking, bright eyes and a drooping, dripping tongue, was requesting that he focus on the job at hand.

"Sorry, pal, but I think it's about time. You will have to go back to work," he said to Toby, who gave him a disapproving look, but obediently followed his boss back to and through the gate.

Ken entered the tomb-silent house, slowly walked down the hall, and stood for a moment outside the door of Lena's room.

He knew what to expect, but a small, irrational part of his brain pictured him back many years, Lena sitting up in bed, looking tired, with a sweaty forehead, but with such love in her eyes, holding their newborn, Sheena.

The thrill that a new life had come from their union was greater than anything he could remember, filling him with the love of something shared that could never be taken from them. It had stained his heart with an indelible glow that had never dulled, even when that love was no longer reciprocated.

Ken quietly pushed open the bedroom door to see Lena lying motionless on her side, eyes closed, lips pursed in what, under more normal circumstances, would have appeared to be a smile at a pleasant dream.

He stood at her bedside, silent, watching her, as though any noise might wake her and somehow disrupt her journey—but also to see, or perhaps hear, if breath remained.

The slight rise and fall of her chest from beneath the thin sheet answered his unasked question. Each shallow breath seemed only to last a second. They came in rapid succession and he knew that each might be the last.

Ken gulped in air, as though drowning in the rising pool of sorrow that overwhelmed him. In that moment, he wished he had let them come and take her back to the Caring Hands Hospice.

Instead, she was lying right in front of him, and it seemed too much for his heart to take. The silent movie in his head was now on fast-forward, with images speeding by so fast that it all became a blur. Gasping for breath, he felt that he had to leave, but his feet refused his demand to run from the room.

"Will you come closer?"

Her whisper was so soft that it was barely audible.

Ken looked at Lena, quite sure that she had asked him to come closer. He didn't know what to do. He thought that perhaps his mind was playing tricks. But he leaned closer to Lena and reached beneath the sheet, taking her hand in his.

"Please …" Her fragile voice faded, but this time he had heard her request clearly. Ken found himself slipping off his slippers, walking around to the far side of the bed, climbing beneath the sheets, and cuddling up against her in a familiar fit.

Lying still beside her, he felt her coldness, and could hear the faintness of her arrhythmic breathing. So he held her close to him, hoping to transfer heat from his body to hers, and closed his eyes. So many nights, they had cuddled together, providing each other comfort, and the power to heal the hurtful cuts inflicted by others upon them during the day.

Her fingers tightened ever so slightly in his hand. "Ken." The whisper of his name from her lips for the first time since she had arrived made his heart skip a beat. "We were good together, weren't we?"

"We were great together," he managed to say through trembling lips and his effort to contain his muted sobbing.

"Thank you" were the last whispered words he heard before she gasped in her last breath, which rattled in her chest and left her still and lifeless beside him.

***

The pastel colours beyond the dark veil became her full focus as she drifted through the opiate fog that filled what was left of her mind. Her senses were carefully packed away in preparation for the last part of her final journey, leaving only one small, candle-like flame that lit the path through the darkness toward the light. But she was not alone.

The boatman, tall and thin, face hooded from view, punted her boat along the river divide between the world she had known and her destination. She felt at peace, and held no fear, only a faint melancholy that seemed to draw her face to a figure standing on the riverbank, watching her.

She tugged at the boatman's long, low-hanging sleeve and pointed at the figure. "Will you come closer?" She asked the boatman, unsure if he would comply. "Please."

When the boatman punted toward the shore, the flame burned a bit brighter, lighting up a man's face—one that she had not seen for what seemed like an eternity.

A warmth joined her melancholy. Her mind was filled with joyful memories of family, friends, sunny summer days, and sweet rain that grew gardens.

She mostly saw her children.

Asher's first diapered steps, and then in his Eaton jacket, one size too big, that morphed into a gown worn by a man receiving his PhD.

She blinked into the milky grey eyes as Sheena, so tiny in her arms, for the first time looked into hers. Then they were riding into the wind, each on horseback. And from within a crowd, she cheered her daughter on as she broke the winner's tape on a high school running track.

And Ken, the wind causing his flowing, dark brown hair to dance, his body tanned and fit, stood at the helm of their sailboat, *forever free*. She was wrapped in a quilt of emotion, a patchwork of joy, sorrow, and unbridled, unconditional love.

She looked into the face of the man who stood before her, puzzled that he seemed so sad. She wanted to reach out and touch his cheek, but the boatman held down her arm.

"Ken …" She could see him clearly now, and her heart was playfully tickled by a silken scarf of passion that she had only known with him, and that had made her feel loved and safe. "We were good together, weren't we?"

She could not hear his reply; she only felt the heatwave from his love, and it warmed her.

"Thank you," she said, wanting the boatman to take her closer. But instead, he punted the narrow craft away from the shore and toward a river of darkness illuminated only by the single flame. Then the boatman was gone, leaving her to drift within a span of time that had no beginning and offered no end.

She drifted alone until the caring, timeless fingers of Creation snuffed the flame and raised her through the dark veil, where countless souls, illuminated by the light radiated by all the stars and galaxies that have ever existed, at all wavelengths from the ultraviolet through the far infrared, during all of cosmic history, welcomed her.

Acknowledgments

It is said that writing novels is a lonely business, and it is, but a finished book is rarely accomplished by one person; although any errors contained within are mine alone. I have lived a very engaged and full life during which I have met a truly eclectic range of characters, all of whom have helped me to embrace humility, tolerance, and the importance of listening to their stories. Above all, they have given me insight into the human condition present within each of us.

The characters within this novel are fictional and thus unattributable to anyone alive or recently departed. Any similarities with individuals who have played a part in my life are unintended. I hope, however, that the story and the overarching themes contained within it will strike a truthful chord and make the reader think about the fact that our common histories are inherited and cannot be changed. But our present condition and where future generations are headed are very much in our collective hands.

Several people stepped up to help me complete this work. Fenella Fownes, who was my constant champion and helped me with the cover design and the marketing of this novel, I cannot thank you enough. Notable among several alpha and beta readers are Sheelagh Chapman and Christina Wilson, both of whom managed to read through the raw, unedited text and still give positive and useful feedback to help me improve this book.

But I must reserve the highest praise for Kenya Gutteridge, who took on the daunting task of editing my writing. You taught me more than you know, and your thoughtful and meticulous attention to detail has made this a much better book. I am truly grateful, and I thank you.

Printed in the USA
CPSIA information can be obtained
at www.ICGtesting.com
LVHW040231260624
784028LV00005B/181